Take Me Over

Libby Waterford

Also by Libby Waterford

Sawyer's Cove: The Reboot

Take Two

Take a Bow

Take it All

Take a Chance

Hot Take in Steamy Shorts: A Kissed by Romance Anthology

Take Another Look in A Kiss at Midnight: A Kissed by Romance Collaboration

Never a Bride

Can't Help Falling in Love

Can't Make You Love Me

Can't Fight This Feeling

Can't Hurry Love

Weston Reunion

Flirting with Her Professor

Her Reunion Fling

Falling for Her Ex

For Arell

"I have loved and been in love. There's a big difference."

— Katharine Hepburn

Sawyer's Cove Credits

Starring
Camille Corsair as Amy Green
Jay Orlando as Parker Wild
Nash Speedwell as Will O'Connell
Darren Silverstein as Noah Rosen
Spencer Crosby as Sawyer North
Ariel Tulip as Lily Fine
Stephanie Mae as Grace Park
Henry Yu as Kai Wild
Glen Michaelson as Danny Rafferty
Trevor Kendrick as Wesley Jones

Produced by
Camille Corsair
Selena Echeveria

Written by
Ryan Saylor
Selena Echeveria

Created by
Ryan Saylor

Sawyer's Cove: The Reboot
Season 3 Episode List

301: The Pancake Breakfast
302: The Hike
303: The Glass Half Full
304: The Borrowed Tiara
305: The Bus Stop
306: The Storm
307: The Proposal
308: The Yard Sale
309: The Wedding Planner
310: The Last Ride

Prologue

This prologue first appeared as the epilogue of Take a Chance, *the previous book in the Sawyer's Cove: The Reboot series.*

Ariel Tulip was starving.

She'd driven to Misty Harbor from New York in one straight shot. It had taken her longer to get out of the city than she'd planned, and her apartment just off Misty Harbor's Main Street had an empty refrigerator. She hadn't been there since Harbor Fest, over a month ago, and she hadn't hit the market to stock up yet. Her pantry held the staples—olives, crackers, and champagne—but she craved something hot and greasy.

Luckily, her apartment was a block from Melba's, the retro fifties diner. She parked, left her bags in the car, and made a beeline for the restaurant. The lunch rush was over, and the early dinner crowd hadn't started yet. In fact, there were only a half dozen customers in the place, including a familiar man sitting at the counter with a cup of coffee and an open laptop in front of him.

"Hey, Loretta," Ariel greeted the server who materialized with a menu.

"Hi, sweetie," Loretta said laconically. "Sit anywhere."

Ariel nodded. She usually asked for a window booth if one was free, but today she went to the counter. "Fancy meeting you here."

Ryan Saylor, the creator of *Sawyer's Cove*, the man who'd hired sixteen-year-old Ariel to play Lily Fine, changing her life with her first big break, looked away from his computer and into her eyes.

The look in his gray-green-brown irises shifted from distracted and wary to surprised, then warm.

"Ariel, hi," he said, swiveling the high-backed stool so he could half stand up and hug her lightly in greeting.

She hugged him back, then dropped onto the stool next to him and surveyed him. He wore brown corduroy pants, and a green plaid shirt under a tweed jacket complete with elbow patch, like an English professor from 1985. The jacket's left arm had been removed and tailored so it ended at the shoulder, due to his limb difference. Ryan had been born without a left arm.

She hadn't seen him in person in years, and there were new fine lines around his eyes. His chestnut brown hair was shorter than when he'd been the precocious twenty-five-year-old in charge of his own TV show, but it still curled around his ears and nearly brushed the collar of his jacket.

"So, what are you doing in my neck of the woods?" Ariel asked.

"Oh, is this your neighborhood? I thought you lived in the West Village."

"When I'm not in Misty Harbor," Ariel agreed. "As of five minutes ago, I live right around the corner until we wrap."

"Still? Didn't you live somewhere around here back in the day?"

Ariel was surprised he remembered. "I did, and I do. In the very same apartment, actually. The first season of the reboot, I made inquiries, but someone else was renting it, so I stayed at the inn. But when the last tenants moved out, the landlord offered it to me. I've been here off and on for over a year now. I like having my own space, and it's handy for Harbor Fest and Cove Con."

"With Jay and Cami and Nash all settled here, it really feels like Misty Harbor is your second home."

"I'm a city girl at heart," Ariel reminded him, "but it's nice to get away from Manhattan sometimes, too. Misty Harbor is a regular Cloudy Cove."

"So I'm learning," Ryan said.

"When did you arrive? Wait." Ariel flagged down Loretta and ordered a grilled cheese with tomato and a chocolate banana milkshake. "You want anything else?"

"No, I ate, thanks," Ryan said. He glanced at his computer screen, which had gone dark.

"Oh, I'm keeping you from your work." She'd been so excited to see a friendly face that it hadn't occurred to her he might not want her company. Story of her life. She went on being her effusive, emotional self, and usually far too late picked up on the clues that she was too much for some people. Most people, actually.

"It's okay," he said quickly. "Just banging my head

against some spreadsheets. Selena left everything in great shape, but I already feel behind. I'm better at words than numbers."

Ariel had been as shocked as anyone when, a couple of months ago, showrunner Selena Echeveria had announced she was turning over the reins of the third and final season of the *Sawyer's Cove* reboot to Ryan, the original creator. Selena had been given a green light to turn her boyfriend Warner Mathis's bestselling mystery novel *Gunsmoke* into a limited series. But studio backing depended on casting one of Hollywood's biggest stars in the role of Jake Wilton, the private detective hero, and the star in question's availability had overlapped with the *Sawyer's Cove* shoot, so she'd had no choice but to step away. Lucky for all of them, Ryan had agreed to take her place.

She already missed Selena and her steady, nononsense hand, but none of the *Sawyer's Cove* family had wanted her to lose out on this opportunity. Plus, it was exciting to have Ryan come back to the show. Ariel was determined that the third and final season was going to be amazing for the cast and crew. They'd been given a gift with this reboot. It had been a chance to renew old friendships, for new relationships to blossom, and for fans to fall in love with the show all over again. It was only when she thought about the end of the shoot, about three months away, that she, typically for her, got weepy.

Once the season was over, the core group of actors wouldn't have any reason to get together with the same regularity they had for the past three years. She was going to miss the camaraderie. On top of which, she wasn't sure which direction she should try to take her career in. Everyone else had their lane, seemed to be cruising along in it, while she was barely keeping up.

It also didn't help that everyone was oh-so-happily paired up. Ryan had only dealt with one on-set romance the first go-round. As she bit gratefully into her sandwich, she filled him in on the rest of the gossip.

"So you know about Jay and Cami, obviously." Their rekindled romance had been all over social media, fanning the flames of excitement for the reboot in the process. "But how up are you on the rest of the *Sawyer's Cove* news?"

Ryan cringed. "Do I really need to know? Surely everyone keeps things professional."

"Sure, we're all pros. But you need to know the basics. Want a quick primer?"

"Will there be a test?"

"Oh, definitely," Ariel said with a wink. "And I'm a very hard grader."

"Then I better pay attention," he said, closing his computer and turning toward her.

She shifted in her seat, suddenly self-conscious. She was used to an audience, but not an audience of one. Ryan was giving her his full attention, and it felt nice— but unsettling.

He'd always intimidated her—he was so smart, so much older than her, more worldly and experienced.

Over a decade later, the age difference didn't strike her as that big a deal anymore. He was what—forty-one? Forty-two? But it was hard not to feel a little nervous around him all the same. He was essentially her boss, even if he was the new kid in town.

"Well, Nash is with Jay's sister, Mimi, who's the head

of the town library. They have this awesome old Victorian house. They did a bunch of work to it and turned the basement into a recording studio for Nash, and the first floor has this library out of a fairy tale, I swear. They're having a barbecue this weekend, if you didn't already hear, so you can see it for yourself."

Ryan's face rippled, but she couldn't read his reaction, so she plowed on. "And of course, Crosby and Darren are together. I'm assuming Darren will be around a fair bit, between directing and things going well with Noah and Will *finally* after all the drama last season. Please don't tell me you're going to break them up, because I might have to hurt you."

"You and every other fangirl," Ryan said, holding his hand up defensively. "Don't worry. Will and Noah will get their happily ever after."

"Excellent. Which means we'll be seeing a lot of Darren, and Crosby will be happy. They're nauseatingly in love."

"And what about you?" Ryan asked.

Ariel took a long pull on her milkshake while he stared at her steadily. "What about me?"

"Who's your significant other? A local hero or a New Yorker?"

Ariel squinted at him, but Ryan didn't appear to be joking. She ignored the stab of sadness his words invoked and decided to keep things as airy as the meringue on the pie in the refrigerated case behind the counter. "Alas, I'm but a poor unattached female."

Ryan's brow creased, as if he didn't understand the concept.

"Somehow I've managed to escape the love curse that

seems to affect everyone else when they get inside Misty Harbor's city limits," she went on gaily. "What about you?"

Ryan took a second to respond. "I'm single, too. Divorced."

Ariel had heard about his divorce. She'd never met his wife, but they'd been married for a while. She wondered what had happened.

"We could start a club," she said. "Sawyer's Cove Singles."

Ryan stroked his chin. "Or we could pair up and appease the Misty Harbor love gods before anything terrible befalls the town."

She grinned at his over-the-top suggestion. "Oh yes, we could make ourselves tributes by dating each other. Great idea."

Ryan's cheeks colored at her acquiescence. "No, I wouldn't put you through that. I'm hopeless at dating. I think I'll just enter my crotchety-old-man phase early."

"Nonsense." Ryan might dress like an aging professor, but he was far from elderly. His clean-shaven face had small lines that made him look distinguished, while his body was as lean as ever. Ariel didn't know what kind of exercise he did to keep fit, but whatever he did, it was working. "I may not be great at dating myself, but I am an amazing wing-woman."

Ryan laughed. "Oh, I don't doubt it."

"I could get you a date to the barbecue by tomorrow," she persisted, feeling as if she had something to prove, even though he wasn't challenging her.

"The barbecue. Nash mentioned it, but I don't know that I should go."

"Why not? Everyone will be so excited to see you."

"I have a pile of work. And you'll have more fun without me."

"What are you talking about?" She was genuinely mystified.

"Just that you're all so close. It's awesome, but I'm like the stuffy dad or the weird uncle."

"Is that how you see yourself? You gave us our livelihoods. You created *Sawyer's Cove*."

"A million years ago. I'm a fossil. Anyway, I have so much work to do I can't—"

"You can and you will, Ryan Saylor," Ariel declared. "I expect to see you at that barbecue, and I'll bring someone nice for you. Even if you just make a friend, you could always use another friend, couldn't you?"

"I suppose." He looked at her thoughtfully. "Does anyone ever say no to you?"

She laughed. "Only all the time. But I'm glad my powers of persuasion work on you, at least."

"You make it easy to say yes."

"Really?" The comment pleased her. She always worked hard to make things happen, in her life, in her career. It was nice to feel a sense of ease around someone for a change.

"And what about you?"

She sucked noisily on the dregs of her milkshake, then peered into the empty glass, but there was no hidden compartment filled with more at the bottom. "What do you mean?"

"Am I supposed to bring a guy for you? Like a *When Harry Met Sally* thing?"

Delighted as she was by him referencing one of her

favorite movies of all time, she shook her head vehemently. "Absolutely not. I don't think you'll be able to find my soulmate in forty-eight hours when I haven't found him in thirty-three years."

"Your soulmate?" His brow furrowed. "I was thinking more like a nice, regular Misty Harbor resident."

"I already know I'm not going to find my soulmate in Misty Harbor," she said. "I've spent so much time here in the last couple of years, I can't imagine I wouldn't have met him already."

"Sorry, but what's with the soulmate obsession?"

"Isn't that the dream—to find the person who completes you? Your other half?"

"Dream?" He scoffed. "It's a fantasy, Ariel, take it from me."

"This from the man who wrote all those beautiful monologues for Sawyer about looking for his soulmate?"

He grimaced. "I was young and romantic. And Sawyer never found his soulmate, remember?"

She bristled. Sawyer had been with Lily Fine for most of season two of the reboot, and she was beginning to think they had been endgame this entire time.

"Nope, uh-uh, you aren't allowed to take this from me. I need something to justify being pathetically alone while all my friends find the loves of their lives in this one-horse town. No offense, Loretta," Ariel said to the server who was picking up her empty plate.

"None taken, hon. Want dessert?"

"The milkshake was enough for me. Just the check."

Loretta slid a piece of paper onto the counter and shuffled away.

Ariel dug out her wallet and removed some cash. "I

will see you at the barbecue. Oh, this is going to be such a bittersweet season. I'm sad already." She sniffed, then brightened. "But finding you a girlfriend, despite you no longer being young and romantic, is a worthy challenge. See you soon, boss."

Ryan chuckled, but when she didn't laugh, he stopped her before she left. "Wait, Ariel—if you're serious about the date thing, I have one rule. No actresses."

"No actresses?" She frowned. "What's wrong with actresses?"

His expression turned sheepish, as if he'd belatedly remembered what she did for a living. "Sorry, it's just a thing I've had since I first got to Hollywood. I don't date actresses."

"No actresses," she said crisply. Well, whatever. It wasn't like she was going to set him up with anyone from the cast. That would be unprofessional.

"No offense," he said weakly.

She channeled her inner Loretta. "None taken, hon." Then she swept out of the diner with all the haughtiness she could muster.

No actresses, indeed.

Chapter One

Sawyer's Cove: The Reboot
Episode 301: The Pancake Breakfast

INT. LILY FINE'S CLASSROOM - DAY

SAWYER looks longingly at LILY. Lily
notices him.

LILY: Do I have something on my face?
SAWYER: Yeah.

Lily wipes at her face.

LILY: Did I get it off?

Sawyer shakes his head no.

LILY: Well, what is it?
SAWYER: Timeless beauty.

Lily rolls her eyes.

A riel despised humidity, and August in New England wasn't the place to be if you wanted to avoid it. Her thick auburn hair hung heavy as an anvil down her back, and she'd already sweated through her favorite peach-colored linen dress. Her second-floor apartment was close enough to Misty Harbor's coastline to benefit from cooling ocean breezes, but a sticky marine layer had settled over the town two days ago and hadn't let up. She'd been mainlining iced tea and obsessively checking the weather app, praying for a break in the oppressive mugginess.

Damp and sticky, she fanned herself with a copy of *Gun Shy*, Warner Mathis's latest Jake Wilton novel. The long-awaited follow-up to his debut mystery, *Gunsmoke,* had instantly hit all the bestseller lists upon its release earlier in the summer. Ariel had picked up a copy in New York before she drove up to Misty Harbor, but hadn't gotten more than a few pages in. She'd been busy since arriving in town. The table read for the first episode of season three of *Sawyer's Cove* was in a few days and she'd been dutifully studying her script. She'd also been distracted by planning a surprise for her Cove cast mates.

In three months, they'd finish filming the final season of the reboot, and everyone would scatter. They might run into each other doing press when the third season dropped, or at Cove Con, the small fan convention that had run in conjunction with Harbor Fest for the past two summers. But there wouldn't be any reason for the five— well, six if you counted Darren Silverstein, and Ariel did

—core Cove actors to be in the same place at the same time after the shoot ended.

She knew the drill—the entertainment business was temporary by design. Actors got close on set, bonding through intense emotional situations and long hours over short periods of time. Then production wrapped, everyone went back where they came from, and you never saw each other again.

She was luckier than most. She'd been able to keep up with Cami and Nash and Crosby fairly well after the original *Sawyer's Cove* had ended nearly fourteen years ago. They'd been so young, they'd become true friends over the initial three-year run. She hadn't been willing to give up her friendships, and she was stubborn enough to keep them in her life. Only Jay, by disappearing from public view entirely when he'd opted to stay in Misty Harbor, had eluded her attempts to stay in touch. Luckily, two years ago Cami had convinced him to give *Sawyer's Cove* another chance, and with it, Ariel had been given the opportunity to cement their friendship. She hadn't squandered it.

In fact, she was meeting Jay in a few minutes to pitch him on her surprise project. She hurried down the stairs and through the street level door. Her apartment was smack in the middle of the long main street that started at the Misty Harbor Inn and ended at the beach. She kept the bare necessities there—her real home base was in Manhattan, in the West Village apartment she'd bought about ten years ago. As she walked, she lifted her mane of hair off her neck, rummaging in her big shoulder bag for a hair tie to put it up with. God, it was putridly hot.

Sweat dampened every cranny of her body by the

time she reached The Cove, the neighborhood bar Jay owned and operated. She'd heard that The Cove had done good business before the *Sawyer's Cove* revival, but nothing like now. The place always seemed full, no matter the time of day. It was too early for dinner, but there were lots of people inside The Cove's cozy brick walls, drinking, of course, and partaking of the upscale pub food.

Jay was a busy man—he owned the bar, he was involved in a lot of local business groups, and he invested in Misty Harbor real estate. He'd renovated another brick storefront on Miller Street, and his longtime Cove manager Danica Brown had turned it into an independent bookstore-slash-wine bar with her boyfriend Ethan Simmons. Ariel admired Jay's business ventures and what he'd done for Misty Harbor. From what she'd seen, and what Cami had told her, his leadership and investments were a big part of why the small town had become a vibrant, tourist-friendly destination.

Ariel stopped at the bar to order yet another iced tea and asked the bartender to let Jay know she was there. While she waited, she checked her phone, responded to a few social media posts, and sent a text to her mom to remind her that Anna's, Ariel's younger sister, birthday was in a few days. Her mother tended to forget birthdays. And everything else. Ariel had always been the one to keep track of her dance classes and homework and theater practice, the one who got herself to auditions and deciphered her contract with her first agent. Her mom had spent three hours getting sixteen-year-old Ariel settled into her new life in Misty Harbor, where she was about to shoot a twenty-two-episode season of television, before returning to their split-level in upstate New York where Anna was a middle-schooler. That was after her mother had readily signed the papers making Ariel an emancipated minor.

She loved her family, but she'd learned early to rely on nobody but herself.

Her iced tea arrived at the same time as Jay.

"Hey, you." He joined her on her side of the bar, looking like an extraordinarily handsome guy trying to stay under the radar in worn jeans, a plain gray T-shirt, three days of stubble, and a ball cap covering his signature nearly shaved head. The effect wasn't exactly subtle.

"Hey. Can we sit for a minute?" She tilted her head toward an empty booth on the other side of the room.

"Sure. Hang on." To the bartender, he said, "Hey, Lee, can I get the new pilsner?"

They settled into the booth and the Cove employee brought the draft beer a minute later.

"What's up, beautiful?"

"I wanted to talk to you about something before we get caught up in shooting. It always gets crazy once the cameras start rolling."

"Tell me about it. I've been trying to get my ducks in a row. I know I signed up for it, but I'm really glad this is the last time we're doing this. Shooting a television show kind of interferes with my day job." He smiled wryly.

His words stung a little. Shooting television shows *was* her day job, but she knew for Jay this was a one-off that had turned into a three-year project. Still, he'd gotten an incredible girlfriend in Cami and renewed interest in Misty Harbor out of the deal. "Anyway, since this is our last go-round, I have an idea for something special we could do to celebrate, and also raise money for a good cause."

"I'm listening."

"Picture this—you, me, Cami, Crosby, Darren, and Nash all together on stage for a live taping of *The Sawyer's Cove Rewatch Project Podcast*. We'd sell tickets and donate the proceeds. The fans would love it, we'd get a really nice memory to wrap up the show, and contribute to a good cause. Win-win-win. The podcast hosts are super nice—Erika and Jules."

"Oh yeah, I know Erika. She's the one dating Henry, right?"

"Yep. They met at the first Cove Con, adorably."

"So I show up, get asked questions by Erika and Jules, and try not to sound like an idiot?"

"Basically." Ariel had been on quite a few podcasts doing press for her last few projects. When done well, they felt like intimate conversations. It would probably be chaotic to do a live show with that many people, but she was confident in the production team.

"My friend Kate Treanor's production company got the podcast onto their network last year. Kate's going to come out and produce it in person. Bonus for me." She saw Kate a fair amount between her visits to L.A. for work and Kate's visits to her in-laws in New York. She and her husband, restaurateur Oliver Mercier, had recently opened a New York location of his signature restaurant, Mercy, and were living in New York temporarily, making it extra easy for her to come up and produce the podcast herself.

"Oh cool," Jay said. "Well, I don't see why not, especially if it's after we wrap."

"Yeah, I have to double-check the schedule, but that's what I'm aiming for."

"Count me in."

"Spectacular. Thanks, Jay."

"I'm sure Cami will be excited," Jay said. "Want me to ask her? Or do you want to do it?"

"You can mention it to her, but we've been trying to find time for lunch, so I'll get her official okay then."

"You ready for the table read? It'll be weird with Ryan there instead of Selena. Like the old days."

"I'm ready," Ariel said, "if I can keep my shit together. I'm already getting emotional about it being the last first table read ever."

"I hope Selena told Ryan to have plenty of tissues on hand," Jay said with a smile.

"Speaking of Ryan, this is kind of a weird question, but you know more people in Misty Harbor than I do. Can you think of any eligible women who might be interested in a divorced forty-something TV showrunner with one arm?"

Jay barked a surprised laugh. "Why? Is he looking?"

"I sort of said I'd help him get something of a social life while he's here. You know, everyone is all paired up like matching socks, and it can be hard to meet new people in a small town."

She'd been regretting her impulsive promise to find Ryan a date since she'd made it. She'd offered to set him up, but his one condition still had her feathers up—he'd made it clear the only unsuitable candidate would be an actress. Apparently, he never had and never would consider one as a potential partner.

Not that she would have volunteered for the role in the first place, but it was the principle of the thing.

Jay shrugged. "I'm not good at this stuff. You should ask Danica. She always seems to know who's single and looking."

Ariel pouted at Jay for a second, but she'd gotten his agreement to do the podcast, so she couldn't be too annoyed. "All right, I'll stop by her place. I can always use another book I don't have time to read, anyway."

"That's the spirit."

"Thanks, Jay."

"You coming to Mimi's barbecue?" he asked.

"Of course. What should I bring?" Besides a date for their boss.

"I'll have Mimi text you if she needs anything."

He refused her offer to pay for her iced tea, gave her a hug, and went back to work—the important business of full-time bar owner and part-time heartthrob.

Ariel left The Cove refreshed by the drink and air conditioning, but the thick summer haze quickly had her fanning herself again on the short walk to the Miller Street Book Bar. The Instagram-ready brick building housed a bookstore in one half and a wine bar in the other.

She pushed open the doors, thankful for the climate control in this establishment as well.

A few customers browsed the books while a slim woman with long brown hair efficiently sliced limes behind a polished wooden bar top. Ariel spotted a romance with a promising cover on a table and grabbed it on her way to the bar. "Hey, Danica. Ariel." She put her hand on her chest in introduction. She didn't know the woman that well, but she'd met her once when they'd shot some *Sawyer's Cove* scenes at The Cove.

"Hi there, Ariel," Danica said warmly, setting the limes in a plastic container. "Can I get you something?"

"Unfortunately, it's so hot a glass of wine would probably put me right to sleep," Ariel said.

Danica nodded. "We're going through a lot of rosé right now."

"Oh, now you're tempting me." Ariel laughed. She did, in fact, have a bottle of sparkling rosé chilling in her apartment fridge. But she didn't want to contemplate yet another evening that began with opening a bottle of wine for one. She was thirty-three with the habits of a middle-aged divorcée, though she hadn't ever been married. She'd never even come close. It had never bothered her until recently, when the happy couples around her began oozing contentment. It was easier to bear her own single status when everyone else in her orbit was unpaired and messy, too. But suddenly they were all lined up like penguins marching into their happy futures, and she was out in the cold. Metaphorically. It was still hot as hell outside.

Maybe she should ask Danica for help with finding *her* a date. But if she fell for someone local, she'd either end up in a long-distance relationship, which she didn't have the stamina for, or she'd be stuck in Misty Harbor. While she loved this little town, she didn't want a small-town lifestyle. Cami and Jay were different—his roots were deep here, and Cami had started handling most of her producing work remotely from Misty Harbor with a work trip to Los Angeles every other month or so. Cami had even stopped acting except for *Sawyer's Cove*.

Ariel didn't want to stop acting. That was the only thing she knew for sure. Otherwise, she was lost, unable to commit to any project after *Sawyer's Cove*, her agent looking for the just-right part that would get her excited. Unfortunately, she had the sneaking suspicion her best parts were behind her. She had lately only been offered boring mom roles. She hadn't been able to bring herself to accept any of them, but she might have to if nothing better came along.

Right now, she had to focus on her mission.

"I have kind of a weird question," Ariel said. "But Jay suggested I ask you, for whatever that's worth."

Danica stopped in the middle of restocking cocktail napkins and looked at her with an intrigued expression. "What's up?"

"Do you know Ryan Saylor? He's steering the ship this season, but he's new to town."

Danica smiled. "Yeah, Jay brought him by a couple of days ago. He seems nice. He practically bought out our entire Hollywood history section, so he's got a friend for life in my boyfriend, Ethan."

Ryan liked Hollywood history? She supposed it wasn't surprising. "Cool. And Ryan is really nice. He's also single. Can you think of anybody he might be a good fit with? Like, romantically?"

Danica widened her eyes. "Wow, I wasn't expecting that. I might have to give it some thought." She looked at Ariel quizzically. "He's looking for a girlfriend here in Misty Harbor? Isn't he from L.A.?"

"He's making a fresh start," Ariel said, not wanting to share too many details. "I...volunteered to help him meet someone new. If you can't think of anyone, that's totally fine. I just thought I'd ask."

"There's always Zelda Won," Danica said, staring out the window as she spoke. "She was seeing Alphonse, the butcher, but they broke up a couple of months ago. And she's terrific. She gets shit done, which I appreciate. She comes to the store's book club, too."

"Zelda." Ariel turned it over in her mind. She was probably in her mid-thirties, attractive, thick black eyebrows accentuating her dark brown eyes. Ariel tended toward curves and a few years ago finally embraced the fact she would never be a stick thin waif and had leaned into her bombshell look by accentuating her hips, ass, and legendary breasts. Zelda, in contrast, was slender, with strong forearms and shoulders from kneading dough and hauling bags of flour. Ariel had no idea if she liked TV or movies, but she'd certainly benefited from the show's effect on the town. "Okay, thanks, that's helpful."

"You're welcome. Come back sometime for that rosé."

"I will," Ariel promised. She paid for her book and headed back to Main Street. It looked like she had to make a stop at the Bakeshop now. She was due for another iced tea, anyway.

Chapter Two

Sawyer's Cove: The Reboot
Episode 301: The Pancake Breakfast

INT. FIREHOUSE PANCAKE BREAKFAST - DAY

AMY: Should we really be encouraging this
relationship? Kai doesn't have the best
track record with women.
PARKER: That's because he has terrible
taste. Unlike me.
AMY: Don't derail me with flattery.
PARKER: How about if I derail you with
kisses?

PARKER kisses AMY

AMY: I'll allow it. This time.

The Bakeshop was blessedly air-conditioned and rather busy for a Friday afternoon. Ariel had seen it with a line out the door, but usually during the weekend brunch and prime weekday caffeine intake hours. Today, she had to wait behind a group of four teenage girls while they ordered complicated drinks that involved oat milk and wheatgrass and sounded honestly undrinkable.

The guy behind the register was taking forever to input everything into the computer—she pegged him as Trevor's replacement. Trevor Kendrick, former Bakeshop employee and town gossip extraordinaire, had gotten too busy to work behind the Bakeshop's counter after he'd landed a small recurring role on the second season of the *Sawyer's Cove* reboot, and had subsequently moved to New York to continue his study of acting. Spencer Crosby's agent had recently taken him on as a client, and Crosby had proudly announced his friend was in rehearsals for his first play—an off-Broadway farce. Crosby had already gotten time off from the production to go back to the city for opening night.

She got to the front of the line as Zelda emerged from the back carrying two salads. Zelda made for the extended seating area in the back of the shop, so Ariel abandoned her chance to order yet another iced tea to catch up to the baker while she delivered the salads to two customers at a cafe table. Zelda made small talk with them for a minute, while Ariel awkwardly stood there waiting for an opening.

When Zelda was finally done and turned to head back to the kitchen, Ariel made her move.

"Zelda, hey!"

"Hey," she said with a quirked eyebrow. "What can I do for you?"

"So funny you should ask," Ariel said jovially. "Can we talk for a second?"

Zelda walked briskly toward the kitchen doors while Ariel scrambled to follow. "I guess. What's up?" She stopped outside the pastry case and pulled out a pad of paper, taking inventory while they talked.

"So, the gang's all here for the shoot, and we're having sort of a kick-off barbecue tomorrow and I was wondering if you were free."

"I can't do catering on such short notice, but I'll see what I have in the freezer—"

"No, sorry, I wasn't clear. Not to cater, although while I'm here I should put in an order that I can bring to the barbecue," Ariel said quickly. "A big order," she added, hoping that would sweeten the deal. "I thought, you know, I've lived across the street from the Bakeshop on and off for two years and you and I have never really talked. I'd like to get to know you better."

Just because she had never thought about getting to know the baker before today didn't make it a lie. Zelda seemed really cool, and Ariel was a firm believer that you couldn't have too many friends.

"It's at Nash and Mimi's. You know them, right? Four o'clock. Please say you'll come. It will be fun, I promise."

Zelda paused her inventory to glance at Ariel questioningly. "That's a really nice invite, but I don't get it. What aren't you telling me?"

"Wow, you have an A-plus bullshit meter," Ariel said,

impressed. "Everything I said is totally true, but there is one more thing."

"Out with it."

"Well, Danica happened to mention you're single right now, and I have this friend who is totally great and new in town, and I could introduce you to him at the barbecue, in a totally relaxed, friendly way, and see if maybe you two hit it off."

"You want to set me up?" Zelda's eyebrows hit her hairline.

"Yeah, but in a casual, no pressure way."

"Uh-huh," Zelda said, sounding patently unconvinced. She chewed on her bottom lip in an uncharacteristic display of indecision. "Wow. You know, in a small town you don't get a ton of fresh blood. I'll bite. Who's the guy?"

Ariel pushed her way through the tiny opening Zelda had given her and decided to lay everything out there. "He's really intelligent, really creative, really...gosh, really *insightful*. He sees into people, and he can take their dreams and their desires and explain them in this beautiful, lyrical way. And he's really attractive, too, if you're into longish hair on a man—his is chestnut brown. He's got these amazing eyes that don't ever decide what color they want to be, and his mouth—" Ariel stopped herself before she finished the sentence with something inappropriate. She hadn't realized how attractive Ryan's mouth was until that moment.

She cleared her throat. "Anyway, there is something you should know, though, in case it's a deal breaker." Her voice grew harder, since she hoped it wouldn't be a deal breaker, but she'd never dated a guy with a visible disability before, so maybe she wasn't one to judge. She told herself it was because it had never come up, but maybe that was just her ingrained ableism thinking. "He has one arm. Born without a left arm. So, that's different." She smiled brightly, hoping to seal the deal. "What do you think?"

Zelda stared at her, mouth ajar. "You want to set me up with Ryan Saylor, the creator of *Sawyer's Cove*?"

"Yes!" Ariel was pleased her description was effective.

"You are nuttier than my cardamom-walnut sticky bun."

"Why? Ryan is a really good guy. And he's new in town, and he wants to meet new people."

"Yeah, but he's from Hollyweird," Zelda said flatly. "What's he looking for—a short-term hookup?"

"No! He doesn't have a home base right now. Who knows what the future will bring?" Ariel said, infusing her voice with tantalizing mystery. "All I ask is that you meet him. Worst-case scenario: you don't like each other, and you get to eat some delicious barbecue. Nash is really good on the grill, I promise."

"Jesus. Well. I am a little bit on the rebound," Zelda said. She looked off into the distance. Ariel wondered if she was thinking about the butcher Danica had mentioned. "What the hell. I'll come. I'll meet him. But no promises after that."

Ariel clapped her hands together giddily. "Yay, oh, this will be fun. I'll come pick you up and we'll go together."

"Fine." Zelda sighed. "And you better buy a bunch of stuff to take to the barbecue. I'm not above bribery."

"Oh, I will. I'll put in an order right now." She'd buy half the store if it kept Zelda happy.

"Teddy can take care of you. He's new, but he's doing pretty well."

"Awesome. See you tomorrow."

"Wait, Ariel—you know I have to ask the obligatory question, don't you?"

"What's that?"

"If Ryan's so great, why don't you date him yourself?"

It was good Ariel was an actress, because her lilting laugh came out perfectly unbothered.

"Oh, well." She cast about for a suitable explanation, while the words "no actresses" echoed in her brain like rumbling from a gong. Again, not that she wanted to date Ryan. Though, having been told in no uncertain terms that she couldn't, it stuck in her craw. "We work together. It would be...problematic." She fervently hoped Zelda wouldn't point out that Jay and Cami were the epitome of partners who also worked together, and it was fine.

Thankfully, Zelda didn't mention the discrepancy. She closed up the pastry case. "Get your order in before the kitchen closes. See you tomorrow."

"See you then," Ariel chirped.

God, she was good. She'd promised Ryan Saylor a date to the barbecue, and she was delivering. She hoped Zelda wouldn't bail between now and then.

After ordering half a dozen of everything on the menu to be picked up tomorrow afternoon, she headed back across the street. She'd have to acquiesce to the incessant humidity, close up her apartment, and crank the AC. But first, dinner. It was one of her many flaws to put off food shopping and rely on Melba's for too many meals, but she was lazy about driving to the chain grocery store near the highway, and even lazier about ordering delivery. Melba's was only a block from her place. And they had milkshakes.

She bounced in and spotted Ryan Saylor himself at the counter, in the same seat he'd occupied the day before.

"This is getting to be a habit," she said, sitting down on the swivel stool next to him.

He glanced sideways at her. "I can't work at Selena's house. It's too big and empty. I work better with chatter in the background."

"What are you working on?" She leaned into his space to peer at his computer screen and the word processing program he had open.

"Episode three-oh-three," he said, using industry parlance to describe the third episode of the third season.

"Ooh, I haven't gotten that one yet," she said.

"That's because it's not done." He closed the laptop and twisted to look at her. "What's up, Ariel?"

"Nothing. Just doing some errands, but I'm ready for the table read, I promise," she said.

"Oh. I thought there was something you needed." He rubbed his eyes and touched his phone screen to check the time.

"I need dinner, but I don't need anything from you," she said defensively. "Can't I say hi without needing something? Am I so terribly needy?" She'd been told she was before. Maybe by asking the question, she proved the point.

"That's not what I meant," he said, frowning.

"Relax, I have good news for you. Remember when I said I was going to get you a date to the barbecue?"

"That wasn't a joke?"

"Decidedly not," she said jauntily. "I never joke about romance. Anyway, I found someone. So you have to be there."

"I already told Nash I'd come, but—"

"Great," she interrupted before he could make an excuse. "We'll see you there." She stood and turned to go, not wanting to give him a chance to wriggle out of it. She'd order takeout.

"Wait." Ryan grabbed her hand to stop her. His hand was big and warm around hers. "Who is it?"

"It's a surprise," she said, deciding to milk this thing for suspense. "You like surprises, don't you?"

He shook his head in exasperation. "This is ridiculous, you know."

"This is fun," she insisted. "I never get to play matchmaker. Maybe you two will spark."

"And if we do spark? What then?" He let go of her hand and she felt suddenly off-balance. She shifted her bag on her shoulder and considered his expression. He looked a little...scared.

"Then you ask her out on a date," she said patiently.

"Sounds simple, but I haven't dated anyone since my ex-wife. What if I've forgotten how to do it?" His eyes widened beseechingly, and she took pity on him.

This was more dire than she thought. She dropped back onto the stool. "Okay, think of it as a scene. You meet this girl; you think she's pretty. She laughs at something you say. Green light. You say: 'I would love to take you out sometime, how about a drink?'"

"Ugh. That's so cliché and boring."

"Well, you're the writer, not me. Juice it up if you want, but it's someplace to start. Now repeat: 'I'd love to take you out sometime.'"

She gave him a hard stare until his shoulders sagged and he acquiesced. "I'd love to take you out some time," he repeated.

"Good. Now I say—I mean, she says, 'that would be wonderful, how about Friday?' And what do you say?" She nudged his calf with her toe to prompt him into coming up with something.

"I'll have to check my calendar," he said stiffly.

She nudged him harder, and he amended, "But I'm sure Friday works."

"Lovely. Until Friday. I'm really looking forward to our date." She smiled at him sweetly, as if she was truly looking forward to meeting him for a date, and Ryan looked dazed. Well, good. She was an actress, after all.

"And scene," she said. "I think you're ready, champ."

He shook his head. "I really ought to be one hundred percent focused on the show."

"We're all giving the show a hundred and ten percent, including you. But we have to have a life, too, boss." She flashed him her most charming smile. "And really, there's no pressure," she added kindly, "we're really just a big, goofy family. You fit right in; I promise."

"You are a menace," he said.

"I know, but a benevolent menace," she said. "See you tomorrow, Ryan."

"See you tomorrow."

When she glanced behind her as she walked out of Melba's, he was back on his computer, typing surprisingly rapidly one-handed. The early evening sun was coming through the plate glass window, gilding his profile and highlighting the golden strands of his hair. He really was an attractive man. Zelda was a lucky woman. Ariel reminded herself she was looking for her soulmate, not a workplace fling.

And besides, she was just an actress.

Chapter Three

Sawyer's Cove: The Reboot
Episode 301: The Pancake Breakfast

EXT. CLOUDY COVE BAR AND GRILL - NIGHT

GRACE: How much have you had to drink?
KAI: Nowhere near enough.
GRACE: Your uncle isn't going to serve you if you seem drunk. And your picture, my friend, is in the dictionary next to wasted.
KAI: Aw, Gracie, you say the nicest things.
GRACE: I know, I'm a treasure. And I'm driving you home.

Nash Speedwell had always been a good-natured guy, but as he welcomed Ryan to his home, a grand old Victorian with native plant landscaping out front and a flagstone patio in the back on which sat a gas grill that seemed larger than Ryan's first apartment, he was positively expansive.

"Ryan, you came," Nash said, slapping him hard on the back. "I'm pumped about this season of the show. Seriously. It's going to be rad. We're so lucky to have you back. Want a beer?"

"Sure." He took the proffered can and opened it one-handed, a technique he'd perfected in college. Having a large hand came in...well, handy. The local brew tasted refreshingly bitter and calmed his nerves somewhat. "Beautiful spot you and Mimi have."

"Thanks, man." Nash rattled on about renovations and improvements they'd made while Ryan took in the gingerbread stylings of the exterior. His grandmother had lived in an old Victorian, too. He'd been convinced it was haunted until he was about fourteen, but that hadn't stopped him from exploring the dusty attic and damp basement, half terrified, half hoping a ghost would take advantage of his solitude and make an appearance. But none ever did. A ghost friend would have been better than no friends at all.

He shook off the melancholy thought. He wasn't a kid anymore. He had lots of friends. He was surrounded by people at that very moment, in fact. If he felt lonely, that was because he wasn't making an effort. He wished Ariel was there—her casual insistence that he was already part of the group had given him a false sense of belonging. But she was nowhere to be seen.

"...better get the steaks on," Nash was saying. "Glad you're here, Ryan."

He nodded as Nash returned to the grill, drank

another quarter of his beer and tried not to feel blatantly alone. He wasn't by himself for long, though.

"Hello, Ryan." A petite, middle-aged woman with curly brown hair walked up and smiled at him. "Do you remember me? Deb Orlando, Jay and Mimi's mom."

She'd been a startlingly young mom when her younger child, Jay, had auditioned for the role of Parker Wild and won everyone over with his authenticity and charisma. She wore the intervening years well.

"Of course I remember you."

"It's so good to see you again. When they said *Sawyer's Cove* was coming back, I was surprised you weren't part of the deal. We've missed you."

"Oh." Somehow Ryan hadn't counted on being missed.

"But you're back now. I don't think you're staying at the inn, are you? I'm a manager there. Do you have a place to stay?"

"Selena and Warner are letting me use their house on Blue Bird Lane. It's way too big for me, but it's temporary, so I'll survive."

"Oh, that's good. I know they're busy with their new project. It seems everyone is so busy these days."

"Mom! Can you help me with the corn?" Mimi Orlando waved from the other side of the patio where a bushel of corn ears teetered on a folding table.

"I'm being put to work, I'm afraid," Deb said.

"Can I help?" Ryan asked, feeling idle. Deb flicked her eyes to the empty left sleeve of his blue T-shirt. He'd foregone his usual tweed jacket in deference to the humid August afternoon.

He tensed, ready for rejection, but she said, "Sure."

Surprised and relieved to be included, he followed her to a table where the corn was being transformed into a mound of husks and a pile of naked corn on the cob. Deb got to work while Mimi gave him a wide smile. "Hi, I'm—"

"Jay's sister, of course. And now Nash's—" He paused. He didn't know their exact relationship status, only that they'd been living together for a couple of years in this place.

"Exactly. I'm Nash's." She laughed good-naturedly. "I'm also the head librarian. Which reminds me, I have some conflicts with the proposed shooting schedule at the library. I used to go to Selena—can you help me?"

Work. A safe topic. Before he could answer, Deb waved a husked ear of corn in front of him. He set his beer down on the table and took the corn, staring at it blankly.

"Can you get the silk off?" Deb asked.

He noticed the small wisps of hair, saw a clean kitchen towel, arranged it so he could set the corn on the towel to give him traction to pluck off the remaining silks. He then added his ear to the finished pile. Kitchen tasks were some of the most annoying when you had one arm; he wasn't much of a cook. He'd taken most of his meals at Melba's since he arrived in Misty Harbor, not only because the atmosphere was better for his concentration than the borrowed house he rattled around in, but because it was easier when he had to eat.

He returned to Mimi's question as he desilked another ear of corn. "No problem. I'll get someone to call you. I'm sure we can work something out." He'd ensure Mimi was happy, even if they had to rearrange the entire shoot. It wouldn't do to piss off a librarian, and Jay's sister, to boot.

"Thanks. So, what's it like being in *Cove*-land again?" Mimi asked.

He glanced around the party. The attractive teenagers he'd hired half a lifetime ago had grown up into fantastically good-looking adults who all excelled in their fields. Jay Orlando had Camille Corsair tucked under his arm as they talked to Nash at the grill, and Spencer Crosby and Darren Silverstein were standing close together, looking at something on a phone and laughing. Crosby's rare, unguarded smile made Ryan's heart happy. And Ariel— where *was* Ariel?

"Surreal," he said finally.

Mimi laughed. "That was a very long pause to get a one-word answer, but I guess I know what you mean. Being *Sawyer's Cove*-adjacent is surreal sometimes."

"Hey, do you know where Ariel is?" he asked as he yanked silk off another ear of corn. After all her haranguing to get him to come to this shindig, for her to bail on him was a bit annoying.

"She'll be here. She said she needed to stop by the Bakeshop for something. I hope it's apple turnovers."

"I hope it's chocolate tarts," a young woman said, walking up to Mimi and giving her a friendly wave. "Can I help?"

"No, we're about done," Mimi said. "Come with me to the kitchen and you can help me bring out the side dishes, though. Pauline, this is Ryan Saylor, the creator of *Sawyer's Cove*. Ryan, this is Pauline Smith. She works at the library and she's my best friend."

"I am?" Pauline, beautiful as the rest of them, despite

her librarian status, blinked. "You're my best friend, too."

Mimi smiled. "That's nice to hear, sweetie."

"I don't think Colin would mind me saying so, since he's got the exclusive place as my partner."

"Where is Colin?" Mimi asked.

"He has a summer cold, but he sends his best," Pauline said.

"Oh shoot, I was counting on him to eat about six of these ears." She gestured to the corn. "That boy can eat. But tell him I hope he feels better."

"I will."

As they walked off to the kitchen, Deb gathered up an armload of corn to bring to the grill. Ryan looked around, then spotted a brown grocery bag. He shook it open with a little difficulty and set it on the ground, then swept the husks and silk into it. Between the two of them, they had the chore finished in a minute. It was nice to feel useful, even if it was something that simple. Deb left to fuss over the buffet, which was growing crowded with dishes Pauline and Mimi were bringing out of the house.

He hovered by the table, not approaching the group by the grill. It wasn't that he was shy, it was that they were all so comfortable with each other. He knew intellectually they were happy he was there, but he couldn't shake the feeling that he was the extraneous relative people invited to things because he was technically family, but not because they actually wanted to spend time with him.

He finished his beer and took it over to the helpfully marked recycling bin, about to resort to digging out his phone for something to do, when he heard a flurry of talking and laughter as people approached from the front of the house.

He knew before he saw her that Ariel was one of the new arrivals. He recognized her voice—the throaty contralto she'd had as a teenager had only gotten mellower and huskier with time. She was partially hidden by the enormous bakery box she was holding, while loose waves of her red hair flew around her as a gust of hot, humid wind buffeted her. She peered over the top of the box, searching for a place to set it down. He felt frozen, impotently standing there while she needed help. But then Jay arrived, helping her deposit the box onto a clear spot on the buffet table. He then took another box from the second new arrival—a slender Asian American woman with dark hair pinned to her head in a loose bun, wearing jeans and an oversized man's Oxford shirt that suited her nicely.

"We made it!" Ariel exclaimed to her audience, which was half the party.

Jay gave her a quick hug. "I didn't know you were bringing us the best part of the Bakeshop. Hi, Zelda," he said warmly to the dark-haired woman, giving her a hug as well.

"God, I need a drink. Anything but iced tea," Ariel declared as she swept the loose ends of her hair into a ponytail.

"Danica sent me a crate of rosé. Sound good?" Jay offered, walking toward the bar.

She fanned herself theatrically. "Please. What would you like, Z?"

Zelda's eyes widened, surprised at something. "Rosé is fine, thanks, Jay."

Ryan watched this scene unfold, sharpening his metaphorical pencil to capture the interpersonal relationships at play. Zelda seemed comfortable with Jay, but less so with Ariel, even though she'd come, presumably, at Ariel's request. Ariel seemed willfully obtuse about Zelda's comfort level, but she was putting on quite the show of insouciance. He had an inkling of what Ariel was up to, and he couldn't decide how he felt about it.

He'd had enough of observing for the moment and sauntered over to where Jay was pouring glasses of wine for the women.

"Can I get another beer?"

"Sure thing." Jay handed him the same again from a metal bucket filled with ice and cans.

"Ryan! Hi!"

Ryan took an involuntary half step backward when Ariel greeted him with a smile. Ariel Tulip's smiles were dazzling on screen. In person, they were incandescent.

"I want you to meet Zelda Won," she said, stepping to the side and presenting the woman with a wave of her hand as if they were at court and he was a nobleman being introduced to an important dignitary.

"Zelda, this is Ryan Saylor."

"Hi, Ryan," she said with a friendly smile. "I think I saw you in my shop the other day."

"Zelda owns the Bakeshop," Ariel clarified. "We're all in love with her amazing creations. During the first run of *Sawyer's Cove*, the only pastries in Misty Harbor were those dry donuts at the gas station."

"Misty Harbor clearly owes you a debt it can never repay," Ryan murmured, bowing slightly. He still felt like he was on display before a queen.

Zelda shrugged. "Feeding Misty Harbor's sugar and

caffeine addictions is a tough job, but someone has to do it."

"So I'm going to run inside for a minute, and you two get to know each other," Ariel said, making a shooing motion with both hands as if to herd them closer. Zelda took an obedient step forward, and Ryan did the same. He was close enough to Zelda now to see the lighter flecks in her dark brown eyes and that she wasn't wearing any makeup on her pretty, fresh face. Ariel seemed satisfied with them and flounced off, her low-heeled sandals clicking confidently on the flagstone patio.

"So," Zelda said, sipping her rosé.

"So," Ryan said, sipping his beer.

Neither said anything for an uncomfortable minute. Ryan ventured into the conversational waters with, "You're a baker. Long hours?"

"Early hours and long hours, both," Zelda said. "It's better now than when I first opened the shop. Now I have a couple of employees who can open the kitchen for me, start the bakes for the day, and I have a good team who can close, so I'm not there fourteen hours a day, seven days a week anymore."

"Jesus, sounds like a shooting schedule," he said sympathetically. "Again, Misty Harbor owes you a great debt."

"I can say the same thing about you. Misty Harbor owes you a lot."

"What? Why?"

She laughed. She had a nice laugh, more of a chuckle, not like Ariel's full-on belly laugh. "Because of the show, of course."

"Oh." Why did everyone want to give him all this

credit when it was Selena and Cami who had brought the show back to life with their hard work and persistence?

"Look, I have to be honest with you, I never watched *Sawyer's Cove*. I was in college when it started, I think. Too busy avoiding class and my parents. Not on my radar at all. Plus, I don't think I saw the appeal. No offense. So when I washed up here, kind of on accident, I had no idea it was part of the town's history. Then Rhonda and Maria started their walking tours, and I figured out why Jay named his bar The Cove, and then I hired Trevor and, well, it was all over. He educated me."

"Trevor Kendrick?"

"He was the best front of the house person I ever had, but he's left me for bigger and better things." She sighed. "And I realized this town had been slowly dying, but the *Sawyer's Cove* fans gave it a jolt of life. Then the revival came along and was a triple shot of espresso to the economy. As a business owner, I thank you."

"I didn't do anything," Ryan protested. He didn't deserve any praise.

She frowned at him. "You created the show, didn't you? None of it would have happened without you."

"I guess."

"Well, anyway. I finally watched a few episodes," she said, smiling now.

"And?"

"Not bad."

He laughed. "Can't ask for more than that."

Her smile grew. "No, it's addictive, actually. Once I started watching, I couldn't stop. I'm kind of bummed this is the last season. I really hope Grace figures things out. She's a sweetie."

Ryan loved what Selena had done with the new characters of Grace, Kai, and Danny. They were on the cusp of adulthood, contemplating their futures as the third season opened. "I'd tell you, but then I'd have to kill you."

Zelda chuckled. "I can't wait." She looked at him thoughtfully. "You know, Ariel's playing matchmaker between the two of us."

Ryan swallowed the beer in his mouth with a cough, the liquid going down with a sharp twinge. He'd tried to convince himself Ariel was joking about the whole thing, but she'd called his bluff by bringing Zelda and thrusting her in his face, almost daring him to mess up the chance to go on his first post-divorce date.

She laughed yet again. "I can see the idea is wild to you. Well. Just wanted to make sure you knew what was going on here. I've never spoken more than three words to the woman, and she came into the shop yesterday on a mission, practically demanding my presence here. She said she wanted to get to know me better—which is nice, but I think she thinks she's some kind of Emma Woodhouse."

"Sorry about that," he said, grimacing.

"So you're not looking?" Zelda asked.

Her directness took him aback. "Well. I wouldn't say that." He let himself consider Zelda as a romantic prospect. She was attractive, successful. She liked *Sawyer's Cove*, but wasn't obsessed with it. And she wasn't an actress.

He steeled himself. His failed marriage was firmly behind him, but he had yet to climb back onto the proverbial horse. He had to do it at some point.

Besides, Ariel would never let him hear the end of it if he biffed this.

"Actually, yeah. I'd love to take you out sometime," he found himself saying, Ariel's voice whispering in his head. "How about..." He ignored the sensible side of him that knew he didn't have time to date when he was essentially married to the show for the next twelve weeks and scanned his brain for his schedule. "Thursday?"

She blinked, as if she hadn't expected him to ask. "Dinner?"

"How about Antonio's?" he said, naming the first restaurant in Misty Harbor he could think of that wasn't the diner.

"I have to open on Friday, so my bedtime is pretty early."

"Early is good. Six?"

"Okay." She smiled. "Sounds fun."

And just like that, Ryan had a date. They exchanged phone numbers, and then Zelda excused herself to partake of the buffet. Nash declared the meat ready and ordered everyone to grab their plates. Ryan staked out a spot at the big table by putting his beer down, then spotted Ariel moving around inside the house through the large kitchen window.

He wanted to share his minor triumph with the woman who'd put him up to it, even if she'd no doubt crow about being the world's best wing-woman or some such nonsense. He didn't mind if she did, as long as she was happy. Somehow, Ariel's happiness meant a lot to him. He didn't dwell on the reason for that as he walked toward the house to seek her out.

Chapter Four

Sawyer's Cove: The Reboot
Episode 302: The Hike

EXT. CLOUDY COVE WOODS - DAY

WILL: Does it feel like all our friends
are heading for the altar? Or the nonde-
nominational venue of choice?
NOAH: Huh?
WILL: Marriage. I'm talking about
marriage. When did everyone wake up and
decide they needed rings?
NOAH: Literally none of our friends are
engaged yet, babe.
WILL: Mark my words. This is the beginning of the end.

Ariel had been trying not to spy on Ryan and Zelda through the window, but the view was so good she'd had a hard time restraining herself. Damn the perfect sight lines of Mimi and Nash's kitchen.

She'd dragged out washing her hands at the sink while Zelda and Ryan talked. For a while, things seemed like they were going nowhere, and Ariel had considered going out and doing damage control, but then they'd pulled out their phones and exchanged numbers. Success.

Then Ryan had looked around and seemed to spot her through the window. She turned around and pretended to be busy selecting an apple from a bowl on the kitchen table, waiting for him to find her.

"Hey, you." He sounded very pleased with himself as he bounded into the kitchen with a boyish energy that made her want to grin.

"Hey, yourself," she said, trying not to tip her hand.

"So Zelda is cool." He shook his head and his hair fluttered as if he were an overgrown golden retriever. "And I asked her out and we're going to dinner on Thursday."

"Oh, wow." Ariel had expected this, had engineered it, even, but the expected flare of pride didn't come. Instead, she felt a nagging sense of—what? Wrongness? She felt itchy, as if she was wearing someone else's clothes. Which made no sense at all. "That's great."

"Thanks for the push," he said, gaze warming. "You're a good friend, Ariel."

"Thanks." The word stuck in her mouth as if affixed there with peanut butter. She swallowed. This was stupid.

This was what she'd signed up for. "Is dinner ready? We better get out there before it's all gone."

"I think there's enough food for the entire block," Ryan said, "but yeah, I'm hungry." He held the door open for her, and they got plates from the edge of the buffet. She watched him maneuver the serving dishes out of the way so he could set his plate down on the edge of the table, then serve himself. He made it look effortless to negotiate a buffet one-handed, but Ariel was struck by how annoying she'd find it to deal with a world designed for two-handed people with only one. She tamped down the urge to volunteer to serve him, feeling somehow the offer wouldn't be welcome. She knew if she were dealing with something similar, she'd be more annoyed if people constantly implied she couldn't do things for herself, even if she actually couldn't. And he was doing fine. Plates piled high, they joined the conversation in progress at the big outdoor dining table.

She found an empty seat next to Nash. Ryan sat between Mimi and Crosby. Zelda was at the other end, near Jay, Cami, and Deb. Henry Yu, another of her castmates, had apparently arrived while she was strategically hiding in the kitchen. He was sitting between Darren and a woman she didn't know, but who she thought was a friend of Mimi's.

"Nash, I need to ask you something."

He raised his eyebrows at her. Since his mouth was full of barbecued chicken, she took that as an invitation to go on. She outlined the plan for the live podcast and asked him if he'd participate.

After swallowing, he asked, "It's a fundraiser? For what?"

"Well, we haven't decided yet. But I was thinking something local to Misty Harbor."

"Mimi and I happen to be working on a collaboration between the library and Rainbow Canyon to open a teen youth center here. A place for kids to hang out after school and on weekends. We'd love an infusion of donations."

"That sounds ideal. So you'll do it?" Ariel pressed.

"I'm in," Nash said. "You know, I thought life would slow down a bit when I moved to Misty Harbor, but it's as busy as ever."

"Wait until you start having kids," Ariel said. Nash's eyes widened, and she realized maybe that wasn't in the cards for them. "I mean, you know, if you guys...never mind," she backtracked.

"Yeah. You're right," he said, with a guarded smile. "Well, send me the info so I can put it in my calendar."

"Thanks, Nash." She glanced over at Ryan, who was shoveling potato salad into his mouth and nodding at something Crosby was saying.

Even if her matchmaking success hadn't left her with the feeling of accomplishment she'd anticipated, she was at least proud of the fact that Ryan seemed to be having a good time at this get-together. Whatever misconceptions he had about the Cove crew, he fit in just as well as any of them.

He caught her gaze over the table, and she was a little flustered to have been caught looking at him. But he only gave her a small smile and went back to his meal.

She shook her head at herself. Why was she such a mess? Literally everyone else at this table had their shit together, even Henry, who was in his early twenties and

had the right to be lost, yet he was in a steady relationship and completing a master's degree in teaching, since
he'd decided he didn't want to keep acting after *Sawyer's
Cove* was over. She was almost thirty-four and still felt
like an emotional, clueless teenager half the time.

Maybe it was a good thing she had no chance of
finding her soulmate anytime soon. She wasn't prepared
for that kind of life-changing experience. She needed
direction. Tomorrow, she'd sort through the scripts from
her agent to see if there was anything that sparked her
joy. And in the meantime, she'd be happy to spend time
with people she loved, people who would soon be more a
part of her past than her future.

Chapter Five

```
Sawyer's Cove: The Reboot
Episode 302: The Hike

EXT. CLOUDY COVE WOODS - DAY

AMY: How late does someone have to be to
take a pregnancy test?
LILY: Holy shit.
AMY: Theoretically.
LILY: Theoretically my ass. Let's get off
this mountain and go to a drugstore
right now.
```

"I'm so glad we're finally doing this—I've been meaning to find time for us to talk," Cami said as she dropped into the chair across the table from Ariel a few days after Nash's barbecue. They'd decided to escape the heat and the hammering as sets were being built on

the soundstage by meeting for lunch at the upscale
restaurant on the harbor.

"It's been so busy with Selena on the other coast right
now," Cami added. "She turned over a lot of the show
admin to me, and it's been good for me to step up, but I'm
also worried I'm going to forget something major."

"You're killing it," Ariel said. "Besides, isn't Ryan
supposed to be in charge?"

"He's handling most of the creative decisions, but he's
a little rusty when it comes to overseeing production. But,
yeah, so far, we're making a good team." A server came to
take their order, and Cami waited until he left before
asking, "So, what's up with you? You're happy with the
script, I hope."

"Oh, the first episode is stellar. I'm already getting sad
thinking about filming the last episode, though." The
table read on Monday had put her through the wringer.
Every time they did something for the last first time, she
wanted to take a mental snapshot and burn the moment
into her memory for posterity, but it was emotionally
exhausting.

"I know what you mean. Another end of an era,"
Cami said. "But we can't hold everyone's careers hostage
indefinitely. I know Crosby wants to get back to theater,
and Selena has *Gunsmoke*, and Nash might do a tour with
his band. What about you?"

"Me?" That was the question, wasn't it? She thought
about giving some bullshit actor-y answer about waiting
for the next right project to come along. But she'd known
Cami a long time. They were the same age, and they'd
come up at the same time. They'd never been in competi-
tion because they were two different types—Cami was

the petite, blonde, blue-eyed girl next door, while Ariel was the buxom, statuesque redhead. Ariel had been relieved when she learned the only other girl in the original *Sawyer's Cove* cast was as genuinely nice as Cami. She'd met her share of showbiz bitches, but she and Cami had become instant friends instead of enemies.

So she decided to go with the truth. "I honestly have no idea. I haven't been getting anything decent from my agent. You all have your careers going in interesting directions and I feel...lost." She'd spent hours the previous weekend poring through scripts, the best of which was for an uninspired procedural in which she'd play a jaded coroner who would no doubt be dressed in improbably low-cut tops under her lab coat.

"Oh, honey. I had no idea. What kind of part are you looking for?"

"That's the thing—I need a new direction and I don't know what it is. I feel too young for the mom parts and too old for the sexpots. Maybe I need to take a break until I age into cougar roles."

Cami laughed. "If you want. You'd be amazing at anything; you know that, right?"

"I know," she said. She had never lacked self-confidence in her acting ability. It was real life where she had lost the plot. "I'm adrift right now. But it's temporary. I have Lily to focus on for the next few months, and I intend to leave everything on the table at the end of this season. She will go out with a bang—no matter what you clever people decide that bang is." She was as in the dark about how the show would wrap up everyone's storylines as the next fangirl.

"I have a few inklings," Cami said mysteriously. "But I

better wait until I confirm with Ryan."

"And in the meantime, I do have a side project. I'm putting together a live podcast taping as a fundraiser, and so far your boyfriend, Crosby, Darren, and Nash are in. I hope you'll agree to join us, too."

"Jay mentioned it. Sounds fun, but when would this epic event take place?"

"Right after shooting ends, but before everyone scatters to the wind. One last hurrah. At least until the next fan convention."

"That should be fine," Cami said. "I'll do it. I just have to watch the calendar because I have some news."

"Oh?" Ariel smelled gossip and leaned over the table. "News you can share?"

"Yeah, actually." She smiled. Ariel instantly recognized the type of smile. She knew what Cami was going to say before she said it, and her stomach dipped in anticipation. "I'm pregnant."

"Oh, sweetie, honey, I'm so happy for you." Ariel didn't even try to stop the tears gathering in the corners of her eyes. Cami knew she cried at everything; it wasn't a secret. She laughed and wiped her eyes, and stood up to give Cami a huge hug. "Jay must be over the moon."

"He's pretty stoked," Cami said, her eyes sparkling. "We waited until twelve weeks; we literally just started telling people like two days ago. His mom is beyond excited. But I haven't told anyone else at the show yet. I'm seeing Ryan this afternoon—hopefully it's not going to be an issue."

"He'll be thrilled for you, but yeah, does this make a

difference to Amy's storyline? Or is she going to get knocked up, too?" Their food was delivered, but she was too excited to eat the seared tuna bowl she'd ordered.

"I don't know. I doubt it'll have an impact. They might have to rearrange some of my shooting schedule. I already feel like a balloon, even though I know I'm not even showing. I didn't exactly mean for the timing to work out this way. We thought it might take longer to get pregnant and surprise! First try." Cami's cheeks were scarlet with exultation.

"Of course. You and Jay are like two baby-making hormones on legs. I'm not surprised. So you're due in—" Ariel did the math in her head. "March?"

"March 9, the doctor says." They spent the rest of lunch talking about pregnancy-related topics. Ariel had been through the drill once with her sister, who had a two-year-old, and her friend Kate Treanor, whose son Maverick was in preschool, so she knew her way around baby talk.

Later, as they gathered their things so Cami could get to her meeting with Ryan, Ariel hugged her tight.

"We're getting a baby in the family. I'm so happy for you and Jay."

"Thanks. I'm so glad you're pleased," Cami said sincerely. "You know, just a thought, but you have experience and expertise in this business besides acting. Producing is really satisfying. You should think about it. No one cares what I look like, which is refreshing. I may never go back in front of the camera, but my career is far from over."

Ariel considered what Cami was saying. She was

happy her friend had found a second act to her career in entertainment, but she wasn't sure the same path would work for her. "Producing is awesome for you. But I'm not ready to give up on acting, I'm just a little stuck."

"Let me know if you need any help getting unstuck," Cami said. "You're like a sister to me, you know."

The happy tears came back. "You can't say things like that and not expect me to start watering up again," Ariel said, "and you're like a sister to me, too."

Cami left to go back to work, and Ariel wanted to be heading somewhere important, too. Instead, she went to her apartment, cranked the AC to its highest setting, and looked at her to-do list. She texted Kate, who called her back instantly, thrilled she had gotten all five of the original *Cove* actors to agree to the podcast. They made some plans, and Kate left her with a few more to-do list items, like liaising with the library and Rainbow Canyon on the best way to position the fundraising portion of the event and double checking their date with the Misty Harbor Inn. Once they had a few other items in place, they could put tickets on sale.

The entire time she worked, she wondered what the hell she was doing with her life. She was happy, honestly. But she hadn't felt this alone since the very first season of *Sawyer's Cove*, an emancipated sixteen-year-old living by herself in this exact same apartment.

The cast hadn't really jelled until partway through the first season. Eventually it had felt like one long slumber party between shooting, halfhearted work toward her GED, on- and off-set drama, press, trying to squeeze a movie shoot into the short summer hiatuses. But initially it was scary to live in a strange small town where every-thing closed at six except for Melba's. Her family had supported her desire to work, but they'd essentially parked her in Misty Harbor and gone home.

She'd managed. But it was still lonely.

And here she was again, seventeen years later, alone in this apartment while everyone around her was cozied up in perfect twosomes, procreating and producing and finding their second acts.

Ariel was desperate for a second act, not because her first act was a failure, but because she didn't want to stand in place, or worse, go backwards. She wanted to grow, she wanted to change. She wanted *more*.

She also wanted dinner. After barely touching her lunch, she was starving. She grabbed her purse and trotted downstairs. She'd go to Melba's, get the veggie melt she'd bugged them to put on the menu, and read her book. She'd live her best life, dammit, even if she was living it alone.

Ryan was about to go on his first first date in a decade.

He and Zelda had made plans to meet at the Misty Harbor Bakeshop five minutes before six to walk over to Antonio's together. He'd arrived with a couple of minutes to spare, so he paced outside, waiting for Zelda to emerge and wondering if he should have brought her flowers, or if that was too over the top for what was essentially a test balloon of an experience.

He hadn't had time to get flowers, anyway, after Cami

had pushed his first-date jitters right out of his head by announcing she was pregnant. After he heartily congratulated her, they'd spent two hours rearranging the shooting schedule to accommodate her doctor's appointments and other considerations. Then when he'd looked at the clock, he only had half an hour to get from the set to the Bakeshop.

He'd wanted to go back to Selena and Warner's house and clean up, but that would have added time he didn't have, so he'd settled for finger brushing his long hair and splashing some water on his face to perk him up. He stared in the mirror and saw a forty-two-year-old man, beginning to gray, more lines on his forehead and at the creases of his eyes than the last time he'd taken inventory. It didn't help his slide toward middle age that he dressed like a college professor, but he'd leaned into the professorial look a long time ago. He could still see the pity mixed with concern on his mother's face when he'd asked her to buy him a blazer. He'd been twelve. Still, she'd gotten it for him, and she'd altered the left sleeve to shorten it and sew it shut, which made it easier to get on and off.

He always had his blazers and jackets altered that way now, and that was how he always dressed. It made it easier to get ready when you knew what you'd be wearing and all your clothes matched. He didn't care about being fashionable, anyway. His hair was really his one vanity. Long hair was almost ludicrously impractical for a one-armed man, but he thought it suited the sharp bones of his face better than short.

There was still no sign of Zelda when his gaze snagged on a familiar face through the window of Melba's Diner across the street. Ariel Tulip's unmistakable red head drew his eye as she sat at the counter. She was wearing a simple light green sundress, and her strong tanned arms stood out against the stark white countertop. She was reading a book. She looked like a fifties pinup for nerds—lush curves, feminine softness, copious amounts of silky hair spilling over bare shoulders, stunning gray eyes focused on a fat hardcover novel.

The picture she made unexpectedly moved him. He'd seen millions of hours of Ariel on film as Lily Fine, but he realized he was looking at someone different, not a character personified. He was looking at a woman he didn't really know at all, a woman who looked oddly—alone.

A woman as beautiful as Ariel Tulip shouldn't be eating alone in a diner with only a book for company. Why wasn't she surrounded by an entourage of acolytes? Didn't she at least have an assistant or something?

Her words from their first meeting in the diner returned to him unbidden. She'd called herself a "poor unattached female," and "pathetically alone." She'd been joking, he'd assumed at the time. Hadn't she?

He was surprised to find he'd taken ten steps toward the diner when he heard his name called from behind him. He turned, and Zelda was in the Bakeshop doorway, smiling at him uncertainly. Her hair was down, unexpectedly long, past her shoulders, and she wore a fashionable jean jacket over a plain white tank top that hugged her body, a dark denim skirt, and sandals. She looked great, and he tried to put his confusing thoughts in order and do the thing he'd come here to do—go on a date with a woman who was not his ex-wife. Who was not Ariel Tulip, either.

"Zelda, hi!" He pivoted and walked back toward her, giving her an uptight little wave.

"Ready to go?" Zelda asked, sounding in need of reassurance herself.

He hesitated for only half a beat, then nodded and fell into step beside her as they walked the scant two blocks to the restaurant.

Chapter Six

Sawyer's Cove: The Reboot
Episode 302: The Hike

INT. LILY'S LIVING ROOM - NIGHT

AMY: I don't think I'm going to need that
pregnancy test after all. I just got my
period.
LILY: Well, that was anticlimactic.
AMY: Yeah. I could have milked it for
more drama, I suppose. But that's not
really my style.

The veggie melt helped. And the milkshake. And the fact that Warner's book sucked her in and wouldn't let her go. Ariel was shocked when she looked up and two hours had passed since she had sat down at Melba's for her solo dinner. She left cash on the counter, slipped the book into her bag, and decided to go for a walk. The August air was still warm, but the humidity had dropped now the sun was on the decline.

She headed to the beach. It was strange—the whole New England coastal aesthetic was a big part of the show's appeal, but she rarely made time to go to the actual waterfront. Tonight, the darkening harbor called to her, and she breathed in the clean salt air, the breeze causing her to dig into her bag for a hair tie. She spied a couple on the boardwalk holding hands as they walked, and she felt like the cliché from a rom com where the lonely girl is faced with evidence of happy couples all around her. But this wasn't a movie, this wasn't even an episode of *Sawyer's Cove*. This was her life.

It wasn't so bad. She'd had a pleasant evening. She liked her own company. But she still couldn't deny the cramp of loneliness that had lodged itself somewhere near her sternum. She rubbed at her chest, wishing there was something she could do about this feeling. Ariel was a woman of action. She'd never gotten anywhere by doing nothing but throw a pity party for one.

She could go home and sign up for a dating app. She could get Cami to introduce her to the first eligible guy she thought of.

But she didn't want to date. She wanted romance.

She'd been spoiled by playing a woman who men would move heaven and earth for. Even Sawyer North, fuckboy to end all fuckboys, had finally realized what a goddess Lily Fine was and had changed his entire life to keep her. There were damn wedding bells in Lily and Sawyer's future, she knew it. It would be ironic if Lily ended the run of the show knocked up with Sawyer's baby and his ring on her finger and Ariel ended the run as single as when she started.

Even Ryan, who had more reason to be morose than she did, given his divorce, was putting himself out there. Thanks to her. Wasn't tonight his big date with Zelda?

Suddenly, the knot in her chest turned from angst to anger. Yeah, she'd helped Ryan get a date with a super cool person while she ate at the diner alone. Ryan, who had put all these childish notions of romance and soulmates and happily ever afters into her head in the first place with his brilliant writing and emotionally fearless storytelling.

She stalked back up the main drag toward her apartment. She had half a mind to call him and demand restitution for all of the heartache he'd caused her by writing such a dynamic, fun character to play, next to whom every script she was sent seemed boring and stale. It felt better to blame him—it was something to do, at least, instead of gazing into the ocean and feeling sorry for herself.

When she got within a block of her apartment, she'd apparently conjured up the man himself out of her anger, because there he was, walking down the street. He must have just come from dinner, but there was no sign of Zelda.

"Hey, you," he said, smiling at her.

His good mood only provoked her further—the date had obviously gone well. She marched into his personal space and made a face. "I have a bone to pick with you, Ryan Saylor."

His eyebrows quirked. "Oh?"

"Yes. How did your date go?"

"Does that relate to the bone picking?"

"Don't be cute. Seriously, I am going through some very major trauma right now and it's all your fault for being a gorgeous wordsmith who's ruined me for all other parts."

He faltered. "I'm...sorry?"

She stepped closer to him, and he took an involuntary step back. "You should be!"

"Hey, it's clear we should talk, but maybe not out here," he said, looking around.

She'd forgotten they were on the street, in *Sawyer's Cove* country. Even if it didn't feel like anyone was paying them any attention, a fan could literally come around the corner at any minute on one of those *Cove*-themed sightseeing tours. It had happened to her before.

"Let's go to my place," she said, brushing past him. She knew he would follow her. Men tended to do what she told them. The problem was, she didn't want to tell a man to stay with her. She wanted him to want to stay with her. And she hadn't yet been with a man who wasn't ultimately overwhelmed by her, either her fame, or her schedule, or herself. Just her. She tended to overwhelm people, even her friends.

She held the downstairs door open for Ryan, then climbed the stairs to her apartment and unlocked the door. Once inside the tidy space, she threw down her bag, trying to hold on to her righteousness, but losing in the face of reality. She scrubbed a hand over her face, feeling tired, and silly for bringing her boss into her own personal issues, and yet still relieved she wasn't alone.

"So, what's on your mind, Ariel?" His voice was concerned, and she couldn't blame him for being worried. She was being that stereotypical actress, more emotion than brains, all ego, no superego.

"I'm just going through some stuff, I guess. And for some reason, it all made sense in my head to blame you." She injected melodrama into her delivery to make sure he knew she wasn't entirely serious.

"How so?" He sounded confused.

"Do you know how hard it is to take lame mom parts and the dumb mob girlfriend after playing Lily Fine? She's a dynamic, three-dimensional, fucking awesome-with-a-capital-A character. That's all I meant by you ruining me," she explained.

"Ah." He looked less confused, but no less worried about her mental state.

"And I really hope you and Zelda hit it off and fall in love and have lots of babies, if that's something you want, but it's hard to be the only one who's..."

It was too humiliating to say the word *alone*, but Ryan seemed to understand without her having to say it. He was intuitive like that.

"I saw you eating at Melba's." He didn't have to say he'd seen her sitting by herself at the counter with a book for her date.

"Oh. So you know how tragic I am."

"It was a rather incongruous picture," he said.

What did that mean?

"Cami told you she's pregnant, right?" She realized too late the change in subject was telling.

He nodded, smiling slightly. "She's so excited. I'm really happy for them."

"It's not going to be too much of an issue for filming?"

Ariel didn't actually care about that. The production would figure it out.

"No, we'll be fine," he confirmed. "Is that what this is about?" he asked tentatively.

"No! Jesus, I'm as happy as anyone for them. They'll make great parents, for one thing. And it completes the whole small-town-life package, doesn't it? My personal meltdowns don't have anything to do with that." But as the words came out, she wasn't so sure she wasn't lying—to herself, if nothing else.

"They will make quite the Misty Harbor first family," Ryan said. "Now all they need is a golden retriever and a station wagon."

"Ha. Watch Jay strap a car seat in the back of his Defender. Though Cami might have to get a bigger car than her Fiat."

"So we're both happy for them," Ryan said, "but that doesn't mean we can't also be a little jealous."

She fluttered her hands. "You're jealous?"

He shrugged his jacket-clad shoulders, and she suddenly realized how warm it was in the apartment. She flipped the air on, shook her hair out of her ponytail and wound it into a messy bun to get it off her neck.

"Sure, a little," he said. "Jay and Cami have been through a lot, from what I gather. They're really good together. Anyone with a heart not made of stone would want some of what they have for themselves. If I believed in soulmates, they'd be Exhibit A."

"There—" she jabbed a sharp finger in his direction. "That word."

"What word?"

"Soulmates. You can't keep bringing it up if you insist they don't exist. What the fuck is that about?"

"It's a fairly common concept, if an overdone one."

"But it's messing me up, Ryan," she wailed. "It's probably messed up countless teenage girls, thinking they aren't doing something right if they don't find that all-consuming, perfect fit, soulmate kind of love. I waited, Ryan, I waited and now I'm thirty-fucking-three and I'd settle for someone who can tolerate me enough so I don't have to eat veggie melts alone."

He blinked. "You're not looking for your soulmate anymore?"

Chapter Seven

Sawyer's Cove: The Reboot
Episode 302: The Hike

EXT. CLOUDY COVE WOODS - DAY

KAI: Dude, have you seen the new librarian? She is unbelievably smoking.
DANNY: Smoking in the library? Sounds like a fire hazard to me.
WILL: I think Kai means she's hot, Danny-boy.

"I used to think the reason I kept striking out was because I hadn't met the right guy. But now I think maybe I'm using the wrong rubric entirely. A rubric I formed on the basis of your stupid ideas." She rubbed her bare arms as if the air conditioning was making her cold. "And then I see Jay and Cami, Nash and Mimi. Crosby and Darren, too. They all found each other, and I can't help but feel like it's just me, that I'm the defective one in the bunch, the one who didn't get the magic soulmate dust sprinkled on me."

Ryan shook his head. "There's no magic soulmate dust. There's nothing wrong with you, Ariel." As he looked at her, his defensiveness at being held accountable for spreading the apparently toxic notion of soulmates gave way to awe. Ariel was a vision of righteous anger, ruby cheeks clashing provocatively with her striking auburn hair. Her flimsy dress didn't provide much armor, but her pose, hands balled into fists and posture slanted forward as if about to launch into battle, made her look like Athena, down to her flashing gray eyes.

"Except I'm too much. I'm emotional and—horror of horrors—*an actress*."

He winced at the obvious reference to his ill-advised gaffe that day in the diner. "Look, that's not personal."

"Sorry, but it felt personal to me. Being an actress and all. Look, I get it. Actresses are crazy people, right? Well, I love being an actress, and you created this incredible character, and I wish I could get you to write the script for my life because some days I feel like I'm doing a shitty job of it myself."

Suddenly, all the fight seemed to go out of her. She blinked, and he realized she was trying not to cry. He's seen her cry countless times, on and off camera. She was a crier. The sight tugged at strings in his chest that hadn't been pulled in a long time.

"Hey." He crossed over to her, put his arm tentatively around her. He wasn't the most physical guy. He tended to give people a wide berth, not welcoming casual touching himself, but if anyone looked like she needed a hug, it was Ariel Tulip at that moment.

She collapsed against his side, wrapping her arms around his waist and snuffling into the lapel of his jacket. He rubbed her back, the material of her linen dress not nearly as soft as the warm silk of her exposed skin. He hadn't touched another person, except perfunctorily, in so long. It felt so good, and it made him realize he was ready for his self-imposed sequester to end.

"There's no script for life," he murmured. "Do you think I would have written a cold marriage and a messy divorce for myself? Would I have wanted to keep Jay and Cami apart for all those years? If I could, I'd write you the happiest, most sickeningly sweet ever after with your six-foot-two underwear model/doctor soulmate and a brood of babies."

Ariel laughed wetly. The sound tugged at different strings in his chest. "I'd settle for one or two, not a brood."

"Noted. But I'm not God. I'm just a writer. I only have control over the world of *Sawyer's Cove*. Which isn't real, sadly. But I understand where you're coming from. When I wrote the pilot, I viewed my fantasy life as a huge upgrade from my real life—dirt poor, hating my job writing jokes for a game show, at which I was terrible, living with wannabe actor roommates who spent more time partying than going out for auditions. No girlfriend. Definitely no soulmate. I created *Sawyer's Cove* because it was a world I wanted to exist. A world I wanted to be a part of, to live in, where beautiful people had first world problems and where the geek got the girl. Of course, it didn't exactly work out that way. Sawyer didn't get Amy."

"No, he got Lily, twelve years later," she said, tipping

her head up.

"That's right." He looked down at her, transcendently beautiful. "Lucky bastard."

She smiled, and he felt shaken, as if he were the only one who felt a 5.0 earthquake. He had an amazing person nestled against him, beautiful and aching for connection, just as he had been all those years ago. Maybe he was still aching for it, had let Heather and work subsume him, to try to make him forget he was looking for the same thing Ariel was—maybe soulmate was too strong of a word, but someone who understood him, who loved him despite his flaws, who was attracted to him despite his unconventional body.

As Ariel looked up at him with her luminous gray eyes, he had the strongest urge to kiss her.

Which would have been disastrous. She was looking for someone, but not someone like him. In real life, the geek didn't get Lily Fine. And they indisputably didn't get Ariel Tulip.

Still, it almost looked, the way she parted her lips and gazed at him, almost as if she expected—almost as if she wanted—

Carefully, he set her away from him, putting precious inches of space between them. Her mouth closed, and he straightened up, looking away. The moment was broken, but the disconcerting desire to kiss her was still there.

She looked slightly dazed herself, and she licked her lips, almost as if they had kissed. But they hadn't.

They never would.

Still, her words of scorn and despair—*I'm an actress*—pinballed in his mind.

"You know what? I'm an idiot. I played by the rules my

whole life and you're right—I still got run off the board. It was completely unprofessional of me to allow you to get involved in my personal life."

"But aren't you glad I did? Zelda's awesome, and you have a shot with her, right?"

Yes. Zelda. The woman he'd gone on a perfectly nice date with earlier in the evening was the woman he should be thinking about kissing, not this tempestuous, tempting person who was both his employee and, barely, his friend.

"Zelda and I had a good time," he said cautiously. "But my private life isn't your problem. I appreciate you making me feel welcome. You've done a great job. But you've done enough."

"Right. Okay. Fine." She stiffened.

Dammit. He'd offended her again, without meaning to.

"Look, Ariel, I get that you want us all to be a big, happy family, but I'm here to work."

"And also have a life," she added.

"Same thing."

"Weren't you saying *Sawyer's Cove* isn't real life?"

"It is to me, I guess, in a way. It's always felt very real."

"Yeah," she said glumly, as if she didn't want to agree with him. "Unfortunately, sometimes real life seems to pale in comparison."

He would have agreed with her on any other day, but at the moment he found himself glad he was plain old Ryan, here with Ariel. Someone he shouldn't want but couldn't help find indescribably appealing.

"Life feels pretty vivid right now."

"Oh?"

"You're like Technicolor, Ariel," he said. "You're pure unadulterated life. You say emotional like it's a bad thing. It's not. You're so very alive. Why would I want fiction when you're here and you're real?"

She beamed at that. "Are you just spinning pretty words again? Because if you mean that, it's the nicest thing anyone's ever said about me."

"It's true," he said simply.

"Thanks, Ryan."

"If you've been waiting for the right guy, then don't give up now. Besides, Misty Harbor isn't exactly flush with eligible bachelors."

She laughed at that. "Manhattan would have better odds, you'd think, but I keep striking out there, too."

"I can't imagine why," he said, flabbergasted at the men of New York and the population in general for letting Ariel Tulip stay single. "You're..." He trailed off as she looked at him expectantly. Every word that came to mind to finish that sentence seemed too revealing. He was suddenly embarrassed by his train of thought.

But the longer he went without saying anything, the dimmer her smile grew.

"Yeah, I know," she said, sighing. "It's okay. I'm not mad at you anymore. You don't have to stroke my ego. I know it's not really your fault that I believe in soulmates, and that I thought I'd find mine by now. I guess I'm partly still the silly girl who first came in to audition, thinking she should be cast as Amy Green and ended up playing Lily Fine."

He remembered it, distantly. She had read for Amy Green, the traditional fresh-faced girl next door, but even then, Ryan had known that would never be Ariel Tulip.

She'd brought a swagger and a playfulness to her read that had him immediately crossing her off as a possible Amy and signing her immediately up for Lily.

"You rocked that audition, but you weren't meant to play Amy."

"You remember?"

"I do. I remember thinking you blew away every other girl we saw that day. You always bring your A game. That's never changed."

"Thanks." She put a hand on her hip and cocked it. "I am a professional."

"I know you are."

She smiled again, small, but it was there, and he felt like he'd done his job.

"Well, now that we've analyzed each other to death, I should let you get home. No doubt you have a busy day tomorrow."

"I do." Yet he found himself reluctant to go back to the comically large and empty house on the other side of town. He wanted to stay in this cozy nest of an apartment and continue analyzing Ariel into the wee hours.

But that would have been dangerous in more ways than one. So he gathered his scattered thoughts and offered her one more word. "I'll tell you a secret. I think timing has a lot to do with all of this love and soulmate nonsense. Your time will come, I'm sure of it."

"I want to believe you," she said solemnly.

He grinned. She was quoting one of the signature lines from the series. "Touché."

"See you around, Ryan."

"See you around, Ariel."

That night, he dreamed of gray eyes and auburn hair.

Chapter Eight

Sawyer's Cove: The Reboot
Episode 304: The Borrowed Tiara

EXT. CLOUDY COVE HIGH GYMNASIUM - NIGHT
The school is decorated for Winter
Formal.

LILY: We didn't go to any school dances
together. I don't think we even ever
danced together.
SAWYER: Will you dance with me, Lily
Fine?

First days never went smoothly, even when you had a pro like David Blakely at the helm. Ryan wanted to tear his hair out by lunchtime—the morning had gone so slowly, they were already two hours behind. It wasn't technically his problem yet, because the director and the first AD could work it out and make the time up some-where else, but he couldn't help being stressed.

This afternoon was a less complicated two-hander with Lily and Sawyer, so he had hopes that would be bump-free.

He hadn't seen Ariel since the night in her apartment nearly a week ago. The night she'd railed at him and cried, and he'd somehow found himself cradling her and wanting to kiss her.

Something had happened to him that night, and he didn't quite know what it was. He'd been distracted ever since in a low-level way, as if his subconscious was perpetually wondering if he'd forgotten to turn off Warner and Selena's expensive coffee maker.

He'd turned it over in his thoughts when he wasn't focused on work and finally chalked it up to a normal reaction to a beautiful woman tucked under his arm. He had simply temporarily fallen under Ariel's spell.

But that didn't explain why he was still thinking about her days later, or why he'd texted Zelda to say thanks for dinner but hadn't asked her out again. He'd made a point to stop by the Bakeshop a day later to tell her in person that he thought they were better as friends, and she'd agreed with comical alacrity. The relief he felt only reinforced that he should focus on work, not dating, right now.

He was talking to David and making audio notes on his phone as Ariel walked onto set in full Lily Fine regalia—knee-high leather boots (faux, at Ariel's request), tight denim skirt that ended mid-thigh, a green corset-like top with frills and flounces that showed her breasts off to perfection. Her hair was brushed straight down her back, a waterfall of color. It shifted with her movements, glimmering under the set lights as if she was about to shoot a shampoo commercial. Her lips were painted berry red, and she was smiling wickedly at something Crosby, outfitted in Sawyer's jeans and a flannel over a white T-shirt, had just said.

Heat flared in Ryan's chest so fast he almost choked on it. He'd been around beautiful people his entire professional life. He'd had a few crushes, taken inspiration from a few of the encounters for scripts and storylines. But he'd never felt like this before—acutely aware of someone, even when they were out of his line of sight, while knowing all of the reasons he shouldn't be feeling this way.

He was delusional if he thought having a crush on Ariel would end well. He needed to get his shit together. There was no room on this set for inappropriate feelings. Not only was he ostensibly her boss, but there were nine years between them. He was practically ancient next to Ariel. He could understand being attracted to her—she was objectively gorgeous, after all. But he couldn't have *feelings* for her. That was ridiculous. Unprofessional. Inconvenient.

And undeniable.

"Ryan?"

"Huh?"

David gave him a funny look. "Everything okay? We're going to move on."

"Yeah. Of course. Sorry. Carry on." He moved to the rear of the stage. He had about five million things to do in his office, but he wanted to watch a couple of takes.

Maybe if he saw Ariel in work mode, he would remember the reason he'd had the no actresses rule for half his life.

He had arrived in Los Angeles twenty years ago with nothing but a month's rent, a stack of cringe-worthy spec scripts, and the phone number of a television writer who was the uncle of one of his college friends. Harry had been gracious, meeting with Ryan, and eventually even getting him his first job in a writer's room. And the first thing out of his mouth at their initial meeting over lunch at Canter's Deli was, "Never date an actress, kid. They're always more trouble than they're worth."

The trouble an actress might create seemed tantalizingly vague to Ryan, but as he gained more experience in the industry, he realized Harry's advice was moot— actresses weren't interested in a one-armed aspiring writer, anyway. When he finally had his own show, it was mostly populated by teenagers, so dating wasn't a consideration. On projects after *Sawyer's Cove*, "no actresses" was a sensible mantra—he had no desire to complicate real life by mixing work and pleasure. Soapy twists and turns were better on the screen.

However, his long-standing rule wasn't having any effect on his current insistent desire to kiss Ariel Tulip, known actress.

As the crew moved around doing their jobs efficiently and professionally, he watched Crosby and Ariel turn into Spencer and Lily the second David called, "Roll tape." Ariel was speaking a line he'd written only a couple of days ago to tighten up the scene. Lily and Sawyer, after years of will-they-won't-they, finally got together over a season ago. They had a few ups and downs, but this was the point-of-no-return moment.

They would either stay together, or they'd break up, and they knew it. She had an opportunity to move out of Cloudy Cove, to teach in London on an exchange program, and she needed to know if he wants her to stay or go.

"Going to London would be running away," Ariel-as-Lily said, voice thick with longing. "Don't let me run. Don't make me start over for the dozenth time in my life. Let me have you, let me have our life here in Cloudy Cove."

"How can I be what you really want?" Crosby-as-Sawyer asked, oblivious to the end.

"Because you're a lucky bastard," Lily said, with her trademark sass.

Sawyer's slow smile was all the answer Lily needed. She threw her arms around him, shrieking with happiness.

Ryan smiled, too, because the scene was a home run, and he was proud of all of them. He was starting to think he wasn't going to make a hash of this season, after all. Ariel was radiant; she shouldn't be relegated to those second-banana roles she'd told him her agent had been sending her. She was a star.

Someone should write her a part—the knockout role she deserved. As he slipped away from the soundstage to his office, he realized he could do it. Maybe he was confusing personal feelings for professional inspiration. Perhaps Ariel was simply awakening his dormant muse.

It had been a long time since he'd been excited about a new project. He and his ex-wife Heather had copro-duced his follow-up to *Sawyer's Cove*, a minor hit about twenty-somethings trying to make it in Hollywood. It ran for five seasons, but when it ended, it had been apparent his marriage was ending, too.

He'd picked the sensible choice in Heather—another writer, someone who made sense for his career, someone who was so bored with him by the end of their marriage that she barely noticed when he came into a room. They had never had great sparks between them, anyway. The sex had been perfunctory and serviceable. It had taken some time in therapy to realize Heather hadn't actually been all that attracted to him. She'd loved him, but not in an all-consuming way. He hadn't loved her that way either, to be honest. Being with her had been easy and safe and had helped him grow up. But eventually it wasn't enough for either of them.

He'd been in a bit of a creative drought ever since, picking up a few script doctoring gigs here and there, renting an overpriced apartment in Century City since Heather had ended up with their house—not to mention their business and most of their friends—in the divorce. His agent had encouraged him to write another teen soap —à la *Sawyer's Cove*—but then Selena had called and offered him a chance to helm the real thing one last time.

They'd met for lunch in Atwater Village, and she'd pitched him on taking over. "Cami can't do everything between acting and producing," she'd said. "We need you, Ryan. Please."

He'd looked into her big brown eyes framed by round glasses and melted. The idea of returning to *Sawyer's Cove* gave him a sickening feeling in his gut, but he decided to interpret the nausea as excitement rather than fear. He'd accepted the offer on the spot.

He'd told himself he was doing it for Selena, for the

actors and crew that had worked so hard to revive the show and make it a hit for a second time. But he was really doing it for himself. To see if he could still do it, to see if he could add something to the special cocktail of love and drama that was the show.

Now it was happening, and he was starting to see the months of preparation paying off. But the nauseous feeling hadn't gone away. Because in a few months, this chapter would be over, and he'd be facing life after *Sawyer's Cove*. Again.

At least he finally seemed to be getting his groove back, thanks to Selena's gift of trusting him with her baby, thanks to Ariel's attempts to bring him into the fold, and thanks to the community his pilot script had spawned over two decades.

He was the lucky bastard, and he knew it.

In his office, he opened a new document and started typing. An idea coagulated out of a swirl of emotions and images: a female-driven drama, the main character an actress, in the mold of the old Hollywood greats. Ariel could certainly have gone toe-to-toe with Stanwyck and Hepburn back in the day. He'd been on a Hollywood history kick lately, and he could see it now—an old-school-style star unable to function in the ordinary world she grew up in. He decided to name her Franny. Her character would be a fish out of water, back in her small hometown, trying to make a new life for herself out of the public eye. There'd be family drama and a love interest or two. He'd learned from his years in the industry you didn't have to have everything planned out as long as you started with a rich group of characters and a compelling setting. The characters would eventually tell him what the story should be.

While his main focus was on *Sawyer's Cove*, it felt good to have this new script in his back pocket, another distraction from the whole crush on Ariel thing. The next few weeks went by quickly, as filming the first three episodes of the show consumed nearly all of his waking hours, leaving a few minutes at the end of each day to decompress and add to his notes about this new show idea.

By the time he'd written a messy first draft of this new pilot, which he was tentatively calling *Lost Stars,* he'd convinced himself he didn't actually want to kiss Ariel Tulip. He just wanted to work with her. That made sense.

There. He'd solved it.

And if he still dreamed about red hair and gray eyes, and woke up with throbbing morning wood, well, he was a professional. He'd never let that get in the way of their working relationship. He had his no actresses rule for a reason.

Chapter Nine

Sawyer's Cove: The Reboot
Episode 304: The Borrowed Tiara

INT. CLOUDY COVE HIGH GYMNASIUM - NIGHT
Gym is decorated for Winter Formal.

LILY: It's a good thing we never really
went for it in high school.
SAWYER: Why?
LILY: High school romances never
work out.
SAWYER: What about Amy and Parker?
LILY: I love 'em, but those two are
freaks.
SAWYER: Does that make us normies?
LILY: Babe, I don't think we're even on
the scale.

Ariel really wanted a scone. The Misty Harbor Bakeshop was the logical place to get one. They sold traditional English-style scones, more like sweet biscuits than the oversized fruit-studded American ones, and served them with clotted cream and Zelda's homemade three-berry jam. Her mouth watered just thinking about them.

Unfortunately, getting a Bakeshop scone meant going into the Bakeshop. And she was strangely reluctant to cross paths with Zelda.

She had no idea if Zelda and Ryan had continued seeing each other after their dinner date weeks ago, but either way, she was self-conscious about having inserted herself into their love lives. At first, it had seemed like a harmless lark, but lately she'd been extra sensitive about her changing dynamic with Ryan. He was literally running the show on the *Sawyer's Cove* production, but it was different this time around.

She'd always been so much in awe of him, this mysterious older man who seemed to have all the answers to the secrets of the universe bound up in his laptop, who poured his massive heart onto the page in dialogue she'd never found the equal to in the years since. Spending time with him this fall, working with him as a peer without the haze of childhood innocence and hero worship—well, it could have gone badly.

But while she didn't think he had all the answers anymore—she understood now that he never had, he'd only been able to wrap up all his own conflicted thoughts and feelings in a compelling package—she admired him as much as ever. His brain worked in a particular way that she found charming. He really cared about the show and the characters the way no one else did. He was the ultimate fan; he loved all his characters more than they loved themselves.

From a creative standpoint, she'd been having a ball being Lily Fine. She'd had a lot of meaty scenes in the first few episodes of the show, and there were more to come. Ryan and the other writers were going all out for this final season, hitting emotional highs and lows in every episode and swinging for the fences. It was an actor's dream, and she didn't want to wake up.

But reality had a funny way of knocking you awake when you least expected it. And there was another reason she didn't want to run into Zelda, scone craving notwithstanding. She was, to be excruciatingly honest with herself, jealous.

She stomped to her fridge and looked inside, willing there to be a decent scone substitute, but all she had on hand was orange juice and a jar of cocktail olives. She slammed the door shut petulantly and looked for her car keys. She could do an actual grocery run instead of hiding out in her apartment feeling churlish.

Ugh. Ariel hated feeling jealous of a cool person who deserved all the happiness in the world. But Zelda was allowed to date Ryan, and she wasn't.

Wait. She was jealous of Zelda being yet another example of everyone else in Misty Harbor being more desirable than she was, not because she was dating Ryan, specifically. Right? That night in her apartment when she'd cried on Ryan's tweed-covered shoulder, he'd held her and called her alive. He'd called her real. And he hadn't made that seem like a bad thing.

But he hadn't meant anything by it.

You wanted him to mean something by it, an annoying voice inside her whispered.

That gut punch of an idea plagued her the entire drive to the grocery store. Was she so pathetic that she latched on to the first available guy who was halfway decent to her? She pressed her foot on the accelerator, taking her frustration out on her poor car.

It occurred to her she'd been hyper-aware of him for weeks now, the way he tucked his hair behind his ears with his long fingers, the way he spoke into his phone to take notes, his sculpted mouth endlessly fascinating to watch. His hearty laugh, his positivity mixed with common sense. She knew what he smelled like from that night in her apartment—detergent and pine-scented body spray. She remembered the comforting weight of his hand on her back.

She'd thought it was safe to allow herself to get closer to him because he'd made it so patently clear he wasn't looking for someone like her, let alone his soulmate. She'd thought maybe, in time, they'd become true friends. But somehow, she'd messed up their straightforward working relationship by finding him *attractive*.

She'd been ridiculously waiting for some dream-come-true guy to sweep into her life and make everything make sense. Ryan didn't make sense, but she was beginning to understand she wanted him, anyway.

Life was a bitch sometimes.

Not only did they work together, which despite that not being a problem for some of her friends, wasn't necessarily a good idea, but he didn't want an emotional, overly dramatic actress. If she'd been a badass high school teacher like Lily Fine, or a baker-slash-entrepreneur like Zelda Won, maybe she would have had a shot. But she was Ariel Tulip. Despite her profession, she really couldn't be anyone except herself. And Ryan would never want her like that.

She parked, found a shopping cart, and started grabbing things nearly at random from the shelves. Pickles. Swiss cheese. Peanut butter. Strawberries. She paused in the baking aisle and surveyed the flours. How hard could it be to make a decent scone? Ha. She knew her limits.

Ariel changed directions and made for the freezer section. Ice cream had never let her down before. She'd have to drown her craving for scones and unattainable men in toffee almond crunch, because it didn't matter that she wanted to be held by Ryan again, that she wanted him to want her. It was never going to happen, and she was enough of a realist to know it. She surveyed the contents of her cart and tossed in a second pint for good measure.

Chapter Ten

Sawyer's Cove: The Reboot
Episode 304: The Borrowed Tiara

INT. CLOUDY COVE LIBRARY - DAY

KAI, GRACE, and DANNY are browsing the
DVDs.

KAI: What do you think—slasher flick or
monster movie?
GRACE: Could you be more obvious about
wanting to get in her pants?
DANNY: Yeah, you could go for a musical
or something and really mess with her
head.
KAI: But I hate musicals.
GRACE: Dude, you aren't going to be
watching it, anyway.
KAI: Oh, right.

"So now's about the time in the season when I start feeling totally burned out and worry I can't make it to the end." Selena's voice came through loud and clear on his computer's speakers. They had just finished up a video call to go over some budget issues. Even if Selena's name wouldn't be on the writing credits this season, she was still an executive producer. Ryan had enjoyed working with her so far, her dry humor and her no-nonsense attitude refreshing. She was a truth-teller, and he loved that about her.

"Are you a mind reader?" Ryan could feel his eyes getting drier by the second as he sat in his office, gazing in despair at the stacks of scripts, notes, and spreadsheets. There was always more work to do, but they'd wrapped episode five earlier that evening on a high note. Cast and crew had already left, glad to escape into the fine early fall weather until shooting resumed Monday morning. As far as he knew, he was the last one standing.

"You should take a break," Selena insisted. "Get some fresh air. You've probably been living at that damn soundstage."

"Gee, it's like you know my life."

She laughed. "I thought so."

"Okay, I promise I'll leave the studio."

"And do something fun," Selena prompted him.

"And do something fun," he parroted back. But what? All he had waiting for him at his borrowed house was a frozen dinner and the temptation to do more work on his side project script.

"I gotta go. We're probably looking at a Fraterday situation. Wish me luck."

Ryan winced. Fraterday was when Friday night's shooting bled into the early morning hours of Saturday, an outcome no one relished. "Good luck." He ended the call, tucked his computer into his bag, and slung it over his shoulder. He locked up his office and headed toward the rear exit, the one nearest the parking lot. There was a light on in one of the small conference rooms. Just as he was about to reach inside to switch off the light himself, the door opened.

"Ryan!" Ariel, framed in the doorway, looked at him in surprise.

"Sorry, thought I was the last one here. Can I walk you out?"

Ariel nodded, turned off the light in the conference room herself, and fell into step beside him, a laptop under her arm.

"I was doing some work on the podcast fundraiser," she said. "I hadn't realized it had gotten so late."

"How's it coming?"

"Good, I think," she said. "Kate's got all the technical stuff covered, and everyone's schedules are clear so far. The inn's been super to work with, and the tickets are going on sale Monday morning. I guess I'm nervous no one will buy one."

"Impossible. It's going to sell out," Ryan predicted. When they got to the exit, he leaned his hip against the bar to release the door to the outside world.

"Thanks. I hope so." Night had fallen, and all they could see of the woods that surrounded the studio were dark shadows limned by an inky blue night sky. With the reverberation of Selena's command that he have some fun echoing in his brain, Ryan found himself asking, "Do you want to do something tonight?"

"Something?" Ariel repeated doubtfully.

"Something fun. It's Friday night. We both could use a night off, no doubt."

It wasn't the most specific of invitations, but Ariel perked up. "Something fun sounds…fun. Like what?"

Ryan cast about for an activity. "A movie?" Misty Harbor didn't have a movie theater, but there was one in neighboring Southville.

"I haven't been to the movies in ages." Ariel smiled at him, which made him feel as if he'd had a brilliant idea. "What do you want to see?"

Ryan used to keep track of movie releases, and at one point in his life tried to see absolutely everything that came out. But with work subsuming his life, he had no idea what was playing. "Um…"

"Let's be spontaneous. We'll go to the theater right now and get tickets for the very next show, no matter what it is," Ariel said assertively.

Spontaneous had never been a word used to describe his personality, but Ryan decided he was capable of being spontaneous if it got Ariel to smile at him.

But her smile vanished before he could agree to her plan. "You don't have a date with Zelda tonight?" she asked, a little anxiously.

He couldn't explain that her matchmaking had come to nothing because he'd been too preoccupied with trying not to want to kiss her to date someone else. Maybe this movie plan was ill-advised. But somehow he knew if he backed out now, she'd be disappointed. And disappointing Ariel Tulip felt as wrong as putting his right shoe on his left foot. "No. We...didn't spark."

"Oh."

He wouldn't have been surprised if she'd pushed for more details, but all she said was, "I want a disgusting amount of popcorn."

"You got it." They'd reached the small parking lot by then, and Ryan eyed his nondescript rental sedan, then Ariel's red two-door Nissan Z parked a few spaces away. "Should we meet there?"

"Oh my God, what's the *fun* in that?" She unlocked her car and reached in to move some things from the passenger seat to the shelf behind the front seats—a sweater, a couple of books, and a computer charger. "Hop in."

He, like many before him, was helpless to disobey a direct order from Ariel Tulip. He hopped in.

~

"This is fun," Ariel said, "as promised." She popped an ice cream bonbon into her mouth and let the sugary cold balance out the salty popcorn she'd had in lieu of a proper dinner.

They were sitting five rows back, waiting for the movie to start. They'd made it to the three-screen Southville theater before the last showing of the night, a horror sequel in a franchise she'd never managed to catch before. They'd had some time to kill before the movie started, so they bought a mountain of snacks that ended up costing more than their tickets, walked around looking at the posters for coming attractions, then finally went into the semi-dark theater to wait for the show.

They ignored the slideshow on the screen advertising local businesses and overdid it on popcorn. They'd each gotten their own, and Ryan's was securely held between his jean-clad thighs. He'd sat on her right side, which meant there was no arm next to her to grab on to in case she got scared during the movie.

Not that it would have been totally professional to grab on to him in any case. But still—Ariel didn't hold back. She immersed herself in the world of the story and she responded like it was happening to her.

"I better warn you, I get kind of into movies," she said. "Like, my reactions can get extreme."

"Really?" He swallowed a handful of popcorn. "Are you going to be okay with this movie?"

"I don't know. Maybe it'll be too silly to be scary. Just warning you in case I try to climb into your lap or something."

He gave her an uncertain smile. "Okay. Thanks for the warning." He took a long pull of his soda.

"So what was the first movie you saw in the theater?" she asked. They weren't on a date, but it kind of felt like one, so she fell back on unofficial first date topics.

He frowned in thought. "Oh!" He glanced sideways at her, a bit diffidently. "You won't believe this."

"Why?" She laughed. "Don't keep me in suspense."

"*The Little Mermaid.* I was eight."

She laughed harder. "You're right. I don't believe you. Eight is kind of old for your first time going to the movies."

"My parents tried to take me when I was four or five, I

think, and I was so scared I begged them to leave after the lights went down. I don't know, it all seemed so intense, so overwhelming."

"That I do believe. I was the same way, actually. But once I got past the fear, I was hooked."

"So what was your first movie theater movie?"

"My parents tell me it was *Space Jam*, but honestly, the first movie I really remember was *The Parent Trap* remake with Lindsay Lohan. I saw this incredible little girl, not much older than me, doing a British accent and wearing fancy clothes and getting to do wild stuff on screen, and I knew then and there that's what I wanted to do with my life."

"Seriously?"

"Seriously. That was it for me." She'd begged her mom to let her take acting lessons after that, and she signed up for every theater opportunity in their town until she felt ready to start approaching agents.

"That's a pretty good movie," Ryan said. "I haven't seen it in years."

"Me either," Ariel said. "But I bet it holds up."

"We should find out," Ryan said.

She glanced at him in surprise. That sounded like an invitation to hang out again. Just the two of them. Before she could answer, the theater darkened, and the trailers started. She barely paid attention to them while she tried to sort out what was happening. It might feel like a date, but it couldn't be one. He'd asked her on the spur of the moment. Everything about this night was spontaneous, which in and of itself delighted her. It had been far too long since she'd had someone to be spontaneous with.

So it wasn't a date, but this also wasn't simply two

coworkers hanging out after a long week at work. Not when she'd admitted to herself her feelings for Ryan weren't strictly platonic. It was why she'd asked about Zelda—she'd never want to poach on someone else's territory, even accidentally. She was a big believer in the girl code.

Her gut response when Ryan had said he and Zelda were better as friends had been relieved, rather than disappointed that all the work she'd done to get them together had come to naught. Did that make her a bad person?

When the movie finally started, she quit worrying, wiped her popcorn-greasy hand on a few paper napkins, then set the popcorn down on the floor. Recliner seats with tables and armrests with cup holders had not yet made their way to Southville. The cold opening was genuinely frightening, and though she'd joked about her raw reactions to movies, she found herself shrieking involuntarily at the first jump scare, then giggling in relief when it was over. Her heart was racing, and she sensed Ryan glancing over at her.

He set down his drink and leaned close to whisper, "Are you okay?"

"All part of the Ariel-goes-to-the-movies experience," she whispered back. "Are *you* okay?"

He nodded his head and turned his attention back to the screen, but as the movie, which turned out to be a clever, nasty horror flick, went on he seemed to be watching her more than the screen as she twitched and jumped and gasped through the whole thing.

She couldn't help leaning closer to him as the movie came to its bloody climax. He didn't have an arm for her to grab, but she found the soft material of his ubiquitous jacket comforting, and she curled her fingers into the fabric at his side, tugging him closer. He seemed to go willingly, reaching across his body to pat her shoulder during a particularly tense scene. She only gave in to the urge to turn away from the screen once, pressing her forehead into his side while her favorite character got chased down a menacingly dark hallway on screen.

There was a thump and a scream, and she jumped when Ryan's hand landed on her back, holding her firmly against him for a long moment. She felt warm and secure nestled against him like that. It was so good to be close to someone, sharing their heat. Her body tightened, as if it was confusing her fight-or-flight response with being turned on. Ryan felt so solid, so male. She was overcome with the urge to slide her hand into the opening of his jacket, to trace his chest with her palm, to feel the rabbiting of his heart through the thin cotton of his shirt.

She couldn't. He wasn't interested.

She gave up her momentary indulgence, released her hold on Ryan's jacket, and slid away, leaving the warm concave of his body. When she moved, his hand fell away, too, settling by his side. She glanced at him once, giving him an uncertain smile. He wasn't smiling, or watching the movie, but staring at her with an unreadable expression, as if she'd been speaking a language he'd heard before but was having trouble understanding.

She didn't know what that look meant, but she figured he was happy for her to stop acting like a silly girl, so she kept a careful space between them for the rest of the movie. She tried to pay attention to the plot—her favorite character got away, killed the bad guy, and would probably need a lot of therapy to get past all the horrors wrought upon her in the film.

When the end credits flashed on screen, she clapped loudly, the way she did at the end of every film she liked.

Ryan didn't applaud, but there was a smattering of applause from some of the other moviegoers. She glanced at him; he was smiling at her, no longer inscrutable.

"Well," he said as they gathered the detritus of their movie theater dinner and headed for the exit, "I don't know about you, but that was the most fun I've had at the movies in a long time."

She laughed in disbelief. "Really? They could put that on the poster."

"It didn't have much to do with the movie, honestly," he said, holding the door open for her.

She passed by him, the night air smelling sweet after the recycled popcorn air of the theater. "Are you saying I'm more entertaining than *Haunted Horror House IV*?"

"I'm saying you're fun to go to the movies with," he said, voice neutral.

She couldn't help the pleasantly fizzy feeling in her belly at the mild compliment. She unlocked the car, and they got in and buckled up.

"It's late," she said as she pulled out of the parking lot. Too late to get a drink? She didn't even know what was around Southville, which was larger than Misty Harbor, but sleepier. The Cove would be open, though, and they had to go back to get Ryan's car.

Without commenting on the late hour, Ryan said, "Are you hungry? Popcorn isn't exactly dinner."

She wasn't hungry at all. She rarely ate after dark—

one of the ways she stayed even marginally slim enough for the camera. But she said, "I could go for a snack. The Cove is open."

"Okay," he said easily, as if they went to the movies and had a late supper all the time. As if they were friends.

Or a couple.

Chapter Eleven

Sawyer's Cove: The Reboot
Episode 305: The Bus Stop

EXT. LOVER'S LANE - NIGHT
Inside Will's sports car.

WILL: Remember the last time we were
here?
NOAH: Vaguely.
WILL: Remember the first time we were
here?
NOAH: That I do remember. Our first kiss.
WILL: I was so nervous.
NOAH: Yeah. So was I.
WILL: You still nervous? About us?
NOAH: They say nervousness is another
form of excitement. And I'm excited as
hell.

Ariel didn't like driving at night, so she took the slower, better lit local road instead of the highway. They talked about the movie they'd just seen, what they'd liked, what had been too ridiculous. Ryan, a bit surprisingly, had enjoyed it quite a bit. He'd been quieter than her, so she'd thought maybe he was bored, but he spoke enthusiastically about the performances and the plot twist at the end.

They passed the town line, and Ariel turned over the question that had been on her mind half the night. She wanted to ask it while she was focused on driving, when she couldn't afford to overreact, no matter Ryan's answer.

Two miles from downtown Misty Harbor, she made herself say it. "Can I ask you a question?"

"Of course," he said immediately, which, again, surprised her. She felt like an open book; he was far harder to read, but perhaps she only had to ask to know what was going on in his head.

"If I wasn't...me. Or no—if I was something else, if I *did* something else. For a living." She thought about Zelda and her ex. "A butcher, or a baker."

"Or a candlestick maker?"

"Exactly." He was making fun, but she didn't care. The point stood. "Would this—could tonight have been a date?"

She lost her capacity to process his answer dispassionately the second she asked the question, so she plowed on before he had a chance to say anything. "I mean, I know you have a very strict no-actress policy, and I'm so very definitely an actress, and I'm not a baker, I can't even make cookies from those dough logs without burning them, and I'm even less cut out to be a butcher, I mean, I'm basically vegetarian, and I absolutely could not cut up animals for a living—ugh. So never mind. I answered my own question. Oh look, we're almost there."

She stepped on the gas, as if once they parked and got out of the car, Ryan's memory of the last five minutes would be wiped clean.

"I can't really answer the question as posed." Ryan's voice was gentle, the kind of tone you used when you were about to let someone down as easily as you could. She tensed, feeling stupid and childish. "As you so conclusively established, you aren't a butcher, Ariel. Or a baker, or a candlestick maker. And if you weren't an actress, you wouldn't be you."

"Right. I figured." It was silly to feel disappointed. It wasn't like she'd ever had a real shot with him, for so many reasons. Besides, she was still holding out for her soulmate, wasn't she? Ryan had made it clear he didn't think much of that goal.

"I'm not—" He stalled and ran his hand through his hair a few times. "Let's set aside the actress thing for a minute, because that's not relevant. It's a stupid rule I made for myself when I wasn't mature enough to know what I really meant was look for people I can trust, who like me for me. I've always had trouble believing that anyone I could be attracted to would genuinely want me back. Doesn't take a psych degree to get why that might be."

He was referring to his limb difference, obviously. She'd known him for so long, it barely registered for her anymore. Ryan was just Ryan. Only not just Ryan—not anymore.

"I guess I understand. I had to learn people might be more attracted to my fame than to me." She'd learned the lesson swiftly and painfully, but hadn't had to learn it more than once.

"Right. We've both been careful because we're smart and we don't relish getting our hearts broken."

"And look where it's gotten us," she said plaintively. "Alone on a Friday night while our friends all bask in their cozy, monogamous domesticity."

"We're not alone," Ryan said in a voice so low it sent an unexpected tremor through her. "And we can't see each other as consolation prizes."

"Aren't I, though?" She parked in the beachside lot across the street from Jay's bar and shut off the engine. "I'm the leftovers, the last one standing. Otherwise, we wouldn't even be together right now." Her bitterness left a sour taste in her mouth. She hated being negative, but she was sick of pretending she was fine with being alone, with so much love to give and nowhere to put it.

Ryan shifted to face her, resting his left knee against the center console, reaching out as if to make contact, but pulling back at the last minute.

She was glad he didn't touch her because she would have been tempted to cling to him and not let him go.

"Ariel, the reason we're together right now is because I can't seem to stop wanting to be around you."

It took a moment for that to sink in. "But—" She hadn't been expecting that level of candor. "Wait— really?"

His jacket rustled as he reached for her hand and followed through this time. His warm palm engulfed her fingers. "For the past few weeks, there hasn't been a moment when I'm not thinking about you or dreaming about you. But I didn't ask you on a date because the nerdy sixteen-year-old that still lives inside me would never presume someone like you would want to go out with me."

The earnest expression on his face made something funny happen to her insides. All of the half-formed thoughts and aborted desires she'd felt stirring since Ryan had arrived in Misty Harbor seemed to grow as fast as a neglected plant given sunlight and water going absolutely nuts in a time-lapse video. Tendrils of hope, attraction, fondness, and care wrapped themselves around her heart with his faint encouragement. She was full to bursting with possibility, with anticipation.

"I would. I mean, I do," she said, matching him for earnestness. "I like you, Ryan. In the classical sense, you know...butterflies and all that wonderful nonsense." Her upper lip bloomed sweat in the close air of the car, and she felt more nervous than at her first audition. "I've been over here cursing your stupid no-actresses thing for weeks."

His grip on her hand tightened. "I had no idea."

"That's good." She giggled a little manically. "I didn't want to be a portrait of a needy, clingy, immature—"

"Stop. If anything, I've been the immature one. I kept thinking I had to be the grown-up, the one in charge who ignored his feelings because—well, it's a long list of made-up reasons."

Her heart leapt with hope. "So you have feelings about me, too?"

"I can't stop thinking about kissing you," Ryan said in an entire register lower than his usual baritone, his eyes dark and gaze fixed on her lips. "Not since that night you brought me up to your apartment and yelled at me."

"You liked that?" she asked, unable to stop her own already throaty voice from descending into Nina Simone territory.

"I don't know if I should admit it was a huge turn-on."

"I'll keep that in mind," she said, filing it away. There was a somewhat awkward pause. If they were following one of Ryan's scripts, they'd be kissing already, but this wasn't a carefully orchestrated first kiss scene.

"So what now?" Ryan asked, the note of desire disappearing from his voice. "I'm still, you know, in charge of the show."

"And I'm still an actress," she put in, hoping he'd say it didn't matter, it had never mattered, because she was worth the trouble.

But all he said was, "We work together, and this show is incredibly important to both of us."

"I'm a professional. I can keep work and my personal life separate."

"Or we could...wait?" Ryan said.

"Wait?"

"The shoot will be over in what—six weeks? Then you'll go home to New York and I'll—"

"You'll go to L.A. for post on the show and I wouldn't see you for months." She contemplated sitting on these feelings for an undefined amount of time and felt anxiety crawl its way into her chest. "And let's say we do wait until the show's over and we're in the same city and we finally go on a date—don't you think the pressure would be outrageous? We'd be so nervous after all the buildup; nothing would be able to live up to whatever we'd spun up in our heads in the meantime. No relationship could survive that kind of stress."

Ryan seemed to consider her words seriously. "You're right," he said finally. "It would be a lot to ask. I mean, it's just a crush. Our feelings might have faded by then."

"Wow. Just a crush. Let's not bother, then." She removed her hand from his gingerly, the sting of rejection erasing her growing anxiety, even though she knew he didn't mean it that way. Not exactly.

"No, I—" He sighed, and ran his hand through his hair again in a frustrated motion. "Sometimes I wish I still smoked."

She laughed sharply at that. "Good to know I bring out the self-destructive habits in you."

"No," he said sharply, grabbing her hand again. "That's not it. You aren't the problem here, Ariel. Please, never think that."

"All right." She let the words soothe the rough edges of the conversation for a moment. "I think we should kiss and get it over with."

Chapter Twelve

Sawyer's Cove: The Reboot
Episode 305: The Bus Stop

INT. THE BAR'S OFFICE - DAY

KAI: How did you know Amy was, like, you
know, the one, dude?
PARKER: Why? You think this girl is
the one?
KAI scoffs, embarrassed.
PARKER: You'll know when you imagine
life without her, and it just seems…
wrong.

Ryan was holding Ariel's hand in her car when she said they should kiss. He was trying to stay in the moment and not fuck this up any more than he already had.

"That way, if it's not good, we can move on and not

waste the next few months of our lives on a pointless crush."

She sounded casual, but he'd picked up on her emphasis on the last two words. Ryan was beginning to understand there was always more to Ariel than met the eye. As outwardly candid and effusive as she seemed, she held herself back a little bit. At least with him. He wondered how magnificent she would be if she stopped holding back. Then his brain caught up to what she'd actually suggested.

"Wait, you think it might not be good?"

She shrugged coolly. "It might be like kissing your sister."

He let out a horrified snort. "God, I hope not."

"Well, let's find out," she said, challenging him with a lift to her chin.

He peered at her, letting himself really see her. So often lately, she'd walk into a room, and it was as if she were wearing a yellow safety vest holding lighted flares, drawing his attention while warning him there was danger in coming too close. But that was all in his head, where he'd built her up as this off-limits creature, as someone who wasn't for him.

Now here she was, asking him to touch her, inviting him to come closer. But he took a moment to get his fill first. He gazed into her gray eyes, granite in this dim light, shadows accentuating the curves of her cheekbones. Her lips were shiny from some gloss she'd put on before they started driving. She'd pulled her hair back into a loose ponytail, but on the drive from the theater, the elastic had come loose, wisps chaotically escaping. The effect was the opposite of the way she was made up for the screen in Lily's layers of meticulously applied makeup, her hair a bright sheen of uniform waves.

She looked softer than Lily Fine right now, a plain sage green cardigan covering her shoulders, a high-necked white T-shirt beneath it. She had very little skin showing, but she couldn't hide her classic hourglass figure that never went out of style.

Ryan had seen her a million times on set, on screens. She'd always been tall and surprisingly robust, with strong shoulders but delicate wrists. But right now, folded into the driver's seat of her sporty car, she looked surprisingly small, almost fragile. He'd never thought of her as weak, not even when she was breaking down into tears over one thing or another. That was how she processed, how she worked through what was happening around her.

She was a beautiful crier, as twisted as that might sound.

But she wasn't crying right now. No, now she was waiting with affected patience, waiting for him to meet her halfway. Waiting for him to take what they both apparently, incredibly, wanted.

She was putting herself in his hands—figuratively speaking, of course. She was trusting him with her body, at least as far as a kiss. She was—she was so fucking *beautiful,* and he wasn't prepared for this. He had popcorn breath, his clothes were stale from the long day, and he hadn't even taken her on a proper date. What kind of a jackass took Ariel Tulip to see a silly horror movie as their first date?

"Stop thinking," she demanded, turning his hand

around in hers so she was gripping him rather than the other way around, "and kiss me."

Time to get over himself. He swallowed and leaned in, closing his eyes, trusting his instincts and his rather comprehensive knowledge of her features to guide him.

The first feather-light touch of their lips made him shiver, even though the car was warm, and the air was stuffy after sitting with the engine off for so long. He pressed in, and her other hand found the lapel of his jacket and urged him closer. The angle wasn't great, and the top of his head kept hitting the car roof. But she parted her lips, the sensation of her hot breath in his mouth so intimately erotic he couldn't help trying to get closer still, until the front of his jacket brushed the firm swell of her breasts, her hand trapped between them as he deepened the kiss and invaded her mouth with his tongue.

She tasted so good, vaguely like a peach. Probably her lip gloss. He wanted to kiss it all off, he wanted to devour her mouth, to strip her bare right there in the car and feast on her body, giving her as much pleasure as he was capable of giving to another person.

Ariel let go of him to slide her hand between his shirt and his jacket, her touch on his back making him twitch. It had been so long since he'd been touched like that—he felt extra sensitive. He mirrored her gesture, slowly but assuredly making contact with her waist, taking in the silky texture of her shirt, the soft give of her torso. He scraped a thumb over the bottom of her rib cage, and she quivered and nipped his bottom lip with her movie-star-white teeth.

He took that as an invitation to deepen the kiss.

Slowly, it melted into something hotter, something baser, as they fought for dominance, tongues and teeth battling.

If the center console hadn't been in the way, if they'd been anywhere near a bed, or, hell, a wall, he would have used his height and weight advantage to pin her down, to rub his entire body over hers. Feeling her against him was a pathological need at this point. But they weren't in a bed, they were fumbling in the dark, in a car, as if they had five minutes before curfew to fit in a messy make-out session.

When he finally gave up, accepting the reality that they weren't getting any farther than that tonight, he pulled away with difficulty, leaving his hand on her waist, but putting air between them.

Her eyes stayed closed and her mouth stayed ajar, as if she wanted to continue being kissed. So he kissed her again and again, helpless against the implicit demand. Would he ever be able to deny her anything now he'd had the ambrosia of her kisses?

He tried to pull away again, but she pouted. "Don't stop."

"Ariel, we can't make out in this parking lot all night." His raging hard-on ached, punishment for his common sense.

She opened her eyes a millimeter at a time. Her lashes were smudges of black, her mouth bitten red. "I suppose not." She shook herself, pulled her hand off his, smoothed down the front of his coat, once, twice. "Well, what's the verdict?"

"I enjoyed the hell out of it. But you tell me. Like kissing your brother?"

Her lips curved wickedly. "I wouldn't know, but I highly doubt it."

"Thank fuck," he said fervently. They exchanged loopy, punch-drunk smiles, but he sobered first. "What do we do now?"

"Like, big picture?"

He nodded. He was in no condition to make sensible decisions, but he'd do his best.

"I have no idea. But right now we should probably go inside and get a drink because otherwise I'm going to want to invite you back to my place and I know that's not the smart option."

"You are very smart," he said gravely.

"I am, actually," she said with a pert smile. "So. Drink?"

"I'm going to need a minute, but then, yeah, a drink sounds good." Something icy cold to counteract the heat that suffused his skin even now.

"A minute?"

He glanced at his crotch in explanation. It took her a second to catch on, but when she did, she giggled. "Oh. Wow. I didn't know."

"Stupid car design," he said, thumping the top of the center console that kept them apart. "But as you said, maybe for the best, because right now I'm not thinking super clearly."

"Cock blocked by a sports car." She giggled again, and it wasn't helping his erection. Everything she did and said was turning him on, and now that she'd activated the permission switch in his brain, it was even more difficult to control himself.

They sat there for a second, until she pulled her bag

from the rear shelf and rummaged around in it. She pulled out a tube of lip gloss, and the scent of peaches hit his nose as she applied it.

"Peaches," he said, like a dork.

She flashed him a now-glossy smile and put the tube away. "Peaches," she confirmed.

"You are smart," he declared once more. "Now your beautiful lips are all sticky. A kiss deterrent."

Her shiny lips curved upward. "I bet I could still get you to kiss me, even with sticky lips."

He chuckled. "Ariel, you could get me to do any damn thing you want."

He worried for a second he was being too revealing, but she rewarded him with a wide grin, and his breath caught at being on the receiving end of such a surprised, pleased smile. The more honest he was and the less he held back, the more she seemed to bloom under the attention and the intimacy.

"Good to know," she said quietly.

A minute later, they finally extricated themselves from the car. He missed being six inches away from her, but it felt good to stretch his legs. They walked the fifty yards to The Cove's entrance. It was Friday night, so even though it was near midnight, there was still a healthy crowd inside.

He gave in to the urge to lace their fingers together as they searched for a free table. When he glanced at her to see if the gesture was okay, she held on tighter and followed in his shadow as they edged through the crowd.

He didn't see an open table, but he heard something that made his heart sink.

"Ariel! Ryan!"

He turned toward the voice and spotted Darren Silverstein at one of the big corner booths, his arm around Spencer Crosby. Trevor Kendrick was there, too, along with Henry Yu.

He hadn't anticipated running into people they knew, which was totally naive since there were only a handful of places to drink in Misty Harbor. He wasn't prepared for so early a test of their nascent relationship. They'd only just changed their status from work friends to work friends who kissed and had romantic feelings for each other. The crashing interruption of the real world was a splash of ice water to the back of his neck.

"Um." He stopped and turned his back on their friends.

Ariel looked at him ruefully, as if she knew the dilemma they faced.

"Should we join them? I wanted—"

"Yeah, me too," she said sadly. "But I guess we can't ignore them."

He looked down at their joined hands, unwilling to be the first one to let go.

Chapter Thirteen

Sawyer's Cove: The Reboot
Episode 306: The Storm

INT. WILL AND NOAH'S KITCHEN - NIGHT

NOAH: Will is going to be the death of
me. He's not taking this storm seriously.
I told him to stay put in Providence, but
he got on the road an hour ago, and now
he's not responding to my texts.
SAWYER: Relax, he's driving. He's probably not checking his phone.
NOAH: You think I want to hear reasonable
explanations? Do you not know me at all?

Ariel was having the weirdest dream. She was
holding hands with Ryan Saylor in a crowded bar
while her lips still throbbed with the sense memory of
his mouth on hers. And one of her best friends was beck-

oning them to the table he was sharing with the nosiest person in Misty Harbor.

She pressed her lips together, the freshly applied gloss evidence of everything they'd just done. It wasn't a dream. She and Ryan had just made out in her car and now they had to pretend like nothing had changed. Fuck.

Slowly, she removed her hand from Ryan's, giving him an apologetic smile. He tilted his head in acknowledgment of their predicament.

"I'll get us something to drink," he said gruffly. "What do you want?"

"Um. Club soda, thanks."

"Okay." He ducked his head and his hair fell into his eyes. She wanted so badly to brush it back from his forehead, but she balled her hands into fists instead.

She took a deep breath and walked toward their friends. Her legs felt weighted down as each step away from Ryan took more effort than the one before.

Darren watched her approach, while Henry and Trevor were looking at something on Trevor's phone, and Crosby was gazing at Darren. The boy was totally in love and it warmed Ariel's heart—truly. She'd known Crosby for so long, and he'd been alone for too much of that time. Since he and Darren had gotten together, he'd mellowed a bit. He smiled more. She was grateful to Darren for that.

"Hey, fellas," she said, hovering by the side of their booth. Maybe she could get away with a quick hello-goodbye.

"Sit down, girl," Darren said quickly. "What have you been up to?"

"Ryan and I went to a movie," she said, using every

ounce of her training to act casual. "What have you been up to?"

"Drinking, mostly," Crosby said, his smile bleary. He was a happy drunk.

"Any particular reason?"

"Darren got a directing job he went out for. So we're celebrating," Crosby answered. "A TV movie. Big stars. He's freaking out, but we're making him celebrate."

"Congratulations, Darren." She hugged him but didn't sit down.

"Hey, Henry," she said. The twenty-four-year-old played Kai Wild, Parker's half-brother, on the show. He was also the boyfriend of Erika Rainwater, one of the hosts of the podcast she was organizing the live show for. "How's Erika?"

"She's amazing, exceptional, and overachieving, as usual." Henry grinned.

"Did you hear the latest episode of her show?" Trevor asked.

"Not yet, but I heard she had a pretty exciting guest," Ariel said, throwing finger guns at him.

Trevor's rouged cheeks went darker still. "It was my first podcast. I think I stuttered over every other word. I can't bring myself to listen to it."

"No, man, it was great," Henry said. "The story you told about going from a fan to being part of the show—it was touching. I teared up, no lie."

"Oh, dear." Trevor buried his face in his hands. "I gushed. I couldn't help it." He lifted his head and glared at Henry. "Your girlfriend is a really good interviewer. She made me spill all my secrets."

"I know. I can't wait for her to get here." Henry looked

wistfully at Crosby's curly blond head, which was now resting on Darren's jean-jacket-clad shoulder. "Long distance sucks."

"When does she get in?"

"Not for a few more weeks. She still has her day job, you know. But she's taking vacation time so she can be here for the last few days of the shoot, and the wrap party, and then the live show, so that'll be really fun."

Ariel's belly fluttered with nerves over something besides Ryan, which was a nice change. She knew the live podcast was going to go well, but she was still nervous about it.

"Tickets for the show go on sale Monday—make sure you all spread the word," Ariel ordered, pointing to each of them in turn.

Darren nodded solemnly, Crosby grinned sleepily, and Henry winked. Trevor was the most animated. "Don't worry, Ariel, it will be a sellout. Promise."

"That's what I told her," Ryan said, appearing at her elbow and making her jump. He'd snuck up on her without her noticing. He handed her a glass with clear liquid inside.

"Thanks. Where's yours?" she asked, then realized he couldn't exactly easily hold two full drinks at once. She felt like an idiot, but before he could answer, a young female server appeared and handed him his own pint glass of beer.

He thanked the server, who flashed him a big smile, winked, and said, "Let me know if you need anything else," before melting away into the crowd.

Ariel felt her mouth pucker sourly at the server's

retreating back. She took a sip of her club soda to mask her irrational jealousy.

"Are you going to sit down or what?" Henry asked.

"Um." Ariel looked at Ryan helplessly. She had been trying to figure out how to get out of this situation and hadn't come up with anything. She wasn't the writer in this relationship.

"Actually, I think we need to take off," Crosby said, looking at Darren meaningfully. "Don't we, babe?"

"Right. Yeah. I guess it's past our bedtime," Darren said, smiling overly brightly at the group as he got out of the booth and helped Crosby out, who leaned against his boyfriend's side as if he might have trouble standing on his own. "Don't worry, I'm sober. Crosby did enough celebrating for both of us. Be good, party people." They headed for the exit.

Henry looked after them and sighed wistfully. "Long distance *sucks*. I'm sure they'll be having a very good night. Me? I'm going back to a cold, empty hotel room."

"That's what phone sex is for," Trevor said, then he glanced at Ryan and clapped a hand over his mouth. "Oops."

Henry laughed. "True that, Trevor. I hope you aren't driving home. Want to split a ride?"

"I live close enough to walk," Trevor said. "But I'll walk out with you, Henry. Sorry to abandon you, Miss Tulip, Mr. Saylor, but this boy needs his beauty sleep."

"Hey, I get it," Ariel said, giving Trevor a hug on his way out of the booth. To Henry, she said, "See you Monday."

Trevor saluted and he and Henry walked out arm in arm.

"Trevor fits right in with this crowd, doesn't he," Ariel commented.

"And we scored a big booth all to ourselves," Ryan said, sitting down and scooting in, motioning for her to join him. She plopped down and shifted close, much closer than necessary given all the room they had, but if anyone was watching them, she didn't care. She'd earned the closeness, she deserved to snuggle with a guy who set her blood on fire, who called her smart, who made her feel good about being herself.

She looked into his changeable eyes. "Hey."

His face creased into an easy smile. "Hey."

Her belly leapt. She'd never felt this way before. Excited and comfortable. Turned on and intellectually stimulated. Ryan was the whole package. And he had feelings for her. Could this be who she'd been—

"Dude, it's Lily Fine!" A figure rushed their table, a bro who reeked of beer. "Can I get a picture?"

"Ah, sure." She put on her friendly celebrity smile, trying not to recoil at the guy's breath when he stuck his head close and held up his phone with the camera reversed. His dexterity was subpar, and he fumbled, unable to snap the pic one-handed from this angle.

"Hey, dude, would you?" He thrust the phone toward Ryan. His eyes widened when he noticed Ryan's limb difference and apparently decided he wouldn't be capable of taking a photo one-handed, either, which was ridiculous. Ariel had seen Ryan do everything on his phone one-handed for weeks now.

"Oh shit, sorry," the bro slurred, retracting the phone.

"Sorry for being a drunken douche?" Ryan said dryly. "Yeah, I would be, too."

"Whatever, man," the guy said defensively.

Ariel wasn't thrilled about posing for a picture with this lout, but it was easier to take it and send him on his way. "Here, I'll do it." She snatched the phone, snapped a picture, and returned the device, pushing the guy away firmly in the process. "Have a good night."

"Yeah. Thanks." He smiled down at the phone and lurched away, apparently not giving them a second thought.

"Wow, that guy sucked," she said, wiping her hands on a napkin. "Sorry about that."

"One hundred percent not your fault," Ryan said. "Maybe we should get out of here. It seems like the crowd's rowdy tonight."

"Yeah. I'm not usually here this late." But she was disappointed to have to cut their hard-won private drink short. She pulled on her club soda. He chugged half his glass of beer.

"Rain check?" he suggested.

She nodded. "Sure."

They left their glasses on the table and made their way out of the bar. They didn't hold hands this time.

As they stood outside in the dark, Ariel wished she knew how to get the magic back from before the bar and their friends and that jerk with the selfie. But it was late, and she was tired, and her heart had been seesawing back and forth between angst, hope, and uncertainty all night.

"So what now?" she asked. "I mean, after I take you back to your car."

Ryan sighed heavily, tucked his hair behind his ear. "So here's the thing. I like you. Obviously. But there are real reasons that getting into a relationship is complicated. So I think I should take my cue from you. What do you want, Ariel?"

She opened her mouth to respond, and nothing came out. He was giving her the power to tell him what she wanted, which meant she had to know what that was.

"You are a very clever man," she said, not entirely happily.

He smiled crookedly. "It's okay if you don't know. We don't have to do anything. Nothing has to change, I mean."

"Oh great, more pining, sign me up for that," she joked, but it was true. She'd tried to not be so utterly aware of him for the past few weeks and it hadn't worked. "And now that I know what a good kisser you are, that won't make the sexual tension worse, not at all."

"You think I'm a good kisser?"

She couldn't help her cheeks getting warm. "It could be that I've had enough of a dry spell I forgot what kissing is supposed to feel like and you're terrible," she teased. "But I don't think so."

"Thanks for giving me the benefit of the doubt."

She waited, but he didn't say anything else. "So, am I a good kisser?" she prompted.

He put his thumb and forefinger to his chin and pretended to think. "Not sure. I think I need another demonstration."

She giggled, the sound bright and embarrassing. "Oh you do, do you?"

"Yeah."

She found herself putting her hands on his chest

again, nestling close enough her breasts grazed the front of his shirt. "What happened to following my lead?"

"You're right. We shouldn't kiss," he said with mock stoicism.

"You idiot," she murmured before she kissed him, on the sidewalk outside The Cove where anyone could see them.

It was different kissing standing up, their bodies pressed against each other from chest to thigh, his hand winding around her waist to hold her in place. He tasted different, too, like the beer he'd drunk half of, but his mouth was just as warm and expert at getting her to open up to him as before.

She liked the way he kissed, purposeful, not sloppy, but thorough, his lips and tongue and even his teeth working in concert to bring her to the edge of arousal in record time. He tasted good; he smelled better. His hair fell forward, and the strands tickled her forehead.

Ariel had the strongest desire to lay him out in her bed, run her hands through his hair, to find out if he had any on his chest, to learn everything about him. She'd never seen him without a shirt on. She had no idea what she'd find underneath his clothes, and she wanted to know what he looked like so she could picture him properly when she was lying in her bed alone, hands wandering around her body, seeking satiety so she could sleep.

It was strange to think of Ryan as someone she was allowed to fantasize about now. She could fantasize about anyone she damn well wanted in the privacy of her own head, but now she knew what it felt like to kiss him, she considered that permission to think about him more intimately.

Did that mean he'd do the same? Would he get out of the shower tonight, slip under the sheets in whichever of the many guest rooms in Warner and Selena's place he was using, and think about her? Would he picture her tits, imagining what they looked like under her clothes, just as she was imagining his bare chest? Would he bring himself to hardness thinking about her body, her face, her hair? The idea was unbelievably erotic. She didn't like to think about random people who used her image in their fantasy lives—it was none of her business, and it certainly didn't turn her on. But Ryan thinking about her, bringing himself off to her, specifically—that had her panties damp and nipples hardening. She wanted that. She wanted him to want her. She wanted him to think about her as he made himself come.

But that was all her fantasy life.

In real life, they were coworkers who had more to negotiate than just tedious details like long distance.

They stopped kissing slowly, as if knowing this might be the last time and not wanting it to end.

As much as they wanted each other, she was going to be an adult. She wasn't going to let the needy emotional side of her dominate and ruin everything. If they tried to date while they worked and she ended up making it uncomfortable on the set or in some other work setting, she'd be fulfilling all his fears about being with an actress. She refused to be a walking cliché.

So that meant one thing.

"Here's what we'll do," she announced. "We both have to focus on work for the next few weeks. So we'll hit pause. We'll be coworkers. Friends. But we'll wait until the shoot is over to do any more kissing or anything in that general area." She gestured to the lower half of her face to illustrate the boundaries.

She waited for his response trepidatiously. He'd given her the power to make this decision, but what if he thought she was being unrealistic or a prude?

He considered silently for a beat, then nodded. "You're right. We should concentrate on work. We can pick this up where we left off when the shoot's over. That is the mature and responsible thing to do."

He didn't sound mad about it. He sounded impressed that she'd chosen this option.

"Mature and responsible, that's me," she said weakly.

"You are many things, Ariel," he said. "And one of those things is worth waiting for."

Her head swam. "Oh damn. This isn't going to be easy, is it?"

"It's going to be hell," he said cheerfully. "But it makes sense."

"All right." They walked back to the car, got in. Ariel tried very hard not to kiss him again, back at the scene of the crime where it had happened for the very first time. "Come Monday morning, it'll be business as usual."

"Right," he said briskly. "Business as usual."

When she dropped him off at his car a few minutes later, there was an uneasy pause before he got out. "I'm going to hug you goodbye because we would have done that before tonight. All right?"

"Yeah. Business as usual, right?" she said, not letting herself cry.

He hugged her, strong and reassuring. "It's going to be okay," he whispered into her hair before letting her go.

She smiled at him, not trusting her voice. After he shut the door behind him, she let out a breath and whispered, "I want to believe you."

Chapter Fourteen

```
Sawyer's Cove: The Reboot
Episode 306: The Storm

INT. LILY'S KITCHEN - NIGHT

GRACE: Everyone already cleared out the
shelves prepping for this stupid storm. I
managed to get some nine-volt batteries
and off-brand blue raspberry popsicles.
LILY: Great, so we can turn our tongues
blue and then shock them.
AMY: Sounds like a party to me.
```

Business as usual sucked.

Oh, filming was good. They were on the sixth of ten episodes, and Darren was directing this one, which was always a good time. But it had been an entire week since the night they'd kissed, and it hadn't exactly been easy to pretend her world hadn't turned upside down.

For one thing, they were professional toward each other in all the ways that mattered, but sometimes she caught Ryan looking at her; he didn't have the decency to look away immediately, then he'd send her unfairly wicked smiles that made her insides turn to goo.

She supposed turnabout was fair play because occasionally, when she wasn't prepping for an upcoming scene and he wasn't on set, she would drop by his office and say hi. She made sure to wear her peach lip gloss and smile a lot as they overly casually shot the shit. It seemed to leave him vaguely amused and frustrated.

Well, good. This whole waiting thing might have been her idea, but she'd only gone for it because she'd wanted him to think of her as a mature, sensible creature, not a woman who gallivanted her way through life doing whatever she wanted.

Which she clearly was not. If she were, they would have already had sex by now.

She had no doubt now, after kissing him twice, that the sex was going to be spectacular. She had thought of little else in her off hours, actually. She hadn't been this low-key twenty-four-seven turned on in her life.

She had never felt this way about anyone else.

When she let herself think about how this felt like everything she'd been waiting for her entire life, she was glad they weren't rushing into anything because the stakes suddenly seemed terrifyingly high. If this was going to be her one great love affair, she couldn't screw it up.

So she smiled, she worked, and every night she went back to her apartment feeling vaguely horny and buzzing with anticipation.

It was hard to hold it all inside—honestly, it was impossible—when everything was so raw and new. Holding things close to the chest wasn't in her nature.

Cami was the first to comment. She and Ariel were in wardrobe doing fittings for costumes for the final two episodes.

"God, I feel like a beach ball," Cami said, groaning and peering at herself in the full-length wall mirror. "And don't tell me I look normal because I don't care how I appear, everything *feels* bloated."

Ariel scrunched up her mouth sympathetically. "I can't imagine. But you look beautiful, my dear."

"At least I stopped throwing up. Everyone says the second trimester is the best, and so far, I have to agree. Anything's better than vaguely feeling like you could hurl at any second."

Ariel wrinkled her nose. "Gross. But I'm glad you're feeling better."

"And I have these darling dresses that won't show a thing," June, the head of wardrobe, declared. "Let me grab them. Ariel, what do you think about these pants for the hiking scene?"

Lily and Sawyer were going hiking in next week's episode. Ariel tried on a pair of fitted trail pants while June flitted over to the other side of the room, which resembled an enormous closet full of racks of clothes, all neatly labeled and organized.

"How are you doing?" Cami asked, once June was out of earshot. "You seem...distracted. Is everything okay?"

"Hmmm." Ariel hadn't talked about Ryan with anyone, which was probably contributing to the bursting-at-the-seams sensation she was experiencing. She felt like a kombucha someone had shaken and left out in the sun, fizzy and ready to erupt. "There is something, but this isn't the best place to talk about it."

She trusted June, but she couldn't talk about Ryan when he could come walking in any second.

"Should we have dinner tonight? Oh, I can't. Ryan and I are meeting to talk about the finale."

"Oh." She turned her face away, but the damn wardrobe room was covered in mirrors and reflected every angle, so Cami couldn't miss the blush uncontrollably sweeping across her face at the mere mention of him.

"What's—oh. Oh! Huh?" Cami sounded as if she'd made a confusing discovery.

"Like I said, not here," Ariel hissed, fanning herself and feeling ridiculous.

"Well, since my bedtime is about eight o'clock these days, it'll have to be over breakfast. Want to meet me at the Bakeshop?"

Ariel winced. She couldn't talk about Ryan at Zelda's place, either. God, she couldn't believe their non-affair was causing so much drama.

"Can we do Melba's instead?" The place would be busy and noisy enough that they could chat.

"I'll be there." Cami cocked her head and examined Ariel's reflection in the mirror. "Those pants look terrific on you, but I'm in total suspense here."

Ariel jutted out a hip and leveled a cheesy smile at herself. "That makes two of us."

Cami was already waiting for her in a booth when Ariel arrived at Melba's, dressed for the suddenly chilly autumn morning in a long hunter green cardigan over a boatneck tee, high-waisted jeans, and Frye boots.

"Hey, you," she said, slipping into the seat across from her friend.

"Hey. I ordered us coffee," Cami said.

"Are you allowed?"

"One lousy cup a day," Cami moaned. "But I think the baby likes coffee, so it's fine."

Ariel shook her head. "Wow. You are such an addict."

"My one vice."

"Fair enough. So, how did the meeting go last night?"

"Oh, good. I'm getting weepy thinking about the end of the shoot, though."

"Weepy? That's my territory."

"Blame the hormones."

"Oh, right." Ariel had almost forgotten her friend was growing a human being inside her body. She hoped when—if—*when* she was in the same position, she'd be half as glowing and graceful as her friend. "Don't talk to me about the finale, or I will start getting sad. I can't believe we've already done almost three seasons—again."

"Yeah, it's gone by so fast. I know why we can't keep going, better to go out on a high note, yada yada. But I can't lie—I'm going to miss this. We all work together so well."

Loretta delivered their coffees, and Cami ordered a veggie omelet. Ariel ordered the breakfast burrito and extra salsa.

"We're like a gold-medal synchronized swimming

team at this point," Ariel said as she doctored her cup with sugar.

"I was thinking Ryan's next project should shoot in Misty Harbor, too. That way, we can keep the local crew employed."

"Ryan's next project?"

"Yeah, the pilot he's working on. I've been consulting on it a bit. I thought maybe he'd mentioned it to you."

"No." Ariel frowned. It wasn't as if they had a lot of time to talk. They'd been trying to keep their distance, in fact, even if every time they were in a room together, it felt like they were the only people there. Her awareness of him was automatic now. She had become oriented to him like a compass pointing north.

"Well, contingent on selling it to the studio. Based on the idea, I can't imagine they won't at least green light a pilot."

"What's—never mind," Ariel said. Ryan would tell her about it if he wanted her to know. This was another sign that everyone else was thinking about the future and she was, what, hung up on a guy? She frowned into her coffee.

"You must be thrilled about the podcast," Cami said. "A sellout in the first twenty-four hours, that's amazing."

"I am." The podcast was something she could be proud of, at least. "It's going to be really fun. I can't wait for Erika and Jules to get here. They're coming into town a few days before we wrap. I told Jules I'd give her a tour before they strike the sets."

"The whole live podcast thing was a good idea. A sensational way to celebrate the finale and give back to the fans. I should have thought of it myself," Cami said.

Ariel allowed herself a warm curl of pride at Cami's words.

"Speaking of," Cami went on, "I know you said you're not looking to get into producing, but Selena and I were talking and we both agree you'd be a valuable addition to our team if you even wanted to come on board part time."

Ariel had to process for a moment to understand what Cami was saying. "Are you offering me a job?"

"I would be in a heartbeat if I thought you would take it. Right now, it's only an idea. We already know we work well together, you're a doer, you have tons of connections. And we have more work than we can handle right now, between *Gunsmoke*, *Sawyer's Cove*, and Ryan's pilot. Think about it."

"But I don't have any producing experience," Ariel said.

"You're producing this live podcast, aren't you?"

"I'm coordinating the guests, and the location, and the tickets, but Kate Treanor's producing the show itself."

Cami swept Ariel's objections aside with an airy wave of her hand. "Sounds like producing to me. You're smart and you work hard—that's basically all the qualifications you need. Anyway, I told Selena I'd plant the idea with you, and I have. Now I want to talk about your mysterious crush, or whatever it is."

Ariel groaned. She was fine with moving off the completely unexpected topic of her joining Selena and Cami's production company, but she felt more than foolish having to tell Cami the reason she'd been a little flighty lately was because of a man.

"I haven't told a single living soul this," she said solemnly.

Cami snorted, presumably at her melodramatic open-ing, but she sobered when Ariel projected her most serious expression.

"And you can't tell anyone. Not even Jay. So if you can't keep a secret from him, I can't say anything at all."

Cami made a crisscross gesture over her heart and widened her big blue eyes until they seemed to take up half her face. "I swear. Your secret dies with me."

Ariel giggled at Cami's gravity, which broke the tension. "Okay, good. Here it is. I'm just going to say it." Her heartbeat sped up involuntarily, and she took a deep breath to steady her pulse. "Sorry, for some reason this is really hard."

Cami reached across the table and patted her hand. "It's okay. Take your time. Or don't tell me. Whatever you—"

"Ryan and I kissed," Ariel blurted out.

"Each other?" Cami gasped, palpably shocked.

"Yes, each other. He kissed me. I kissed him. On the mouth. In my car. And outside The Cove."

"Wow." Cami took a gulp of coffee. "I'm going to need more information."

At that moment Loretta arrived with their breakfasts, so between bites, Ariel told Cami about the impromptu movie date and the feelings she'd been having since reac-quainting herself with Ryan. "I told him I'd help him find a date in Misty Harbor, so I set him up with Zelda."

"So that's what that was about," Cami said. "Wow, I can kind of see them as a couple. You're a good matchmaker."

"Yeah, thanks," she said dryly. "Anyway, the problem was I started seeing him not as my boss, but as, ugh, a *man*. And it didn't work out with Zelda, so it's not like I tried to mess that up, but then we went to the movies and it was kind of pathetic how much I wanted it to be a date, so I sort of asked him if he could ever see me that way, and he said he had feelings for me."

Ariel was mildly surprised when Cami didn't say something like, "He does? Why on earth would he have feelings for *you*?" Instead she said, "Go on."

"And so we kissed, and it was good. It was very, very good." Her lips tingled at the memory. Or maybe it was the salsa on her breakfast burrito.

"What's happened since then?"

"Nothing. We decided we should wait until the shoot is over to pursue a relationship."

"Whose boneheaded idea was that?" Cami asked, waving Loretta over for a refill.

"I thought you were supposed to only have one cup," Ariel said. "And it was my boneheaded idea, thank you very much."

"This is an emergency," Cami said, giving Loretta a grateful smile. "And why would you want to wait? If you have feelings for each other, and the kissing is good, it seems like the logical next step would be dating, sex, all that fun stuff."

"If you hadn't noticed, Ryan is the showrunner of the show we're on. He's in charge of the production. Hello? It's an HR issue. Plus, he's always had this thing about actresses and not dating them, and I didn't want to give him any reason to—well. I really like him." She buried her face in her hands so she didn't have to see Cami's pity at her utterly woeful state.

"I've never seen you like this about anyone. I'm so happy for you, honey!"

Ariel peeked through her fingers to see Cami's smile, big and genuine.

"I know the sexual politics are kind of a gray area, but you two can figure it out. I'm just happy you found each other."

"What do you mean?"

"You deserve to be with someone amazing," Cami said forcefully. "And I happen to think Ryan is amazing. Good choice. I won't tell anyone. But, honestly, Ariel, you should go for it. Have some fun, enjoy each other."

As they finished their breakfasts, Ariel considered Cami's advice. She'd wanted to prove to Ryan, and to herself, that she was a grownup who could delay gratification and focus on the work they both loved. But was she acting out of prudence, or just fear? If they never acted on their feelings, then she couldn't be hurt when Ryan inevitably decided she wasn't worth the trouble.

The temporary pause button they'd hit suddenly seemed in danger of freezing them in place permanently.

Chapter Fifteen

Sawyer's Cove: The Reboot
Episode 306: The Storm

INT. THE BAR - NIGHT

PARKER: Dude, you need to call Noah. He's been blowing up my phone. He thinks you're dead in a ditch somewhere.
WILL: Shit.
PARKER: What is up with you?
WILL: Do you think we should get married?
PARKER: Dude, I love you, but I don't think Amy would be cool with it.
WILL: Not you and me, jackass. Me and Noah.
PARKER: Ouch. Break my heart, why don't you?

R yan stood in the middle of the woods questioning all his life choices up to this point.

They were about to wrap filming on the seventh episode of the season. Only three episodes left, and he was feeling the pressure of keeping so many balls in the air. The L.A.-based editors had already sent rough cuts of the first two episodes for notes, he was doing a final polish on the script for the last episode, for which the stakes felt astronomically high, and in every spare minute he was working on the pilot script for his new show about an actress named Franny.

He had no business writing something else when *Sawyer's Cove* took up so much of his energy, but he knew he had a good concept and the words were coming easily. He'd even talked to Cami about it, and she'd been extremely enthusiastic about the idea. It was a long shot to get something made in Hollywood that wasn't based on an existing IP—original television shows were unicorns—but even if nothing came of it, he had to get it out of his head and on the page.

But writing a script for Ariel Tulip was a pale substitution for what he really wanted to do with her.

She had bewitched him. There was no other word for it. What else would you call it when she walked into a crowded room and made it seem like everyone else vanished? When she laughed and it felt as if he'd been punched in the stomach, unable to catch a full breath?

Their timeout, if you could call it that, had served its purpose. They had stayed focused on their work. He'd been so invigorated that the days flew by, and he'd gained the confidence he'd lacked at the beginning of the season

—he believed he could actually steer the ship in Selena's stead.

Meanwhile, he felt like he was experiencing a second adolescence, sexually speaking. He'd fall into bed exhausted at the end of the day, expecting to fall asleep immediately, but he'd be bedeviled by the memory of kissing Ariel, of the knowledge that he hadn't had sex in so long he barely remembered what it felt like.

But he could imagine all too well what it would be like with Ariel, her smooth, luscious body, her cascade of hair, her giving, peach-scented mouth. And his body would respond instantly, throbbing with need until he stroked himself to completion. In the morning, he'd wake up hard all over again and have to indulge in another quick jerk-off session just to calm down enough to start his day. He hadn't touched himself this much since high school.

But as much masturbation as he indulged in, it didn't take the edge off seeing Ariel in person. Every time he saw her, his skin tightened, and he started sweating. It couldn't have been particularly attractive, but she still threw him these mysterious, mocking smiles that made it seem as if she knew exactly what he was thinking, that said she remembered that night, too, and she was waiting impatiently until they could pick up where they'd left off.

The logistics of exactly how they were going to do that were still unclear. He was expected in Los Angeles right after the end of the shoot to work on postproduction. But still, he had to believe they'd figure something out.

In the meantime, he wondered if what he was feeling for her was real, something they could build an actual adult relationship on, or if it was all hormones and lust. Ariel was extremely sexy, and he was in the longest dry spell of his life. But she wasn't a convenient object for his masturbatory attention. She was unique, and fascinating, and she was a staggeringly good actor.

Today was a case in point.

They were making history on *Sawyer's Cove* today, shooting on location in the woods behind the Misty Harbor Inn.

Sawyer North, the titular character, the one Ryan had naively envisioned as his own avatar way back when he wrote the pilot as an angsty recent college graduate, but who had morphed into a completely different character with his own set of foibles and successes over the years, and who Spencer Crosby brought to beautiful life, was proposing, after years of will-they-won't-they and the last season and a half of monogamy, to Lily Fine, badass feminist warrior princess, misunderstood and overly sexualized as a teen, now teacher and mentor to the reboot's new batch of Cove kids.

They were getting engaged, and as a fan of the show, Ryan couldn't be more excited. As the showrunner and one of the writers, he was terrified they weren't going to get it right.

He'd worked on the dialogue for days, polishing and tweaking, until Crosby himself said, "Dude, you've got this. I've got this. We've got this. It's going to work," and practically wrestled the script away from him.

The location had already been set up by their exceptional crew—lights, sound, makeup, and wardrobe were all in place. Crosby was ready to go, holding the prop engagement ring Ryan had picked out personally with the help of Theresa, the head of the props department, and Ariel was outfitted in practical-yet-sexy hiking clothes. Samantha Diaz was directing the episode. She had a light touch with the actors, and she trusted the seasoned crew to do their jobs.

He found a spot to watch from, where he'd be out of the way but on hand if anyone needed to consult him. They rolled sound, rolled camera, and then the Steadicam camera operator followed Crosby-as-Sawyer and Ariel-as-Lily through the woods.

They hiked, spoke a few lines of dialogue, and then Crosby dropped to his knees on the trail.

"Cut," Samantha called. She conferred with the camera operator, and they made some adjustments, Crosby and Ariel waiting patiently for them to reset.

"Back to one," Samantha said.

They did it again, and Crosby went to his knees, then launched into his speech. *The* speech. The one Ryan had been laboring over for days.

"Lily, I love you. I think by now you know how much. I know I'm getting by far the better end of the bargain in this relationship. I once thought my life wouldn't be complete until I met my soulmate. Now I don't know if there is such a thing as soulmates, but if there are, I'd want my soulmate to be someone who understands me, who challenges me, who turns on both my brain and my body, who makes me better and has patience with me when I'm not good enough. You check all the boxes with your big red teacher's marker. Call it what you want, soulmates or not, it doesn't matter. A rose by any other name and all that stuff. I know I'm lucky to even share the same air as you, let alone a life. But that's what we're doing.

We're sharing our lives. You have, miraculously, chosen to share your life with me. I'm humbled by it. I'm grateful for it every damn day. And I want to make it official, babe. I want to marry you; I want the world to know how lucky I truly am. Would you do me the honor of marrying me?"

Crosby reeled off the heartfelt monologue, nailing every nuance of every line. Ryan hoped the camera got all of that because his performance was a masterpiece.

The camera held on the tableau for a moment and then, at Samantha's signal, everyone broke to set up the next shot, which would capture Lily's reaction.

Ryan looked at Ariel, who had tears streaming down her face. Most of the time, Ariel kept a lid on her outward expression of passions when she played Lily, who was more buttoned-up as a rule, but he had to agree, seeing the stoic Lily crying in response to Sawyer's words made a big impact.

She was, as ever, beautiful when she cried.

With the late fall sunlight filtering through the orange and gold canopy, Ariel was bathed in an almost holy glow that no human-manufactured lighting could achieve. She looked like a heartbroken Madonna in a Patagonia jacket. His heart constricted painfully tight looking at her. He realized how true his words, Sawyer's words—whose words were they, and did it even matter anymore?—were. He was lucky to simply breathe the same air as Ariel, and lucky that she seemed to want so much more. Was that why he'd jumped on her offer to wait, because he was scared of how very much he felt for her, how quickly it had swept over him, how potentially heartbreaking and world-changing this relationship could be? Was he even worthy?

He had to try. If she was giving him a shot, he'd be a fool not to take that chance and run with it as far as he could go.

He wanted to cross the leafy floor of the woods, drop to his own knees, press his cheek into her belly, and beg her not to change her mind, to give him the chance she'd offered so freely, so hopefully, weeks ago.

He wanted to pledge himself to her, like a medieval knight, to live the rest of his life in her honor.

Since he had to let the scene finish shooting, and she was in the zone, ripping off her return lines with the aplomb of an old Hollywood leading lady, he sank as far into the background as he could, hunching into his jacket, glad he'd brought a scarf, wishing he'd brought a hat. It was getting cold.

Fall was wearing on, and they'd be done with the shoot soon. He should be focused on nailing every single scene from now until then. He should be thinking about the next script, the pilot he'd had simmering inside him for weeks.

He was sick of should. He'd done what he should do his entire career—played it safe. He'd had some hits, some misses, but he was still in the game. But he was afraid of playing it too safe this time. Suddenly, his world was full of possibilities, and if he didn't say yes to some of them, they might disappear.

All he knew, as Samantha called a wrap on the scene, and on Ariel Tulip for the episode, was that he wasn't going to waste another second. He was going to tell Ariel he was ready, that they should try this, for real, right now, because they weren't getting any younger and he wanted her too much. His patience was plumb out. He'd been tested, and he'd worn his own self-discipline thin with wanting.

But before he could corner her somewhere in these woods, she found him. Only she wasn't alone—Crosby and Jeff, the sound guy, flanked her.

"Ryan," she said ebulliently, "wasn't that incredible? We're celebrating at my place. Game night. Wanna come?" She held up her hand, with the diamond and emerald prop ring he'd picked out himself.

Seeing the jewels winking on her ring finger did something strange to his stomach, making it pop and fizz with desire, jealousy, a need to claim her for himself.

"A girl only gets engaged every so often, you know." She laughed, exhilarated, and he knew it was the comedown from the scene, not that she was actually confusing herself for Lily, but it still tangled his stomach in a complicated knot.

"Game night?" he echoed stupidly. He didn't want to socialize with a group—he wanted to grab Ariel and kiss her until she allowed him to strip her bare and touch every peach-pink inch of her.

"Yeah, come on, it'll be fun," Ariel said, emphasizing the last word as if it was their secret code.

"Okay, sure. Game night. I'll be there." He was done playing the waiting game. Tonight they'd play something else.

Chapter Sixteen

Sawyer's Cove: The Reboot
Episode 306: The Storm

INT. WILL AND NOAH'S BEDROOM - NIGHT

WILL: Timing is everything.
NOAH: You're telling me.

Ariel flew around her tiny living room, making space for the extra chair from her bedroom and dragging her game collection out from the chest at the base of her bed.

She'd invited Crosby, who'd invited Darren and Trevor. Jeff the sound guy was coming, and Stephanie Mae, who'd recently turned twenty-one and had been in the prop room when Ariel had gone back to return the engagement ring like the responsible person she was, even though it was so pretty she'd wanted to surreptitiously keep it forever. Stephanie had called Henry, and

Ariel had put the two of them in charge of the booze, since she had no idea what young people liked to drink these days.

Now the game night was an episode wrap party-slash-birthday party for Stephanie. She'd already called and ordered a slew of pizzas, and she'd raided her cupboards for olives and the cute paper cocktail napkins with "Girls just wanna have fundamental human rights" printed on them that a fan had given her at the last convention.

She'd invited Ryan, too, but she wasn't sure if he'd actually show up. She wasn't sure she wanted him to, honestly. It was too hard to be around him and not want, well, everything. But she could handle it.

The first knock at her door had her smoothing down her hair. She expected it to be Darren and Crosby, or maybe the pizza guy, but it was Ryan.

"Oh, hey."

"You sound surprised. Was that not a real invitation before?" Ryan said, perceptive bastard.

"No, I mean yes. I mean, of course, come in." She held the door open for him and he entered, suddenly halving the space.

"I brought some whiskey." He held out a paper bag, and she took it gingerly. "But you don't have to drink it."

"Thanks." She pulled the bottle out of the paper sleeve and set it on her makeshift bar.

They stared at each other for a minute and then Ryan said, "This isn't working."

Her heart started beating even faster than it had when she'd opened the door to find him there. Did he mean them—the possibility of them? It was suddenly hard to breathe. "What isn't working?"

"You're incredible and I'm so lucky you're even giving me a second look. So if you still want to—to try, with me —I don't want to wait any longer. I know the timing is probably worse now than when we decided to wait, but I don't care. I want you. Now."

He practically growled the last word, and she felt it in her gut.

Her smile felt embarrassingly big, but her joy was involuntary. "I still want to try. And not waiting sounds good."

"Oh, thank God," he said, then he put his hand on the back of her head to pull her in for a deep, long kiss she felt to the soles of her feet. She was breathless when he let her go, her entire body awakened by the kiss, her first instinct to drag him down the hall to her tiny bedroom.

"I've been wanting to do that every single second since the last time," Ryan whispered, as if he were confessing something naughty.

"Me too," she admitted. It was mind-boggling not to be alone in this, to know that her feelings, big as they were, were matched by this man's, that he could understand the depth of her need, the breadth of her desires. "I'm sure we have stuff to figure out, but let's not—"

The knock at the door was an unwelcome thunderbolt of reality.

"Oh shit," she said apologetically. "The party."

"The party." He winced. "Right."

She couldn't send everyone away, not without raising concern. "I can't cancel. But we probably shouldn't—"

"No," he said quickly. "Should I go?"

It would be easier to fake her way through game night if he wasn't there, teasing her, tormenting her with his mere presence. They were obviously not ready to go public yet. "I hate to send you away, but maybe it's best."

"I'll come back," he promised. "Text me and I'll come over. I don't care if it's one AM, text me."

"Yes, I will," she said, thrilled by the passion in his voice.

She opened the door, breaking eye contact with him with difficulty. God, how was she going to survive another few hours without touching him?

"Hi." It was Jeff, the sound guy, holding a six-pack of beer. "Am I early?"

"Nope, right on time, Jeff," Ariel said. "Ryan, I'll text you."

"You aren't staying, man?" Jeff said.

"I have to do...something else," Ryan said awkwardly. "You guys have fun."

"You too," Jeff said.

"Pizza delivery." The person from Harbor Pizza crowded behind Jeff in the hallway as Ryan tried to slip out.

"Oh, can you come in?" Ariel asked, stepping aside so they could bring the six pies inside.

"Think you got enough, Ariel?" Jeff said. "That's like a whole pizza per person."

"I don't know about you, but I can do my part," Ariel said. "Getting engaged makes a girl hungry."

Ryan turned around and gave her an unreadable look. She pulled her eyebrows together and asked him a silent question, but he just shook his head and left. She heard him greet Darren, Crosby, and Trevor on the landing, explaining to them he couldn't stay, and then, finally, more footsteps on the stairs and he was gone. The pizza person left, and then Stephanie and Henry appeared, and she shut the door, turned to the group, and said, "Food first, then games?"

She was met by a chorus of agreement. She helped Henry unload their package store haul of tequila, margarita mix, ice, and limes.

"Margaritas! Oh, you two have my number," Trevor said.

Ariel laughed and said, "You have the run of the kitchen. Go to town."

She grabbed herself a slice of veggie pizza and a napkin and settled on her couch out of the way of the rest of her guests descending on the food and drink like locusts.

Darren settled next to her, mouth full of pizza, when he said, "So you got engaged to my boyfriend today, huh?"

"Hey, I saw him first," Ariel said. "Speaking of which, are you two going to make it official anytime soon?"

Darren glanced over to the kitchen, where Crosby was filling cups with ice for the young people. He leaned close to Ariel and said, "Actually, I have been looking at rings. But it's a secret. I was thinking I'd wait until after the show wraps."

"Oh my God. Seriously?" She had mostly been joking, but if they were really getting engaged, she couldn't be happier for them.

"Well, we've talked a lot about starting the process of finding a surrogate. We both want kids. Getting married seems like a logical first step. Besides, I'm stupid in love with the guy."

Her heart swelled with elation for her friends—and at

the prospect of adding another kid to her honorary niece and nephew list. She blinked hard. "Stop, seriously, I'm going to break down and then your surprise will be ruined."

Darren laughed and rubbed her back. "Don't cry, babe."

"What are you guys talking about?" Crosby called from the kitchen.

"We're talking about Ariel's pathetic love life," Darren threw back. He winked at her and in quieter tones said, "Gotta throw him off the scent."

"Don't mess with my fiancé, dude," Crosby ordered.

Ariel snort-laughed at the irony of Crosby's words and felt some of her pizza go up her nose, then glared at Darren.

"Well, it might not be so pathetic anymore," she said before she thought better of it.

He raised his eyebrows. "Oh yeah? You have something you want to tell me?"

She stuffed her mouth full of pizza. "Not really," she mumbled around her food.

He cackled. "Oh no, that's not going to be good enough."

She swallowed, feeling her throat close up. "It'll have to be, Darren, seriously."

His smile dropped. "Okay. Fine. Are you all right?"

She was giddy with carbs and the news that Darren and Crosby were following Jay and Cami down the stepping stones of adulthood. The memory of Ryan's stubble on her cheeks was fresh, and it hit her with a wallop— she was getting laid tonight.

"I'm going through some stuff," she said carefully,

"but it's good." She smiled in what she hoped was a reassuring way. It *was* good. She was doing adult things, too. She had a secret soon-to-be-lover, and even if she was no closer to finding her soulmate or figuring out what she was going to do after *Sawyer's Cove* was over, that was at least more than she'd had six weeks ago.

Darren put his hand on her shoulder. "Okay, well, let me know if you need anything."

"Will do." She stood up and clapped her hands. "Okay —everyone loaded up on food and drink? Let's play a game."

Hours later, she was in a heated game of hearts with Stephanie, Henry, and Trevor, while Jeff, Darren, and Crosby were arguing over the finer points of their house rules Monopoly game.

"Where did you learn this devil game?" Henry complained as he picked up the queen for the third game in a row. He'd started the night as a complete newbie and he was struggling. Ariel hadn't missed an opportunity to unload her worst cards on him, but she had to keep an eye on Steph and Trevor, who were both worthy hearts opponents.

"I learned it from my grandmother," Trevor said. "She's the kind of grandma who takes those buses for old people to Atlantic City and comes home with more money than she started with."

"Oh, I want to be her when I grow up," Stephanie said. Her cheeks were scarlet from excitement over the game and the single margarita she'd been nursing all night. It was a watery mess in the bottom of her glass, but

Ariel wasn't going to offer her another, trusting the girl to know her limits. Steph put down a seven of diamonds. Interesting.

"I learned on set," Steph said. "On my old show." She'd been the lead on a popular kids' show on cable for years. "We shot in the summers, so there was no school or on-set tutor needed. In our downtime, we played cards."

"I totally missed out," Henry said, sweating over being forced to put down a ten and take the trick.

"How did you learn, Ariel?" Trevor asked.

"Ryan taught me," she said, the memory coming back to her, suddenly unlocked like a video game level finally won. The first season of *Sawyer's Cove*. Early days. Everyone still trying to find their place, both on the show and behind the scenes.

She'd bonded early with Cami and Nash, while Jay and Crosby were harder nuts to crack. Jay because he had no acting experience, and Crosby because he was Crosby. Slowly, the chemistry was gelling. But one episode, four or five, she thought, things were not going well on set. An electrical short forced them to redo a bunch of set-ups, and they were coming up against turnaround. Everyone's tempers were short. She was nervous about an upcoming scene, in which she had a fairly long chunk of dialogue. Even though she'd memorized it, she was still worried about the words flying out of her head once the tape started rolling.

Ryan had seen her pacing and told her it would be at least another half an hour before they needed her. Nash and Crosby were in the scene, too, and he pulled the three of them to the side, produced a pack of cards from somewhere, and they played hearts. Crosby was always good at games, but Nash, like Henry here, struggled. Ariel loved the ruthless elegance of the game and caught on quick. She remembered Ryan's approving smile the first time she ended the hand with zero points, and she remembered being impressed that he was able to hold thirteen cards in one hand. He had a system for setting his cards down and extracting the one he wanted to play without disturbing the others.

She'd looked up to him so much. He was so smart. So intense. Aspects of all the *Sawyer's Cove* characters were rolled up into one mysterious long-haired man she occasionally caught smoking behind the soundstage.

Her heart seized with a confusing mixture of emotions. She knew him better now. He was still intense, but he wasn't so mysterious. He was just a guy. A guy she liked very much. A guy who turned her on, mentally and physically, a guy who made room for her feelings, who seemed to get that she needed to experience things in a big way before she could settle into an approximation of normalcy.

She supposed it was a good thing she hadn't seen him as a potential romantic partner back then. She had been a teenager, after all. He was nine years older than her. It would have been inappropriate. But if he was truly her soulmate, shouldn't there have been some indication of it? Shouldn't her heart have recognized him even then?

Or maybe she was being overly dramatic and Ryan was just a great guy who turned her on and she should stop overthinking everything.

She and Ryan would probably have sex, date for a few months, and then decide to go their separate ways.

Oh God, she was going to die alone.

She shook off the morbid thought.

Henry took another trick.

She narrowed her eyes at him, looked at the cards she had left. "You little sneak."

"What?" He sounded genuinely confused.

"Oh no." Steph groaned.

"What?" Henry said again, taking another trick. "I'm losing."

They played the final hand, and Ariel laughed. "You shot the moon, Henry."

"I did?" He looked shocked. "How?"

Trevor shook his head. "We weren't paying enough attention."

"I don't think I could have stopped it anyway," Steph said. She scribbled down the scores, giving the three of them 26 and Henry zero. "Congrats, Henry."

"Thanks!" He looked pleased, if confused. "Does that help my score?"

Steph examined the pad. "You're still losing by about sixty points. But good job!"

Everyone laughed. Trevor got up to get some water, and Henry asked Steph if she was ready to go back to the inn.

"Sure. I need to take a bath," she said. "My leg is hurting a bit."

"Oh, I'm sorry, is there something I can do?" Ariel asked. She hadn't noticed Steph being uncomfortable, but she'd seen her on set with a physical therapist helping her in and out of her prosthetic leg and knew it bothered her sometimes.

"No, it's fine. I just get tired by the end of the day," Steph said. "It's pretty excellent to be able to walk around on this thing, but sometimes I like using my crutches better."

"Hey, hop on," Henry said, crouching down and pointing to his back. "I'll give you a ride downstairs."

Steph rolled her eyes, but clambered onto Henry's strong back with help from Trevor. She waved from her perch. "Fly, Pegasus, fly."

Henry mock galloped out of the room. "See you guys Monday!"

"I guess they didn't want the rest of their tequila," Trevor said.

"Please take it with you," Ariel insisted. She certainly wasn't going to drink it, and it was a good way to tell her guests it was time to head out.

She ended up sending Trevor home with the rest of the pizza, the tequila, and the remaining limes. Jeff took off with a wave, shooting dagger eyes at Darren, who'd apparently somehow won the Monopoly game even though every time Ariel glanced over, it seemed as if all three of them were transparently cheating.

Crosby and Darren were the last to leave, helping her tidy up before they tossed on their coats.

"Thanks for the party," Crosby said. "And good luck with your love thingy."

"What?"

"You know, what you and Darren were talking about before. Is everything okay? Do I need to step in?"

"No, everything's fine." *Or it will be once I get you out of here.* "You two drive safe."

"Will do," Darren said. He leaned in to kiss her cheek and whispered, "And let me know if you need to talk."

"I will. Take care of my fiancé, won't you."

"Oh, that I can do," Darren said, waggling his thick, black eyebrows. "I'll take care of him all night, if you know what I mean."

Crosby blushed and sputtered while Ariel giggled and pushed them out the door.

"Get out of here," she said, slamming the door firmly.

Finally. She whipped out her phone. It was barely eleven o'clock. She should be worn out after the intense outdoor shoot, the impromptu party, and all the energy she'd expended holding onto her patience and not exploding at her guests and telling them all to get the hell out so she could get laid. But she wasn't tired in the least. She was wired, jumpy, and anxious.

ARIEL

They're gone. You still want to come over?

Ryan's answering text came less than a minute later.

On my way.

Well, that answered the question of if he was still interested.

She did the math in her head. Warner's house was about a ten-minute drive, plus the time to get to the car and find parking near Main Street. She probably had at least fifteen minutes, but was that enough time to take a shower? She had washed her camera make-up off hours earlier, but she had pizza breath and wasn't wearing anything special, jeans and a fuzzy pink sweater that clashed with her hair, not that she cared. She knew she looked best in jewel tones, deep purples, dark greens, ambers. But she liked to wear pastels anyway, powder blue and cotton-candy pink, baby chick yellow. They did nothing for her complexion, but sometimes she just couldn't resist.

She decided she didn't have time for a shower, but she brushed her teeth, feeling kind of silly since he would be able to tell she'd done it as soon as they kissed. But it was the polite thing to do. She dug in her bag to find her peach lip gloss, smiling as she put it on. God, she was so nervous. She knew nothing *had* to happen tonight. Maybe they'd make out and talk. Or maybe the magic pull they'd felt toward each other would disappear.

Or maybe not.

She checked her bathroom drawer for condoms and found a small stash. She used birth control, anyway.

The timer was running out on her internal clock when the knock came on her door.

Showtime.

Chapter Seventeen

Sawyer's Cove: The Reboot
Episode 307: The Proposal

EXT. CLOUDY COVE WOODS - DAY

LILY: I guess we can't risk doing it in
the woods.
SAWYER: I didn't think this through. I
forgot about proposal sex.
LILY: Race you to the car?

"You changed," she blurted when she greeted Ryan
at the door.

"Yeah." He smiled faintly. "I showered."

"Oh, I was wondering if I should, but I didn't have
time."

"That's okay."

They stared at each other, suspended for a moment,
before Ariel remembered it was her turn.

"Come in," she said, moving out of the way.

He might have showered, but his outfit wasn't much different from his usual uniform. Jeans, shirt, tweed jacket, sneakers.

She wanted to take everything off him.

"Do you want a drink? We didn't open your whiskey."

"Are you having something?"

"No. I just brushed my teeth."

He smiled. "Oh yeah? Me too."

"Cool." She faltered. "A glass of water, then?"

"Water, okay, thanks. How was game night?"

She crossed to the kitchen area and filled a glass with tap water. "Fun. We taught Henry hearts and then he shot the moon, the fucker."

"Hearts? I love hearts."

"I told them how you taught us back in the day."

"Oh, yeah." He looked like he was remembering. "You caught on quick, as I recall."

"It was nice of you to teach us. I remember thinking you were so fascinating and mysterious back then."

"Not anymore?" He sounded mock offended.

She laughed. "It's different. You're much more approachable now. Warmer. I like it."

"I guess I've mellowed in my old age." He pressed closer. "I remember you blowing me away every time you were on camera. But that hasn't changed."

She pinked up at the compliment.

"Seriously, Ariel, today you were magnificent."

"Crosby was the real star today."

"He blew it out of the water. He was perfect, as always. But you—you were real. I—I have to say, I was really affected by it."

"How so?" She was curious what he meant. She rarely got real-time feedback on her performance. She usually had to go by the reactions of the director and her scene partners to reinforce her idea of the way the character would act.

"I think it was the ring," he said softly. He reached out and took her left hand in his. He swept his thumb over her knuckles, rubbing against her now-bare ring finger. "Seeing you wearing that ring—I don't know. It brought up a lot of stuff for me. About us. About what we're waiting for."

"I liked the ring," she said softly. "It was so beautiful."

"I picked it out for you," he said, but then he seemed to realize how that sounded, and he tacked on, "For Lily. For the scene. But it suits you right down to the ground."

"You made a good choice," she said carefully, not wanting to tell him she hadn't wanted to take the ring off at the end of the day.

He encircled her ring finger with his index. She shivered. "I was irrationally jealous that Crosby got to propose to you."

"Sawyer proposed to Lily today," she reminded him. He was beginning to make her a little nervous. He hadn't fallen for Lily Fine, had he? She'd had men confuse her for her character before. It wasn't a nice feeling.

"Oh, I know," he said, voice clearing. "I spent so long on the speech, I practically have it memorized. It was worth it, though. Crosby nailed it."

"It's going to be the best season of *Sawyer's Cove* yet," Ariel said, not blowing smoke, just stating fact. She'd been there for all six of them and this one was elevating the art form to a perfect storm of storylines, performances, and production value. She figured it was probably because they weren't leaving anything on the table. They were wrapping up all the storylines the way they hadn't had a chance to the first time around. It meant everything was extra satisfying. It all meant so much to so many people, and they were delivering.

"I grew up in a town like this, you know," he said, seeming to change the subject. He didn't let go of her hand and she didn't move away. "Cloudy Cove was basically the fantasy version of my life."

She'd heard him talk about that in interviews, how the kid from coastal New England reimagined his ordinary world for a soapy teen drama about relationships and different kinds of love.

"And Amy Green—smart, beautiful, approachable. She was my dream girl."

She pulled her hand away, not exactly thrilled to hear his dream girl was her antithesis. He chased her, didn't let her go.

"But Lily Fine, she was my fantasy goddess."

She supposed fantasy goddess beat dream girl, but still, the words didn't sit right. "Not real, then."

"Extraordinary in every way."

His answer disappointed her. You couldn't actually be with a fantasy, and goddesses were bad news, everyone knew that.

"But you, Ariel, are better than any fantasy goddess. You're real." He kissed her knuckles, brushing his lips over them sensually. "You're here. You're so vitally alive. And somehow you want—"

He broke off, and she smiled, encouraging him to complete the sentence, but he seemed stuck.

"You," she finished. "I want you."

"I don't understand it," he said. "But I'm so grateful for it."

"Me too," she said. It really was as simple as that. They didn't have to understand it. They only had to appreciate their good fortune. "It's late. Should we go to bed?"

Chapter Eighteen

Sawyer's Cove: The Reboot
Episode 307: The Proposal

INT. SAWYER'S CAR - DAY

SAWYER: So, how long before the Cloudy
Cove gossip machine gets wind of this?

LILY looks at her ring.

LILY: If you didn't want people to know,
you shouldn't have put a ring on it.
SAWYER: Oh, I want everyone to know.
Maybe the ring will stop you from getting
hit on at the bar.
LILY: I should have thought of that
before and gotten a fake one.

S he led him to the bedroom, the only other room in the apartment, small and cozy, decorated in generic muted tones, but with a fluffy green plaid quilt over the queen bed.

She lit the single lamp, which sat on the small table next to the bed. It also held a towering stack of scripts and books.

Ryan was in Ariel Tulip's bedroom, and he didn't know what to do.

They were taking this step because they couldn't seem to not take it, but he was still out of his depth. He wanted her so much, but this was well outside his realm of experience. He'd never been with someone so outrageously beautiful. He felt self-conscious in his ordinariness. He supposed his body wasn't strictly ordinary, but he was still just a man. Ariel Tulip, even if she was more real than Lily Fine, was closer to transcendent human perfection than anyone else he'd ever touched.

"Get comfortable," she said. She took a jar candle and a box of matches from the bedside table drawer, lit the candle, and doused the lamp. The semidarkness helped. She was already barefoot, and she arranged herself on the bed, sitting with one leg tucked underneath her, leaving him plenty of room to join her.

He toed off his shoes and shrugged off his jacket, laying it over a simple straight-backed chair.

"Wow, sometimes it feels like I've never seen you without that thing." She nodded to the jacket. "I wasn't sure you weren't made of tweed."

"My signature."

"Like my hair," she said, shaking it free of the messy bun she'd had it in.

"Not an equivalent analogy. Have I told you how much I love your hair?"

"I love your jacket, too," she claimed. "It's cozy."

He shook his head. "You're strange."

"Yeah, I am," she said, matter-of-factly. "So, you want to sleep over?"

"Yeah," he said, his voice suddenly rough. He joined her on the bed. "Yeah, I do."

"Good." She kissed him.

This they'd done before, a few times now, and though every time made him feel like he was dissociating a little bit, looking at himself from outside his body, marveling at kissing this too-good-to-be-true woman, it also grounded him in the basest physical sensations. His body grew hot, achy, as blood rushed to his hardening cock.

She wrapped herself around him, nestling in close as she possibly could, until she had to throw a leg over his hip to get even closer. They had never been in this position, and the possibilities were intoxicating. With his hand twined in her hair, he lost his balance, but she just went with him when he collapsed against the pillows on her soft, girly bed. She kissed across his cheek, down the line of his jaw. Her hands hovered over his shirt.

"Can I?" she asked, biting her lip and looking at his chest as if he were an ice cream sundae she wanted permission to dive into.

"Anything."

She took her time unbuttoning every button on his plain blue Oxford shirt. He usually only unbuttoned far enough to fit it over his head, to save on time fastening buttons one-handed, but she undid them all. She pushed the shirt down his arm, tossed it in the vague direction of the chair. That left him in a gray tee. She didn't hesitate, grabbed the hem, and pulled it up and over his head.

He was naked from the waist up, and she looked at his torso for a long minute. He waited for her gaze to move to his left shoulder, to take in the lump of flesh that represented the arm and hand that never developed. But she seemed riveted by his pecs.

He glanced down at himself, wondering if he'd acquired an interesting scar or a tattoo in his sleep. But all he saw was his regular chest, a healthy amount of soft brown hair down the middle, currently erect nipples a shade darker than the hair. His pecs were fairly well-defined, and his belly was flat—no extra fat. He did a lot of upper body work in the gym—Warner's home gym, these days—to keep his strength and mobility up. Not to mention the three-times-a-week yoga class he took remotely with his longtime Los Angeles-based instructor. He'd discovered yoga was one of the best ways for him to stay in touch with his body and keep it tuned up.

"You're so cut," Ariel said. "Work out much?"

"Yeah. Well. Exercise keeps my mind clear. Stress relief. I need to keep my flexibility up, too. Yoga is essential."

"Well, you look great," she said, tentatively touching his chest with her soft fingers.

"Thank you," he said politely. The suspense was killing him. Why didn't she seem interested in his stump? Every other woman he'd been with—and admittedly, the number of those could literally be counted on his single hand—had needed an adjustment period before they felt comfortable touching him there. If they ever truly got comfortable. It had been a deal breaker for more than one. And that was fine. He didn't need to convince anyone they were attracted to him. Either they were, or they weren't. The reverent gleam in Ariel's eyes proved to him that she was in the "attracted" camp. Thank fuck.

"Here," he said impatiently, taking her right hand and placing it over the stump. "Get it over with, okay?"

"Get what over with?" she said, her attention finally on that part of him, the part he'd long ago made peace with, the part he barely even thought about most days as being something to think about.

"I need you to not ignore this part of me."

"Okay," she said, with no defensiveness. She stroked him, looking at the lumpy flesh there, then glanced at his face. She smiled. "You're so beautiful, Ryan. I've always thought so. I wondered what you kept under all those layers, under all your tweed. You aren't made of tweed, after all. You're gorgeous."

"I'm glad you think so," he said, surprised his voice came out gravelly.

She cradled his stump in her palm for a second, then let out a little gasp. She put both hands over her mouth, hunched over. She let out a breathy "sorry."

"Sweet—what's wrong? Are you—" He was afraid for a terrible moment that she'd been putting on an act all this time and was realizing now she couldn't handle the reality of being intimate with him.

She was crying, her eyes gleaming with tears. "I'm okay. I'm just—I'm really happy and it's kind of overwhelming."

Oh. His breathing resumed. "It's okay, darling." He

thumbed a tear off her cheek. "You know, you're really beautiful when you cry."

Her smile was watery. "Is that a good thing?"

"It is to me. You feel a lot, and you aren't afraid to show it. And I think that's amazing."

"Thanks."

"And if you're happy when you're with me—that makes me so very happy, too."

"Well, look at us. Two happy fools."

"Yeah." He kissed her and tasted salt. "It's pretty great."

"It's hard to trust, I guess. What if we do this and something happens?"

He couldn't promise her that nothing would happen. "Something probably will happen. Something we're not expecting, something that makes this hard. Or harder than it already is. But I still want to give it a shot." He thought about what he could promise her. "But there's one thing I do know for sure—if something happens, I'm not going to hold it against you. I'm not going to take your friends, or the show. I'm not going to take what belongs to you. You don't have to worry about that."

She looked curious about his declaration, but simply said, "Thank you."

"And I'm very aware that the workplace politics of us doing anything like this together are not ideal. You don't have to give me any explanation if you want to stop, ever. I would never want this to be something you were afraid to end."

"I appreciate that, but I'm not worried. You're honorable."

"I would have thought you'd be more jaded after the career you've had."

She laughed without humor. "I've seen plenty. That's how I know I don't have anything to worry about with you."

He took it as the compliment it was and tried not to think about the bad experiences she must have had over the years.

"And now that we've gotten the fine print out of the way, can we have sex now?" she asked.

He laughed. "You're right. I've taken the romance out of the moment. Sorry."

"That's okay," she said. "I can fix that." And she pulled her sweater up and off, leaving her in a jade green lace demi-cup bra. His brain went offline as he attempted to take in the newly revealed swells of flesh. She was round and soft everywhere, and his mouth suddenly watered at the prospect of getting to taste her.

"Yeah, well done," he said, voice even rougher than before. "Come here." He shifted so he was propped up on his arm and she was lying against the pillows. She'd seemed pretty obsessed with his chest, and he had to admit he felt the same about hers. "May I?"

"Please," she said.

He lowered his head to nuzzle along the line of her collarbone, breathing in her fresh female scent, soap and sweat and that damn peach flavor that seemed to cling to her no matter what.

He'd imagined this so many times—actually he'd tried not to imagine it, tamping down on the details in his brief fantasies—but he'd been looking at her for years and the reality of her was entirely different than he might have expected. Normally, she projected sturdy confidence and robust femininity. She rocked shit-kicking boots and could pull off faux leather and flannel or lace and frills with equal aplomb, whether she was costumed as Lily or not.

But in this bed, in which he felt like an oversized, lumbering man, off-balance about everything except how much he wanted her, Ariel was petite, soft, delicate.

She was very nearly fragile. He took a shaky breath and internally vowed not to break her.

He kissed his way to her breasts. Nudged down the cups of her bra to reveal her nipples, large and smokey pink. Licked them. His cock swelled to full hardness as he explored soft peaks with his tongue. She really had tremendous breasts. He stayed there for a while, indulging, because she seemed to like it, too, based on her breathy sighs. She put a tentative hand on the back of his head, keeping him there. He reached back and encouraged her hold. She complied immediately, bunching his hair up in her fist, making him feel the sting of it. He groaned, suckled her harder, and she let out a single, devastatingly gratifying word, "Yes."

He switched to the other breast when he felt he'd worried the first tight bud past the point where it could have been comfortable, and she arched into him eagerly. He paid the other nipple the same attention, not quitting until she started to squirm violently underneath him. He pulled off her, and she dropped her hand from the back of his head to his shoulder, yanking him toward her for a filthily deep kiss.

"More," she rasped, pushing him back down.

She had somehow gotten rid of her jeans while he'd

been preoccupied with her breasts. Her panties didn't match her bra. They were simple black cotton, and he stripped them off one-handed after a nod from her. Her bush was tightly groomed, red hair so dark it was practically brown. She was fully spread out on the bed now, her long hair pillowed all around her, her body paler against the dark quilt than it appeared under the set lights.

She licked her lips, watching him. "You want to get more naked?" she asked.

"I want to make you come," he said, confused by her priorities.

"It's just that you look kind of uncomfortable," she said, nodding to where he kneeled on the bed beside her. His pants tented obscenely, his erection about to pop through the fabric. Suddenly, he became aware of how close he was to losing it. He was a forty-two-year-old man who hadn't been laid in two years. He'd perfected the art of one-handed masturbation when he was a teenager and had plenty of practice, lately especially, but she was right. He didn't want to blow in his jeans like some hapless *Sawyer's Cove* guest star trying to make it with Lily Fine. *Ugh*. He needed to stop thinking about her character, about the show. That was fiction. This was real fucking life, even if it felt too heavenly to be true.

He struggled with the button for a second, and then Ariel launched herself at his crotch. "Let me," she said.

She had him unbuttoned, unzipped, and pushed his jeans off his hips in about three seconds. He had loose boxers on underneath, dark blue. She hesitated when it came time to decide if the boxers would come off with the pants.

He closed his hand over hers, helped her slide both

down. He tipped to the side, and she drew them the rest of the way off, then stripped off his socks at his approving nod.

"There," she said with satisfaction. "Much better."

Her gaze snagged at his crotch, her eyes glittering. He supposed she had a right to stare. He hadn't stopped switching from her face to her breasts to the vee of her mound since she'd removed her clothes. She was staring at his erection like it had the secrets to the universe. He glanced at himself. He was rather ordinary, about average size, in that department, he'd always thought. His sac was heavy, but drawn up, ready to go, the hood of his foreskin dark with blood. Brown curls a shade darker than his hair. No grays down there yet, thank God.

He'd always been grateful for his normal equipment. Women tended to know what to do with that part of him.

But Ariel stared as if she'd never seen a cock before.

"Everything okay?" he asked, a shade nervously.

"Everything's..." She swallowed and finally looked him in the eye. "I've never been with an uncircumcised guy before."

"Oh. Is that okay?"

"Sure. You're absolutely gorgeous, you know that?" she said, her hand gliding from his chest, down his flat belly, to his cock, which she palmed softly. He wrapped his own hand around hers, showing her how firm he liked it, and she got with the program right away, stroking confidently.

"Fuck, Ariel, that feels so good. But I wanted you to—"

"This feels good to me," she interrupted. "God, you're so..." She kissed him, tongue spearing into him, and the sensation of that combined with the way she kept purposefully jacking him had him shuddering.

"I'm too close," he said, stilling her hand. "It's been a while for me."

"Yeah, me too," Ariel said. "Not to mention you've been edging me for weeks."

He laughed at her exaggeration. "Sorry about that."

"It's okay. We'll just stay in bed all weekend until we build up our stamina."

He let himself imagine it—neither of them leaving this bed for days, making love over and over again until they ran out of food and water and were forced to go down to Melba's for grilled cheese and milkshakes. "You have really good ideas." Her answering smile made him feel like the luckiest man in the world.

"So if it's been a while for you, and it's been a while for me, and I'm on birth control, do you think we could go without condoms?" She sounded sweetly hopeful.

He blinked. He hadn't been expecting that. He and Heather had dispensed with them once they'd gotten that sorted out. But if he didn't use a condom with Ariel, it felt like one less layer of protection for his heart, too.

"It's okay," she said when he didn't answer her question. "I understand. It's totally fine to use them."

Why was he resisting? He trusted her. He wanted this, too.

"No, if that would make you happy. Of course."

She frowned. "I don't want this to be a thing you're giving me because it's what I want. It's too important."

He smiled. "We're such a pair. Darling, it's okay."

"I just feel like I want our first time to—I don't want to feel anything between us. Which sounds psycho, probably." She smiled self-consciously, though she didn't seem self-conscious about being gloriously naked and touching his cock while they debated condoms.

He examined how he felt about it. What if they never made love to anyone else for the rest of their lives? They'd always remember this first time, how it felt to be with each other completely, fully.

What if this was the only time? He'd have the memory of what it was like to be inside her with not even a millimeter barrier between them.

"Darling." He kissed her. "I don't want anything between us, either."

Despite the prolonged condom debate, he was still rock hard. He laid her back down on the bed. She parted her legs, and he slipped his fingers in the gap, lightly feeling out her folds, and the addictive heat of her pussy with its gathering of moisture. His fingertips came away slickly wet.

"Ryan. I need you inside me."

He bent down, licked a stripe over her sex, and tasted salt and musk. His cock grew impossibly harder.

She bucked into his mouth when his tongue dipped into her pussy. "Ryan. Not what I meant."

He lifted his head, smiling wickedly. "Oh, sorry."

"Don't stop," she complained, almost whined.

He returned to his task, reveling in the sheer hedonism of burying himself in the dark, hot nooks and crannies of this exceptionally beautiful person.

Her cries grew breathy as he switched back and forth from her clit to her pussy, then finally she broke, and her hand went to the back of his head, the way it had when he'd suckled her breasts. This time she didn't hold back

—she gripped his head assertively, grinding his face down on her sex while she writhed and shook all over. He lost himself there, her musky wetness the only thing he'd need to survive for the rest of his life.

Finally, her shaking reached a crescendo, the grip on his hair painfully tight.

"Ryan, fuck, I'm coming," she said, her voice gone throatier than usual.

He held her hip and licked her through the orgasm shaking her. His cock was so hard it felt like it was punching a hole through her quilt, straight into the mattress.

When her body seemed more sensitive than responsive, he let go of her, used his undershirt to wipe the moisture from his face. She lay on the bed, twitching, eyes glassy.

"Holy fuck." She pushed herself up to her elbows. "Fuck," she said again.

"Is that good?" he asked, though he was pretty sure he knew the answer.

She responded by pushing him down on the bed and climbing on top of him, kissing him, her mouth scalding hot. For a second, he was overly aware of her scent, which no doubt clung to his mouth, but she kissed him as deep as ever, unbothered by her own flavor. She straddled him, her pussy sliding along the ridge of his erection. He gasped as she caught his cockhead in her opening, all the while kissing him, and then sank down slowly over his entire length.

He was inside Ariel, bare, her legs squeezing his thighs, her hair swinging down into his face, her tongue inside his mouth. His entire body tightened, his arm circled her waist, lifting her up, encouraging her to move.

She pulled out of the kiss with a dirty pop and obliged, riding him with slow, confident motions, just like she'd jacked him earlier. He was so close, but he didn't worry about that as much since he'd made her come once already.

"Fuck, Ryan, you feel so fucking good, oh my fucking God."

He distantly registered that he'd never heard her swear so much in a single sentence. "Ariel." It was the only word he could think of.

She set the pace, slotting against him as if they were made to be together that way, a hand in a glove.

"Ariel, darling. I'm going to come," he said, warning her. Promising her.

She moved faster, her strong thighs pumping up and down, her breasts swinging in time, hypnotically heavy and full, teasing him by being so close and yet so far away. Then she cupped them, somehow keeping up her rhythm and holding her own breasts out to him, like an offering, as she cried out, her mouth round and pink, her hair a tangled mess.

She was coming again, he could tell, and his body responded instinctively, the orgasm he'd been holding at bay through sheer willpower suddenly galloping through him, a runaway horse of pleasure that had him arching into her soft, sweet body, pumping into her what felt like an endless stream of his release. She pitched forward, keeping her seat, but curving so her breasts ended up in the vicinity of his mouth. He turned and suckled the nearest one, her cries turning high-pitched as he worried her nipple and she kept moving, shuddering, coming down from her second climax while he felt the post-orgasm haze of lethargy steal over him from his toes on up.

Gently, he released her breast, then shifted to kiss her mouth. She moved and there was a gush of wetness between them where her body was letting him go. He had an irrational desire to stay connected to her all night, to nest their bodies, to keep the feedback loop of pleasure going indefinitely.

She didn't seem anxious to break contact, either. She grabbed a fistful of tissues from a box by the bed, swiped up the mess, and threw the tissues in the general direction of a waste bin, then pushed down the green quilt to reveal soft white sheets.

"Get in," she said. She hadn't put on any clothes, so he didn't either. No condom. No clothes. They didn't need anything between them, not anymore.

It was more than he deserved, and more than he expected, and he was greedy enough to hang onto it with every fiber of his being for as long as she'd let him lie with her in this bed, their bodies wrapped around each other.

Chapter Nineteen

Sawyer's Cove: The Reboot
Episode 307: The Proposal

INT. CLOUDY COVE COFFEE SHOP - DAY

LILY: Guess what?
AMY: You're pregnant.
LILY: Jesus, no. What, you have babies on
the brain or something?
AMY: You won the lottery.
LILY: Sadly no. One more guess.
AMY: You invented a time machine and are
going back in time to see The Beatles
perform live?
LILY: That would be cool, but no.

S he and Ryan were under the covers. The candle had
been blown out. A faint glow filtered under the door
from the lamp left burning in the living room, but other-

wise it was dark. It was late, she'd had a long day, and their round of sex had been protracted in the best possible way, but Ariel didn't feel tired. She was thrumming with energy, the blood Ryan had awakened running through her veins at double speed. She felt jittery, as if she'd drunk three cups of coffee and eaten one of Melba's prune Danishes. Thank God she didn't have to work tomorrow, because she definitely wasn't getting her beauty sleep tonight.

She wouldn't easily drift off to dreamland with a naked man in her bed.

Having him there was strange, but not unwelcome. They'd negotiated the space once they were under the covers. She usually slept closer to the right side of the bed, but turned out, so did Ryan. It made sense—that way he could reach whatever was on the night table by the bed more easily. So she'd taken the left side. A simple adjustment, but it still felt odd.

She was naked, too, but as alert as she was, she was too lazy to get up and put on her usual sleepwear of a big T-shirt and sleep shorts. Nothing existed to her outside of this bed.

"Are you comfortable?" she asked, whispering into the dark.

Ryan hummed. "Yeah. Thanks."

"Are you tired?"

There was a moment of silence. "I'm guessing you aren't." There was a trace of humor in his voice.

"I feel high," she admitted. "Sugar and caffeine and sex."

"Endorphins." He turned over and she could make

out the glint of his multicolored eyes. "You want me to leave?"

"No. You want to leave?"

"No."

"Okay. So what happened with your ex-wife?"

Ryan's laugh was shocked, but he didn't get out of bed. Rather, he touched the tip of his nose to her shoulder, kissed her arm. "Do you need a bedtime story?"

"I need—I want—oh, I just feel so good, and I can't sleep, and I thought since we're doing this, maybe we could talk."

Ryan sighed, but not in a put-upon way. "I guess this is as good a time to talk about my relationship failures as any, when you're still in the post-orgasmic afterglow."

"How did you meet?"

He laughed again, but not surprised this time. Fond. "We met at a party. Introduced by mutual friends. Nothing cute about it, just industry people. We found ourselves alone, and she liked Ginger Rogers and Fred Astaire movies. We dated for a year, and then I asked her to marry me because we'd been talking about moving in together and I was kind of old-fashioned about it, I guess. I was going to be thirty-three, and it seemed like a good time to get married."

"I'm thirty-three," Ariel said quietly. "Not to make it about me," she added as an afterthought.

"I thought I was getting old. And I was never any good at dating and it was just a relief to have it over with."

"Sounds like a solid foundation for a marriage," Ariel said in what she hoped was a teasing tone. Privately, it seemed like the darkest, saddest way she could imagine embarking on that kind of commitment. Even if she wasn't head over heels for someone—no, scratch that. She'd like to think she'd *only* marry someone she was head over heels for. And if that meant she stayed single until she was forty-three or fifty-three or a hundred and three, so be it.

"We tried," he said. "We worked well together. But eventually what small flame we had between us died out, and I could see she wasn't happy, and then she pointed out that I wasn't particularly happy myself, and I realized I'd spent most of the decade waiting for things to stop being rote. I thought we'd have kids, and we'd be too busy to dwell on how lukewarm our feelings for each other were. But we kept finding reasons to put it off. Thank goodness."

"You don't want kids?" Ariel tried to tell herself his answer didn't matter.

"No, I do want kids. I mean, it might be too late, but I always saw myself having a couple. I think Heather wants them, too. Just not with me."

He didn't sound upset about it, only resigned. She ignored the fizzy soda feeling in her stomach. "You'd make a good dad," she said, instead of offering to have his babies. She wasn't delusional.

"Thanks," he said, instead of running for the hills. "So, did my sad little bedtime story put you to sleep?"

She did feel calmer, her body heavier, and she was growing accustomed to his weight at her side. "So, does your limb difference make it easier to spoon? Your arm can't fall asleep."

He chuckled. "Yeah, actually. One of the perks. Wanna see?"

"Yeah." She scooted closer, slotted her ass against his

groin, feeling the tickle of his pubic hair on her backside, the length of his soft cock pressed between them. He wrapped his arm around her middle securely, kissed the back of her head.

"Did you ever think about getting a prosthetic?"

"I've tried, a couple of times. I know if I put in the work and was really consistent with it, it might make a difference, but I'm too set in my ways, I guess. I have my own ways of doing things and I'd have to completely retrain myself. It's hard going back and forth. I really admire Steph for spending so much time in hers."

"I know it hurts her sometimes, but she feels like she has to."

"It's not the most comfortable thing to have a piece of machinery attached to your skin," Ryan said. "But she's got a different situation. She lost her leg as a child, and I was born without an arm. I've literally never known anything different."

"I hope you'll tell me if I ever accidentally do anything hurtful, or make an assumption that's wrong," Ariel said. She hadn't worried overly much about it, but she was aware she'd probably make mistakes.

"Sure. I'll let you know if something's bothering me. I guess it's like I said before—I don't want you to pretend there's nothing different about me, but I don't want you to fetishize it or anything. Some kind of happy medium would be awesome." He kissed her hair again.

"Sounds good," she murmured, wondering what he meant by fetish. She was already so attracted to him, and the limb difference didn't add or detract from his appeal. This was how she'd always known Ryan, from the very first moment they met. She'd always thought he was cute, and now she was allowed to think he was beautiful, to be turned on by him. She was also self-aware enough to know she felt a little bit superior to any woman who'd seen him, been with him, and hadn't been attracted to everything about him. And grateful, too, for all the other shallow people, to his ex-wife—who probably wasn't a bad person, but sounded too cold for Ryan's warm heart —so she had a chance to be with the most interesting man she'd ever met.

"Can I ask you one more question, and then I promise I'll let you go to sleep?"

"You can ask me as many questions as you want, Ariel."

There he went, indulging her again. He'd spoil her if he kept on like this.

"Why didn't you want to be involved with the reboot until now?"

"Ah." He splayed his hand over her belly and she wriggled closer. If she talked enough, maybe he'd be up for another round. That way, she could sate both her libido and her curiosity tonight.

"I know Selena asked you, is all," she went on. "She would never have gone ahead with the project without your okay—I know she wanted to work with you on it."

"She did ask me," he said. "It was when things with Heather were falling apart. I didn't have the bandwidth to think about the show, and I also felt like I'd had my shot with it, and it had ended—"

"Don't say badly," she said. "That wasn't your fault."

"Abruptly," he finally said, as though he'd struggled to find the right word. "However it ended, it was over, and my time was finished. Selena had all this energy, this vision for the show. I knew she didn't need me, and I was right. The smash success of the reboot is all down to her and Cami and the crew and you guys for trusting her with these characters."

"I thought maybe *Sawyer's Cove* was too childish for you, when the stuff you've done since has been more serious."

"That might have been part of it. But I've had so much fun on this shoot, maybe I should accept that soaps are more in my wheelhouse than drama, and my destiny is to write about people falling in and out of love."

She laughed. "You might get a bigger audience that way, too."

"I know, I know, my last show was a little self-serious."

"I think *Sawyer's Cove* takes itself seriously; it's never making fun of its characters. But it's not so lofty in its pretensions as some other unnamed shows," she said.

"Thank you for that charitable reading," he said, tickling her ribs until she squirmed against him, giggling.

He kissed her shoulder, her upper arm, her hair. His cock thickened. She turned around to face him, kissed him on the mouth, his jaw, his Adam's apple, the hollow of his collarbone. His hand found her breast and squeezed hard.

This time it wasn't careful, it wasn't slow. He was hard when she guided him to her entrance, throwing her leg over his, canting her hips so they were joined together while facing each other under the covers, a hot, sweaty cave that smelled like sex, which only turned her on more. She didn't care that it was messy—it felt amazing to be messy with someone else, to share the mess, to share the pleasure, to share anything, really.

He used his powerful thighs to thrust satisfyingly deep, and then she was coming. She'd regret orgasming so soon, except she believed this was only the beginning for them. Two tally marks and a million to go. He grunted as he came, his forehead tipping to hers, his hair falling into her face.

She pulled him closer when he tried to pull out.

"Stay," she whispered.

He stayed.

Chapter Twenty

Sawyer's Cove: The Reboot
Episode 308: The Yard Sale

EXT. SAWYER'S FRONT YARD - DAY
Setting up for the yard sale.

WILL: You aren't going to give me one bit
of credit for calling this?
NOAH: Fine. You said all of our friends
were going to get engaged. One couple
down. Happy now?
WILL: What do you think? Should we be
next?
NOAH: Don't joke about that. I know
you're Mr. Anti-Marriage.
WILL: I'm serious. Would you marry me?
NOAH: Hypothetically? Yeah.
WILL: And non-hypothetically?

"All right, we have two episodes to go. Let's finish strong, everyone," Ryan said, completing his pep talk to the department heads with a dorky fist bump. Not that he'd regret it—nothing had been bothering him lately. Every problem that cropped up at work was a challenge to be met with a jaunty smile and a burst of energy.

After a weekend spent in Ariel's apartment, alternating making love with long talks, a shared shower experiment that led them to realize her little apartment's correspondingly small shower wasn't practical for two people, eating takeout, and making a dent in Ariel's stores of bubbly, he felt like a new man.

Sex-filled weekends should be prescribed for anyone who felt rundown and listless. Forget Vitameatavegamin. Copious amounts of hot sex with a girl so beautiful it hurt to look at her might cure anything.

They'd decided at the end of that first weekend not to make any formal announcement about their changing relationship status to the cast and crew, but if it came up privately and they needed or wanted to tell someone, it was all right. Ariel told him she'd already talked to Cami about them. It made Ryan feel better that she had someone she could confide in. He was aware of how lonely she'd been. He didn't want to isolate her from her friends just because they were dating. As for the crew— they had each other's backs—no one would spread gossip.

He was riding too high on endorphins to care about gossip, anyway. At times he felt like one of his characters, someone who doesn't see how sex with the object of his desire is going to lead to his downfall—but he was too smitten with Ariel to consider any negative consequences a deterrent. In fact, at this point, he'd welcome his downfall as long as it meant he didn't have to stop being with her.

Every day they left work separately, only to meet up at one of their places. The visitor would spend the night, then frantically speed back to their home turf in the morning to shower and change for the day. He liked Ariel's cozy bed better than the one in the impersonal guest room he was staying in at Warner and Selena's mid-century mansion, but they agreed the oversized whirlpool tub in the upstairs master bathroom was preferable to her tiny shower. Pros and cons.

Everyone filed out of the conference room to tackle the tasks of preparing the sets, costumes, lights, props, etc. for episode nine of ten. In twenty minutes, he had a meeting with the West Coast editors to go over the rough cut for an earlier episode. They were operating on the same compressed timeline Selena had established in the first season—shooting everything back-to-back, plus editing the first episodes concurrently so that they were ready to launch the show on Christmas Day. This would be the third and final Christmas with new *Sawyer's Cove* as a gift to the fans.

The only one who lingered was Cami.

"You okay?" he asked. He didn't have a lot of experience with pregnant women, and though his instinct was to insist she sit down and take it easy, he knew the suggestion would be met with scorn.

She sat on her own volition, and he joined her. "I'm fine. I can't believe we only have a few more weeks of shooting, but besides that, things are good."

"I know. It's gone by so fast."

"Like a bullet train. Have you been able to work on the script for the new pilot?"

He hadn't touched the document on his computer since the night he and Ariel had sex. He'd been too busy working...and having sex. But he'd thought about it. When things calmed down, he'd refocus.

"No new writing, but it's there, waiting for me to pick it up again."

"Sounds good. No pressure. We're all caught up with other stuff right now. I just wanted to check in with you. You seem...happy."

"You make that sound like a bad thing."

"It's not. Really. It's nice to see you smiling. When you first got here, you were much dourer. Now it's like you're a Christmas tree and someone remembered to plug in your lights."

He wanted to say that sex with a beautiful woman had a way of lighting a man up, but decided to save it for a script instead of saying it to his producer and star actress. "Why do I hear a caveat coming?"

"Because I've been in the behind-the-scenes relationship that's going suspiciously well until the shoot is over and everything suddenly falls apart. I don't know if you and Ariel have talked about it, but I don't want that to happen to you guys. When the season is over, the series is over—consider planning ahead."

"We know it's not going to be easy," he said, not sure how much to reveal.

"Long distance is hard, is all. And Ariel's really special, but she's not as tough as Lily Fine."

"I know that." He was well aware of the differences

between the girl he'd been sleeping with and the girl she brought to life as a job.

"Okay. Well, I'm here for both of you if you need to talk."

"Thanks, Cami." He was overwhelmed by an unexpected wave of gratitude for the fact that these people cared about him at all. *Sawyer's Cove* was a family, and he no longer felt like the outsider. He was one of the inner circle and it felt good to have people care about him. He hadn't even realized how isolated he'd been since his divorce until he'd been blanketed in warm concern from everyone in Misty Harbor. He'd miss it once the shoot was over. Now he understood why Cami and Nash had decided to make Misty Harbor their home base.

It was hard to leave once you found a place you truly belonged.

Did he and Ariel belong here? She loved New York. He liked Los Angeles, had lived there for so many years. But besides work, there wasn't much left for him there.

He supposed this was something he should discuss with Ariel herself, but was it too much, too soon? They seemed to be doing everything out of order, unable to be grownups and progress through the usual stages of a relationship. He'd never even taken her on a proper date. That night at the movies didn't count.

This weekend. He'd take her out, do it right. Bring her flowers, the whole nine. She'd like that, even if she wouldn't ask for it. She liked the trappings of femininity, of tradition.

"Do you know what kind of flowers Ariel likes?" he asked before Cami left to conquer the next production crisis, because there was always a next production crisis.

Cami paused on her way out the door. "Ironically, not tulips—not that she doesn't like them, but it's not the most original choice."

"And not lilies, I suppose," he said wryly.

She laughed. "No, she likes whatever's in season. There's that florist across the street from the bookstore on Miller Street."

"Excellent suggestion, thank you."

"Good luck, Ryan," Cami said.

Her tone indicated she thought he was going to need it.

Chapter Twenty-One

Sawyer's Cove: The Reboot
Episode 308: The Yard Sale

EXT. SAWYER'S FRONT YARD - DAY
Will waits anxiously for Noah's answer.

NOAH: Yes.

Ariel and Ryan hadn't spent a night apart since game night, and after he texted her Friday afternoon to say he wanted to take her out that night, she got giddy at the prospect of going on an actual date with the man she'd been sleeping with for two weeks. She was so happy it scared her. How could anything this good last?

She wasn't even supposed to be in Misty Harbor this weekend. She didn't have many scenes in the current episode, and the break in her schedule meant Ariel could have gone back to the city for a few days. She had made plans to do so—staying in town meant she'd had to cancel a pedicure and massage at her usual spa near her apartment in the West Village, as well as coffee with a friend and a meeting with Mona, her New York-based agent. But she didn't want to leave Misty Harbor when things with Ryan were still so fresh.

She wanted to say it was because things were going well and she wasn't going to turn down regular sex with a hot guy, especially one who treated her like a queen. And that was true. But part of her decision to stay close to Misty Harbor was the feeling that she didn't want to miss a single moment of the honeymoon period, in case this was all they got.

They hadn't talked about what would happen once the shoot was over, but the day was fast approaching when Ryan would fly to Los Angeles to work on the show's postproduction and Ariel—

Well, Ariel still hadn't figured out what on earth she was going to do.

She'd been thinking about Cami's suggestion that she join her and Selena's production company. She'd been watching Cami the last few weeks, juggling her acting job on the show, constantly communicating with Ryan and the director of the current episode, taking calls from the suits at the studio who were putting up the money, liaising with the studio's PR people who managed the press, dealing with fans. Oh yeah, and she was in a committed, loving relationship with a man who had his own small business, and they were going to have a baby together. She was in awe of her friend— Cami had the energy to power a small country—but it was still a lot. At least Cami had finally hired an assistant, a knife-sharp woman named Tori, who was a hard-edged complement to Cami's cotton-candy approach.

Every time Ariel had hired an assistant, she'd always ended up becoming friends with them and encouraging them to pursue their own dreams—which never consisted of supporting an overly emotional television actress—so she'd eventually given up.

She wasn't anyone's goal, anyone's high point. She was just a stepping stone, for the men in her life, for other people's careers. Sometimes she was sure Ryan would leave, too, when it got too hard, no matter how good it was now.

A new script had come in from her agent—one of the things they had been supposed to discuss at the meeting. They'd have to do it over the phone. She wasn't going to take the part, anyway. She knew Mona was frustrated with her, but she couldn't sign up for a project she was lukewarm about just to have something to do, not after the dream experience of *Sawyer's Cove*.

Damn, was she going to be measuring everything against this show for the rest of her life? It was so special, and she would never find something like this again, working alongside close friends with a warm on-set vibe. Even the town, which she wasn't as in love with as some of her costars, still made her feel like a local when she was here.

Since she had some time before Ryan would pick her up for dinner, she went for a walk down Main Street, avoiding both the temptation of one of Melba's milk-shakes and the Bakeshop. She'd been avoiding the Bakeshop for ages now. Or more specifically, she'd been avoiding Zelda. She knew things hadn't ended badly between Ryan and the baker—he'd insisted they'd never really started. One dinner and a hug did not a major romance make. But still, it felt a bit unseemly that she'd stepped into the part when she'd been the one to convince Zelda to give Ryan a shot in the first place.

She passed the insurance agency and the consignment shop, then turned onto Miller Street. The bookstore called to her like a brick beacon. This afternoon, the shop had quite a few people in it, which made her happy to see.

The weather had turned chilly overnight, it seemed, and she'd dug a scarf out of her closet to pair with her tartan coat. She ordered a hot tea from Danica to warm her while she browsed the aisles and killed time until Ryan picked her up.

"So how are things?" Danica asked as she rang her up.

"Really good." She smiled. "I can't believe how fast this season has gone by. Only a couple of weeks left."

"It's wild," Danica said. "I'll be sad when it's over."

"Really?"

"There's always a boost to the economy when *Sawyer's Cove* is in production. But the holiday rush is coming, and we'll stay busy with local shoppers."

Ariel was so self-centered. She'd only been thinking about how the end of the shoot would affect her—she'd forgotten that *Sawyer's Cove* was a local institution. They had Cove Con, the annual fan convention held in town in the summer, but there would be no more production. The soundstages on the outskirts of town could always be used for another show, but who would choose out-of-the-way Misty Harbor over better-established shooting locations like Vancouver or Atlanta?

"So you don't mind the chaos we cause?" Ariel asked.

"When the show came back, it took some adjustment, I won't lie," Danica said. "But I got used to the street closures and Jay being more than just my goofy boss. And it sets Misty Harbor apart from other small seaside tourist towns. It makes us special. For businesses like ours that depend on foot traffic and tourism, it's a godsend."

"I bet," Ariel said. "Well, I'm glad you guys are here, too. Every town needs a groovy wine bar-slash-bookstore." She made a mental note to take out her phone and snap some pictures to post to social media later. She supposed it wouldn't hurt Miller Street Book Bar if she dropped a mention of them into her feed with its two million followers.

Danica handed her a paper cup with the bookstore's logo stamped on it. She let it warm her hands as she browsed the bright, open aisles. She didn't glance over when the door chime indicated a new customer, but she recognized the newcomer by her voice.

"Hey, Danica, is it too early to get a glass of red?" Zelda asked.

Ariel froze, intently studying the fantasy novel she'd picked up at random.

"Never too early for you, Z," Danica said. "What's up? Starting the weekend early?"

"I have to go to a baby shower tonight. I need fortification. And a gift. You have a kids' book section, right?"

"In the back. Looking for anything in particular?"

"No, I'll take a look in a minute. Oh!" Zelda said, sounding a little surprised.

Just because Ariel had gone still didn't mean she was

invisible. She turned around slowly and smiled at Zelda uncertainly.

"Hi!" she said in an overly bright tone.

"Hi." Zelda's voice was completely normal.

"That looks good," she said, indicating the wine Danica was setting in front of Zelda. "Making me rethink my order." She took a sip of her really quite yummy herbal blend.

"Yeah, TGIF," Zelda said, raising her glass in a mock toast. Ariel tipped her paper cup toward her, and they mimed clinking glasses from across the room.

"I'm sorry I haven't been in the Bakeshop lately."

"You've been busy, I gather." Zelda's dry tone made it seem as if she was talking about something besides work.

Ariel winced.

Zelda immediately stammered, "Oh shit, I didn't mean that the way it sounded. My stupid sense of humor."

Ariel waved the apology away. "I have been busy," she said. "And I've also been avoiding you a tiny bit. Sorry."

"Hey, there's nothing for you to be embarrassed about, really." This time, Ariel could pick up the undercurrent of kindness in her voice. "So Ryan and I didn't work out—it's not your fault, okay?"

"Well, I'm sorry I meddled. Turns out matchmaking is not for me." She took a deep breath. "And there's another thing—uh, I sort of started seeing Ryan. Very recently," she hastily added, to make sure Zelda knew it was well after their aborted attempt at dating.

Zelda was silent for a beat, then she laughed, clear and bright. "Oh, that explains so much," she said through her laughter.

Ariel smiled uncertainly. It didn't sound like Zelda was laughing at her, but she still didn't get the joke. "What does?"

"The night we had dinner—maybe this is telling tales out of school, but Ryan could not stop talking about you. It was a little weird, but now it makes sense. I could tell his heart wasn't really in the date—which is fine, whatever, I've had way worse dates. Like seriously, way worse." She sobered, and then brightened. "But it seemed strange. Now it turns out he was just hung up on you. And you got together—that's terrific." She sounded genuinely happy for them, and Ariel found her cheeks heating with a blush of relief.

"Oh, wow, thanks, that's so nice of you," she said, feeling a stack of George R.R. Martin books lighter.

"Is that why you haven't been coming in?" Zelda asked, sipping her wine. "I thought it was because you thought I was a failure as a woman or something."

"No! God no," Ariel said. "It was stupid. I just thought, in case you had wanted things to go differently with Ryan —I didn't want to hurt your feelings."

"Well, don't worry about me," Zelda said. "So, things are going good?"

"I think so," she said. "They are right now, anyway."

"Live in the now," Zelda advised. "That's all we're guaranteed, anyway." She took a big swig of her wine.

Ariel looked at her sensible tea, then walked over to the bar. "Can I join you?"

"Sure." Zelda waved at the open seat next to her.

"Danica, do you have anything with bubbles back there?"

Zelda clapped her hands. "Now you're talking."

. . .

"So then I said, 'well, we have a tip jar,' and he walked out."

Ariel gasped. "Wow, what a cheapskate."

"Celebrities better watch out—service workers never forget who's a good tipper and who's not."

Ariel was at the end of her glass of Prosecco from the bottle Danica had opened for her, and she and Zelda, with Danica chiming in when she wasn't helping other customers, had talked for the last thirty minutes nonstop. It turned out Zelda had grown up in Manhattan, worked at a fancy bakery, and experienced her share of celebrity encounters even before she came to Misty Harbor, where they were a dime a dozen. And she wasn't afraid to spill the tea and name names, keeping Ariel in constant laughter.

"Oh my gosh, it's getting late," Zelda said, checking the time on her phone.

"And you have a baby shower to get to," Ariel said.

"Don't remind me."

"Whose shower?"

Zelda scrunched up her face. "Well, to tell you the truth, it's for my ex's sister. Shelly and I are still friends. And he's probably going to be there. Hence the wine."

"Your ex the butcher?"

"The very one."

"You could bail," Ariel suggested.

Zelda toyed with the stem of her empty glass. Her cheeks had taken on a pretty red blush as she finished her wine. "No. I can't. Besides—I don't want to. It's not Shelly's fault I'm a mess. She's married to her best friend and they're going to have their first kid. I'm really happy for her. It's just hard sometimes."

"I know exactly what you mean," Ariel said. She thought about Cami and the end of the show barreling down on them. The only thing she'd managed to do in the last few weeks was, okay, knock it out of the park at work, finalize the arrangements for the live podcast fundraiser happening in a few weeks, and start sleeping with a guy who tied her up in knots but who had no known address, except he'd probably end up on the West Coast while she went back to New York to begin the downward slide of her career into police procedural guest spots and mediocre holiday movies.

It wasn't as if she had nothing going for her, but she for sure didn't feel like she had anything figured out yet.

"And the worst part is—" Zelda stopped, put her hand over her mouth, as if she was trying to hold something in.

"What?" Ariel leaned in closer to her, well, friend. She was going out on a limb and saying they were friends now.

Zelda squeezed her eyes shut and whispered, "I miss him."

"The butcher?"

"Shush!" Zelda hissed, looking around. There was a man browsing self-help and two women chatting at the other end of the wine bar. Zero people looked their way.

"Sorry," Ariel whispered. "The butcher?" she said in a tiny voice.

"Yeah," Zelda said sadly. "Am I pathetic for wanting to get back together with him?"

Ariel had no knowledge of their relationship or why they'd broken up in the first place, but she knew one thing. "Zelda, you are the least pathetic person I know. You're a rockstar. You own a thriving business, you're a baking genius, and you're gorgeous and funny and smart to boot. If you want the butcher, go get the butcher. As long as he deserves you."

"I think I got scared that things were too good. Like, if we're this happy right now, it can't possibly last." Zelda stared into the distance, then her expression changed as she spotted something through the Book Bar's front window. "Hey, isn't that your guy?"

Ariel followed her line of sight and spotted Ryan disappearing into the building across the street, the flower shop where the production team sourced flowers for *Sawyer's Cove*.

"Yeah." She looked at the wall clock above the bar; it was later than she thought. She was supposed to meet Ryan at her place in less than an hour.

"Honestly, I don't have any chips in this game," Zelda said. "So don't be a stranger in the Bakeshop, okay? I gotta get that baby gift and take off." She got up and walked to the kids' section.

"Anything else for you, Ariel?" Danica asked.

"I better not, thanks. Can I get both of these?" She indicated Zelda's empty wine glass and her own.

Danica smiled. "Sure thing."

While Danica totaled the bill, Ariel peered across the street, but she couldn't see Ryan anymore. Was he at the flower shop on an errand for *Sawyer's Cove*?

Zelda came back to the counter with a handful of board books. "Add these to my tab, Danica."

"Ariel covered your wine. I'll ring these up in a second. Want them wrapped?"

"No, I have a gift bag in my car. And thanks, Ariel, you didn't have to do that."

"No worries. I'm going to go, too." She hadn't found a book, but she'd found something better—understanding with Zelda. And a mystery—what was Ryan doing across the street?

Ariel signed the credit card slip, adding a large but not embarrassing tip. Zelda walked out with her, calling over her shoulder as she waved to Danica. "See you at book club."

Outside, the evening air was crisp and clean. "Good luck at the baby shower," Ariel said, giving her an impulsive hug.

Zelda looked momentarily surprised, but then she smiled. "Thanks. Good luck with...everything."

Ariel laughed. "Thanks."

Zelda went to her car, and Ariel debated going straight back to her place, or waiting around until Ryan reappeared. She took one step toward her apartment, but then Ryan emerged from the shop. He had a huge brown-paper-wrapped bouquet tucked in the crook of his arm, and his ubiquitous messenger bag strapped across his chest. He caught sight of her and leveled her with a smile.

"Hey, you," he said.

Chapter Twenty-Two

Sawyer's Cove: The Reboot
Episode 308: The Yard Sale

EXT. SAWYER'S FRONT YARD - NIGHT

SAWYER: The thing about Lily is that she
understands that I'm messy sometimes.
PARKER: Well, that's true.
SAWYER: Thanks for that. Like Amy's never
had to pick up after one of your messes.
PARKER: I didn't say that. But we're
talking about you and Lily.
SAWYER: Yeah. Lily isn't afraid to get
her hands dirty. Thank God.

"Hey, you." Ariel inclined her head toward the flowers. "Need any help with that?"

Ryan looked at the bouquet and his smile turned into something of a grimace, but he didn't answer.

"I was just at the Book Bar. Heading home now, if you want to meet me later and pretend we didn't run into each other."

"No, that's—that's silly. Here." He shifted the bouquet so she could take it from him.

"They're gorgeous," she said as she glanced inside the wrapping to see asters with tiny purple starburst flowers, golden yellow black-eyed Susans, and dusty pink cone-flowers all mixed together in a voluptuous bouquet. She loved wildflowers, local beauties that hadn't been flown halfway around the world out of season. "Do you need to take them back to the set?"

"What? Oh, no. They're for you."

Embarrassed pleasure swept through her, heating her cheeks and making her stomach leap. "Oh." She looked down again at the flowers, now with a sense of owner-ship, and she felt the flush spread through her whole body.

She looked at Ryan, who was watching her carefully. She blinked back grateful tears. "You got me flowers," she whispered.

"Overdue, I thought," he said. "Flowers are always a solid date opener, I think." He seemed to be asking for some kind of reassurance.

"Oh, I couldn't agree more." She buried her face in the flowers indulgently, breathing in their spicy, fresh scent before raising her head and giving him a kiss on the cheek. "Thank you, Ryan."

"You're welcome. I'm glad you like them."

"They're stunning. The people in this shop know their business, don't they?"

"Oh yes, they took me well in hand, luckily. I'm not

exactly a flower expert."

"These are just right for me."

"I'd hoped so. Now, date step two. Dinner at Harborview. You said you hadn't had good seafood in ages, so I thought—"

"That's so considerate, but I got caught up at the bookstore and I'm not dressed. Do we have time to go back to my place?"

Ryan looked her up and down. "You look wonderful."

Her jeans, boots, and sweater would fly for weekend brunch, but not date night dinner at Misty Harbor's second fanciest restaurant. "No, I have something else to wear. It won't take me long to change. Do we have a reservation?"

"Six thirty."

"Plenty of time, let's go."

"My car is—"

"Is it in an okay spot? I feel like walking." She held her flowers like a trophy, feeling conspicuous in a good way walking down the street with the man she was seeing, holding the flowers he'd given her because they were going on a date.

They spent the short walk catching each other up on the events of the day. She left out the part about her heart-to-heart with Zelda—maybe she'd tell him later when they had more privacy than Main Street afforded.

When they got to her apartment, she pointed him in the direction of the kitchen and a big glass water pitcher that doubled as a vase, then went to the bedroom. She stripped to her simple black underwear and bra and debated taking a shower while she got her dress out of the closet. She'd brought the form-fitting sheath dress in a fit of optimism that she might need something semi-formal and sexy during her stint in Misty Harbor.

I love being an optimist she thought as she laid the dress out on her bed while she grabbed her black velvet heels.

"Hey, how much water—?" Ryan came to the door of her room, froze when he saw what she was wearing. "Sorry, I'll come back." He turned around to face the hallway.

His sudden reticence to see her semi-naked made her laugh. "It's okay."

He turned around, giving her a bashful smile. "You have to forgive me—there's still a part of me—never mind."

"What?" She walked up to him, curious. She slipped her hands between his jacket and shirt to encircle his waist and give him a hug. It felt good to rub her nearly naked body against his clothed one. He kissed the top of her head, hugged her back, the brush of tweed and cotton waking up her bare skin.

"I guess I forget sometimes that you're an adult, that I'm allowed to—"

"See me naked?" she finished.

"Well, yeah. I have so many mental images of you as a teenager—and I was so careful never, ever to get confused at the time about thinking you were an object of desire. I think I still have a little hardwiring to that effect. Sorry if that's gross."

She tipped her head up to meet his apologetic gaze. "No, Ryan, it's not gross. It makes sense. I never thought of you as an object of desire back then, either, if that makes you feel better. You were like the older brother-slash-boss. But that was a decade and a half ago. Almost half my life." She rubbed her cheek against his chest, held him tighter. "I'm glad you didn't perv on teenage me, but I'm giving you carte blanche to perv on me now, all you want."

He laughed lightly. "Good to know."

"I'm serious, like, perv on me right now." She glanced up at him again through her lashes. "I want you to."

His eyes darkened, and he dropped his hand from her back to her ass and squeezed over her panties. "Now? What about dinner?"

"I can be quick," she assured him, hands dropping to his waistband and unfastening his trousers. She felt him harden against her belly, and she reached inside his boxers, gave him a few strokes until he was like steel in her hand.

She liked being on top as a general rule, but just now she wanted to feel him surrounding her, so instead of leading him to the bed, she flipped their positions so her back was to the wall and he crowded her against it.

While he shoved his pants and boxers roughly down his legs, she shimmied out of her underwear, then moved his hand to her tit, which he kneaded the way she liked— firm and confident, rolling her nipple between his thumb and forefinger.

She was wet already, had practically been wet since he'd told her the flowers were hers, a gesture that showed he'd been thinking about her, that he thought she was worthy of such a tribute. She needed him inside her, needed the point of connection that amazed her every time with how good it felt, how easily he filled her up, how in tune they were to each other's pleasure. She guided his erection to her pussy, canted her hips while he made the angle work.

He let out a bone-deep groan when he breached her, and she sighed in response.

"You feel so good," she said as he sank in to the hilt. He ground into her, making her feel it deep, overwhelmed by how good it felt to be joined that way.

It turned her on that he was still wearing most of his clothes, fucking her because she'd asked him to, because she needed him, and he needed her. They needed each other. As much as she liked it, she perversely wished she had access to his chest, his shoulders. He wasn't moving, just pinning her to the wall with his cock; she wanted to bite into his flesh, to spur him into giving her the rhythm she craved.

Finally, *finally*, he began to move, pulling almost all the way out before slamming back in, jolting her entire body as he speared her to the wall, rattling the watercolor seascape near her head.

"Again. Ryan. Please." She was being loud. Maybe they could hear her down the block at Melba's. She didn't care.

He kept up the steady rhythm, every time seeming to reach deeper than before, until she felt like her entire body had been consumed by him, that she was a vessel for him to fill up, again and again and again.

"Ariel," he gritted out, his hand gripping her ass, "please say I can come."

She was so close, and she didn't want it to end, but she trusted him. In that moment she felt she could spend her life like this, urging him to take what he wanted and, in the process, getting everything she ever wanted, too.

"Please," she sobbed. "Harder. Come in me."

He growled and began hammering into her even harder, the sparks of her orgasm immediately blazing into a wildfire so intense it took her an impossibly long time to realize he'd lifted her off her feet, one-handed, between the wall and his cock, shouting as he poured himself into her.

There was a distant crash, and she shouted, too, his name, she thought, as her eyes squeezed shut and she gave into the sharp, hard pleasure of coming while he finished inside her.

"Fuck." It was all she could think to say.

He slumped over her, setting her feet gently to the floor, slowly slipping out of her. Her thighs were tacky with the wet smear of both of their contributions. Out of the corner of her eye, she spotted the framed watercolor on the floor, dislodged by the force of Ryan's thrusts, but it looked unharmed.

He breathed on her for a while. She didn't mind the weight of him pressing her into the wall while he came back to himself. Eventually, he pushed away and raised his head. His hair was a flyaway mess. She must have run her hands through it while he was fucking her. She couldn't quite remember, but it looked like she had.

"You're going to need to do something to your hair before we go out," she said.

He laughed hoarsely. "Can I borrow a comb?"

"Anytime."

"Fuck, Ariel, that was—incredible seems like a cliché, and maybe it's unimaginative enough that I should be ashamed of myself as a writer, but that's what it was."

"Yeah." She kissed him. "I'll take incredible."

"You're so—" He stared at her, unrelenting. She squirmed under his gaze for a moment, then forced herself to still, as colors shifted and swirled in his eyes. She picked out the brown, the gold, the hint of blue. A universe in those eyes, one she wanted to spend the rest of her life exploring. "You're so perfect it's unreal."

His word choice disappointed her somehow. She felt far from perfect, and she wanted to be real. She wanted *this* to be real. She wanted him to see this was the realest thing they had going.

Ariel bit her lip. "Let's go eat. You must have worked up an appetite fucking me into a wall."

"I didn't hurt you, did I?"

"No—I'm...perfect," she answered, with a hint of sadness.

Chapter Twenty-Three

Sawyer's Cove: The Reboot
Episode 309: The Wedding Planner

INT. SAWYER'S KITCHEN - DAY

LILY: I know we just hired this person,
but I think we need to fire them.
SAWYER: Oh, I'm so glad you think
so, too.
LILY: Call me looney tunes, but what if
we skipped the rigamarole and eloped?
SAWYER: I love you so freaking much.

Ryan was buzzing from one too many cups of coffee and nerves. Selena Echeveria would be there any minute.

It didn't matter that he technically had more experience than Selena. She was now the heavier hitter in the industry, with more recent successes, more clout, and hell, clearly more talent. And the big boss was flying in to check up on him.

Selena had a break in her *Gunsmoke* schedule just as they were starting to shoot the tenth and final episode of *Sawyer's Cove*. He'd briefed the cast and crew about her arrival, but no one had greeted the news with what he felt was the proper amount of gravitas. He was the only one who seemed to be anxious. Then again, they'd all worked with her closely for a couple of years, while he still felt like he was on probation, waiting for her to come in and take the show away from him. It didn't matter how many times Cami reassured him he was doing an outstanding job, that the powers that be were thrilled with the early cuts and the fan buzz around the final season, he still felt the lingering trauma of having to end *Sawyer's Cove* so abruptly the first time.

So yeah, he was nervous.

At least the director of this episode, David Blakely, was a pro who'd directed more *Sawyer's Cove* episodes than anyone else and had everything well in hand, but it didn't help that Ariel was back on set today after nearly a week off. He had mixed feelings about it—he loved working with her, but he didn't need the added distraction of their romantic entanglement right now.

It would be a good test, he supposed, of their professionalism. Or his, anyway. Hers had always been impeccable. He was the one who had to remember to keep his eye on the ball and not on the gorgeous creature who deigned to let him touch her.

Instead of stewing in his office, he decided to check in with June, the head of wardrobe, about storing costumes once the shoot wrapped ten days from now. It was hard to believe in a week and a half the sets would be struck and the production dismantled as if it had never existed.

The dressing room was chock full of people and abuzz with conversation when he walked in. The entire original *Cove* cast was there—Nash and Crosby, Jay and Cami, plus Darren, June, and of course, Ariel.

"Congratulations, man," Darren said, pumping Nash's hand and slapping him on the back.

"And you, too, Uncle Jay," Crosby said, smirking at the man whose arms surrounded Cami as she rested her back against his chest, her baby bump surprisingly noticeable in the pink T-shirt she wore. She had months to go yet, but the growing curve was a tangible reminder she was going to have an actual baby in the near future.

"What's going on?" he asked.

"Our little bean is going to have a cousin," Jay said, dimpling hard. "My sister Mimi is pregnant, too."

"And I'm the father!" Nash said with a wide, unironic grin.

Ryan had never seen the man look so happy. "That's amazing! Congrats you guys."

Crosby peered at Cami. "So are you ticked Mimi's stealing your thunder?"

She smacked him on the arm. "Don't be silly. I'm excited. She's two months behind me, but it'll be so cool to have kids roughly the same age."

"Deb must be kvelling," Darren said. "Two grandkids at once. It is only two, right? Neither of you are having twins?"

"Nope," Nash said, unbothered, still practicing his proud papa face. "One kid, due in May. We just started telling people, so please keep it to yourselves a little longer."

There was a chorus of agreement. Ariel hadn't said anything, though she was smiling happily at Nash.

Ryan wanted to go to her side, to share the moment with her as they celebrated their friends' happiness, but he stayed by the door, holding himself clumsily apart from the group. They weren't exactly hiding their relationship—last week at dinner they'd even kissed in the Harborview dining room. At the time he was certain he'd sensed a surreptitious phone camera aimed at them, but he didn't have social media, so if anything had been posted online he'd never know. Even still, they hadn't made a formal announcement, and now certainly didn't seem like the right time to make a declaration, even one as passive as standing next to each other.

Or maybe he was just a coward.

As congratulations were still being passed around, Darren whispered something into Crosby's ear, Crosby shook his head, and then Darren whispered something else. This time Crosby looked around the room and nodded.

"Um, guys," he said, clearing his throat while the room quieted. "In the thunder-stealing department, we have something we wanted to tell you while we're all together like this."

"We're getting married," Darren said.

Someone gasped, but Ryan didn't think it was Ariel. She still had a smile on her face, but her eyes were getting that pinched, pre-tears look.

"You bastards," she said, voice watery. "Making me cry and messing up my makeup. Lavon is going to kill you when she has to fix me." She gave Crosby a huge hug while the rest of the group started chattering and congratulating the couple.

"We were going to wait—actually, *I* was going to wait to propose," Darren said, a painfully large smile stretching his face. "But the ring was burning a hole in my pocket, and I have no chill, so."

"It was way more romantic than he's making it sound," Crosby said, giving his fiancé a fond look. "But yeah, we're engaged. And we're hoping you all can be there when we do the deed, so I guess we need to factor these baby arrivals into wedding planning."

"You better," Cami said. "I'm not missing your wedding."

Ryan added his voice to another round of congratulations, but his gaze never left Ariel. Her eyes were wet, but she wasn't sobbing or anything. She seemed her usual effusive self, but he remembered her state of mind a few months ago, her sense that everyone was moving on with their lives while she was static. Here was tangible proof. Since he'd been dominating her social life, she'd completely stopped talking about the terrible scripts she was being offered. Was she thinking about the future at all?

He suddenly felt incredibly selfish. He'd been taking up her time while she could have been making progress toward her goals. He'd been putting off thinking about what would happen when the shoot ended, but the finish line was no longer way in the distance. Ten days from now, they'd be toasting to the end of the run, and they'd go their separate ways.

He edged his way into the crowd until he was close

enough to Ariel to touch her elbow. She flinched, as if she hadn't expected the contact.

"Hey," she said. Her eyes were red and luminous, her lips glossy.

"Hey," he said quietly. "Can I walk you to makeup?"

She wrinkled her nose. "I know. I must be a mess."

He wanted to say she was the most beautiful thing he'd ever seen, but that would have definitely taken the vibe in the room in a weird direction.

"Here's where you're hiding." A new voice came from the doorway. Ryan glanced over and there was Selena, with her big hair, big glasses, big grin.

Already buzzing with the excitement of the various happy announcements, everyone greeted Selena with a joyful hubbub, shamelessly talking over each other until she put out her hands in supplication. "Hang on, one at a time. What did I miss?"

Cami reached her first. "Oh my God, Selena, Mimi's pregnant—"

"And I'm the father," Nash put in unnecessarily, still overwhelmingly proud.

"And Darren and Crosby are engaged," Cami went on as if she hadn't been interrupted.

Selena clapped her hands happily. "Anything else, or can I dole out the hugs?"

Cami glanced at Ariel and Ryan standing next to each other, but she shook her head. "Nope. Hug away."

"All right." She started with Cami and worked her way around the room. When she got to Ryan, she said, "Hi, there."

"Hi," he said, his nerves returning for the briefest of moments before she grabbed him in a rough hug.

"You're killing it," she said in a murmur. "I know you're busy today, but I also want to talk to you about the *Lost Stars* script."

"What? You read it?"

"Cami sent it to me," she said. "We want to—well, later." She turned to Ariel before he could respond, which was just as well because his mind had gone momentarily offline. Cami had sent Selena his under-baked, practically stream-of-consciousness script?

"Hey, you, missy," Selena said, embracing Ariel, who hugged her back tightly. "Aren't you due on set?"

"Yeah."

"Someone get this girl to makeup, stat," Selena said. "Hey, June." She gave the wardrobe head a hug for good measure.

Cami glanced at her watch. "Sorry, Ryan, I know we're messing up the works."

"It's okay," he said. "It's just going to be one of those days, I think. Can you tell David we have to push by fifteen?"

"On it," Cami said. "Selena, come with me and we'll distract David while Ariel gets fixed up."

"I'm not that bad, am I?" Ariel said nervously.

"No, but I'll take you down to makeup, okay?" Ryan said, suddenly needing a moment alone with her.

She looked at him curiously, but nodded. "See you in a minute, Crosby."

Ryan escorted her out, hyperconscious about touching her, not touching her, people watching them, no one paying them any attention.

Makeup was on the next hallway in the warren that made up the backstage area.

"What a morning," Ariel said, when they'd turned the corner and found themselves alone. "Are you okay?"

"Am I okay?" Ryan repeated. "I was going to ask you the same thing."

"It's just that I know you were a little nervous about having Selena here. But things are going great."

"Oh, that." He'd talked Selena's visit over with Ariel a few days ago. He supposed he shouldn't be surprised that she remembered, and that she cared. "Yeah, it's okay."

She bumped his hip with hers. "Remember, you've got this. She's not here to grade you, just check in."

And she wants to talk about my script. He wanted to ask Ariel about that, to get her reassurance about that, too, but he hadn't found a chance to bring up the script with her yet.

"My mind has been more on you, honestly."

"Yeah?" She smiled at him, as if the idea of him thinking of her pleased her.

"Just all your friends and their good news," he said stiffly, not sure how to phrase his concerns about her delicately. They stopped outside the makeup room.

"I'm, well—it's a little overwhelming, but it's good, you know? Also, by the way, they're your friends, too."

He shook his head. He'd never feel like one of the fold the way she was. "Well, that's good. You have a busy day. I won't keep you any longer."

"Okay, thanks for your concern." She glanced around the hallway, but they were still alone. She pecked him on the cheek. "See you later."

"See you."

She went into the makeup room to get touched up, and he wandered slowly back the way they'd come. She made it seem so easy, but he felt completely insensitive. What had he done to deserve her concern, her kisses? What made him so special that she was wasting her love on him? She'd told him from the beginning—from before the beginning, back when he'd known better, when he could have stopped himself from going down this damned road—that she was looking for her soulmate. That she wanted the kind of all-consuming love she'd read about and watched unfold on TV screens for years.

He'd known that she wanted something deep and wide, and she deserved that. And he was wasting her time.

Mulling over his options, he was still only halfway to the set when Ariel overtook him in the hallway. "Hey, slowpoke," she said, smiling at him, easy and effortless and so beautiful it made his heart hurt. Her eye makeup had been refreshed, and she'd been de-shined for the camera. He didn't know how he was going to explain to her that he had to let her go. Or maybe he could pretend he deserved her for the rest of their lives and hope she never caught on?

No, he couldn't do that to her.

"What's wrong?" she asked. "Bad news?"

"No. Uh." She had to act in one of the most important scenes of the final episode in a matter of minutes. He couldn't sabotage that by bringing any of this up now. "Maybe we could talk later, though?" If he didn't rip the band-aid off, he'd never let her go, and she'd wake up one day and realize she'd lost her chance to find her soulmate and hate him forever.

"Okay, sure. If we wrap on time, we can talk this afternoon. I have dinner with Erika Rainwater tonight, remember?"

"Oh yeah, the podcaster. Fun. Go knock 'em dead."

"Always do," she said, winking at him.

She hustled past, but turned around at the last second and gave him a heartbreakingly tentative smile. "It's nothing bad, right? What do you want to talk about?"

He took a deep breath. He didn't want to lie to her, but he didn't want to ruin her scene, either. Before he could answer, Jason, a PA, ran up to Ariel. "There you are. You're needed on set right now."

"It's my fault," Ryan called to Jason as Ariel allowed herself to be pulled away.

This entire mess was his fault.

Chapter Twenty-Four

Sawyer's Cove: The Reboot
Episode 309: The Wedding Planner

INT. LILY'S CLASSROOM - DAY

NOAH: So if you don't want your wedding
planner, can we have her?
LILY: Why?
NOAH: My marriage-phobic boyfriend
proposed. And I'm sure as shit not planning a wedding alone.

Ariel pushed her disconcerting non-conversation with Ryan to the back of her mind, compartmentalizing as best she could while she and Crosby knocked out three quick back-to-back set-ups. She had a break while they set up for a group scene. The camera would have to work around Cami's belly, so they'd gotten creative with blocking during rehearsal.

She went to the drinks station and got a hot tea. Her throat had felt scratchy since that morning, not like she was getting sick, just from overuse. She had a lot of dialogue to deliver and had to protect her vocal cords.

Darren came up and poured himself a cup of coffee. "How's it going, babe?"

"It's going. So when am I going to get the full story of the engagement? I thought you were going to wait until the end of the shoot."

Darren grinned. "I can't tell you the full story because I gave my word to Crosby I'd keep it between us, but know that it was very romantic and we both cried and yes, you can be one of my groomspeople."

She made a face. "Ugh, you did it during sex, didn't you?"

"No comment. But nudity may have been involved, which is why the story isn't for public consumption."

"I suggest you make something up that you can tell during interviews because I'm not going to be the only one who wants details."

"Good idea, smarty. I'll get the writers to work on that."

"Well, I'm colossally happy for you two. And to think, two years ago you hated each other's guts."

"Hey, I never hated Crosby," Darren protested. "And he didn't hate me, either."

"You know what I mean. Who would have thought the two of you would turn out to be soulmates?" She sighed. She couldn't even be jealous of Crosby and Darren's happiness because things were still red-hot with Ryan—though their looming talk made her frown. Vague talks were almost never good things.

"Soulmates, yeah, sure, I guess." Darren took a bite out of a chocolate chip cookie.

"What do you mean 'you guess?'"

"Well, if you want to label it. I mean, we love each other and make each other really happy and want to be in each other's lives forever. Does that make for soulmates?"

"Yes," Ariel said decisively.

"Oh well, then, yeah. But what was that frown? Trouble in paradise?"

"What? Oh. No. It's going well. Or I thought it was."

Darren had asked her what was going on with Ryan last week, claiming the heart eyes between them were too obvious to ignore, so she'd given him the short version— that they were quietly dating and having a great time. He'd seemed surprised, but supportive.

"What if it's not going as well as I think? He said he wants to talk later."

Darren winced.

"See?" she wailed, then coughed and took a sip of her tea. "Talking is code for something bad, right?"

"Hey, don't worry. Things have been wild around here, with all the news and the series ending. It's a lot. Maybe he just wants to be on the same page with you. Maybe he wants to go public soon, or something."

Ariel's stomach churned with nerves at the idea of going public with their relationship. If they told the outside world and they broke up, she'd have that on her public record forever. She'd be the actress who dated Ryan Saylor for all of five minutes.

"Yeah, maybe."

Darren put his hands on her shoulders and squared

her to face him. "Look, remember when Crosby and I first got together, and everything was going so well, and I was freaking out? Do you remember what you told me?"

"Not really," she said, thinking back to the snowy Christmas they'd gotten together. "But it was probably something insightful and brilliant."

"Exactly right. You said all that matters is we make each other happy, and the rest is overthinking. You're overthinking this."

"And I turned out to be right, didn't I? I said you'd fall in love and live happily ever after and now you're engaged!" She sniffed. "Oh shit. I can't mess up my eye makeup again."

"Don't they know enough to use waterproof stuff on you by now?"

"It gives me a rash, so they can't. I swore to Lavon I wouldn't turn on the waterworks unless it was for the camera."

"Okay, well, you were right, but that means I'm right, too. Don't overthink, just enjoy your man."

She wanted to take her own advice and listen to her friend, but doubt niggled at her like a fish tugging on a line. "I—I think I'm scared because we've reached the point in all of my relationships when the guy realizes my personality isn't cute anymore and he'd be stuck with me for the long haul."

"What are you talking about? Whoever made you think you weren't glorious the way you are is a full-on idiot."

"It's not that I don't have self-confidence. It's never been that I'm not enough. It's usually that I'm too much. What if I'm too much for Ryan, too?"

"Seriously, where are you getting this?" Darren looked at her with lines of concern etched on his face. "You're dazzling, babe, in the very best way. You're never too much for me. If Ryan can't handle the muchness that is you, it's his loss."

She smiled sadly. That could be true, and it could also be true that she might never find someone who could handle all of her muchness. Did she want to be alone, or did she want to try to tamp down her natural inclinations? She wanted Ryan, and she wasn't saying she had to have him only on her terms, but it would be nice if he felt like she didn't have to change. Was that too much to ask?

"Thanks, Darren." At least she had awesome friends. She could be one of those elegant New York women who threw fabulous parties for their coterie of friends and never married or had kids. She could be the cool aunt to Darren and Crosby's adorable kids and be totally happy. "Now, I just have one more question. Did you propose before, during, or after penetration?"

"You absolute sicko." Darren laughed. "I swear, Crosby will kill me if I tell you. Maybe you can get him drunk enough at the wrap party to spill the beans."

"That's the best idea you've had yet."

Chapter Twenty-Five

Sawyer's Cove: The Reboot
Episode 309: The Wedding Planner

INT. THE BAR - NIGHT

PARKER: So you pulled the trigger.
WILL: I might use a less violent
metaphor, but yes. What about you and
Amy? Want to make a trifecta of it?
PARKER: There's no rush for us. Besides,
we're going to be a little busy with the
baby for a while.
WILL: What the hell? What baby?

Buoyed by Darren's confident optimism that she
wasn't over her skis when it came to her relationship with Ryan, and the satisfaction of a job well-done,
Ariel was bouncing with energy after her wrap for the
day. She'd finished before expected, as they'd cut some of

the set-ups to make time for a more complicated scene with Darren and Nash, so she went to find Ryan in his office.

He smiled when he saw her, and she immediately relaxed. She'd totally overreacted to the notion of them "talking." He probably just wanted to check in with her after all the revelations of the morning.

Now that her work for the day was done, she allowed herself the luxury of observing him, his dear face, his sexy hair, his tweed jacket that she'd come to adore—so much a part of him that it was impossible to love the man and not love the jacket.

Wait.

Back up.

She loved Ryan?

She loved Ryan.

She loved her friends, too. Maybe because she was sleeping with Ryan she was getting confused?—but no, she had no doubt. She tended to love easily and simply, but this kind of love had completely snuck up on her, not a swan dive into an ocean of emotion, rather a slow and steady buildup, the kind of love that felt sturdy and strong enough to withstand a windy day or a big bad wolf at the door.

This wasn't fleeting infatuation or loving the idea of love, not only friendship, or companionship, or the idea of building a future with him. It was all of those things combined. It was the whole package. The elusive damn package she'd been seeking for thirty-three years, and she'd found it in Ryan Saylor. And he was looking at her as if he was about to break bad news.

"Hey, you," she said, closing the door and locking it

behind her. Whatever he had to say to her, they'd need privacy. "Is now a good time?"

"Sure." But his smile dimmed. "How did it go?"

"Aces," she said, surprised her voice was even when she was bubbling over with her discovery. She loved him, but that was only half the equation. "How's it going with Selena?"

"I've barely seen her. She and Cami have been holed up together most of the day. But it's okay, I think. No disasters."

"No disasters is good." She perched on the edge of his desk, summoning her courage. "So, lay it on me."

"What?"

"Whatever has you so down. Bad news?"

He dropped the smile entirely and sighed, heavy and sad. "I forgot how insightful you are."

Her heart sped up, and she thought she might be sick. "You're easy to read, Saylor," she said, trying desperately to keep things light. Maybe if she wasn't serious, he wouldn't be, either.

"It's not bad news. It's just, I've been thinking."

"First you want to talk, now you've been thinking. Next you're going to say it's not you, it's me."

He winced. "Not exactly."

The urge to throw up receded and was replaced by an icicle of fear piercing her gut. "So it's me, not you?"

"No—no. Of course not. Ariel—you've always been honest about what you're looking for in a relationship, and now I finally get it. You want what Darren and Crosby have. What Nash and Mimi have. What Jay and Cami have. And I don't want to hold you back. I can't be the person who keeps you from finding what you're looking for."

She blinked at him. He wasn't serious. He couldn't be serious. Wait, was he serious?

"Are you fucking serious?"

He grimaced at her again, like he couldn't help being the bringer of bad news, as if he was telling her some self-evident truth.

"I have found what I'm looking for," she said. "I found it with you."

He stuck his hand in his hair and chewed on his lip. She wondered how badly he wanted a cigarette right now. "So you're just giving up?" he asked fretfully.

"On what? What are you talking about?"

"On finding your soulmate?"

The words, said so casually, felt like someone had poured liquid metal into the hole the icicle had made. She went from cold to hot in an instant. "Fuck you, Ryan."

He blinked at her.

"Are you being purposefully obtuse?" she asked, waving her hands around. "Do you seriously not under-stand what's going on between us?" Her ire made her forget that she'd only realized what she felt for Ryan was as serious as real, true love a few minutes ago.

"I know things have been good between us, but I also know I'm not the guy who's going to be able to give you that soulmate kind of love that you've been waiting for. And you deserve that. You deserve to get everything you want, and I don't want to mess up your chances because I'm too selfish to let you go."

"Why would it be selfish for you to give me what I

want when what I want is you?" She felt like they were speaking two completely different languages.

His hand was back in his hair. "Because I'm not—you don't—I mean. You don't think being with me is a waste of time?"

"Do you think I'm stupid?" She was so angry she was astounded she wasn't crying. Maybe she was too angry to cry.

"Of course not."

"Then do you think I need a guy to tell me when I'm wasting my time?"

"No," he said. "That's not what I'm saying. Or at least not what I mean. I'm sorry. I'm going about this all wrong. I guess I'm having doubts."

"You don't want to be with me anymore?" She was half afraid of asking the question, half furious he was making her ask it.

"I don't want to feel like you'll wake up one morning and regret the time we've spent together. I don't want you to wake up one morning and hate me."

She pushed off the desk to stand with her legs apart and her arms akimbo, what she thought of as her powerful warrior stance. "I don't hate you, Ryan. I love you, you idiot."

"You—you what?" His eyes went round and his eyebrows shot up. He could not have looked more surprised unless he'd been a cartoon character with his jaw literally on the floor.

"I'm in love with you. I don't know about the soulmate thing—maybe I was wrong to fixate on that, or maybe we are soulmates and my definition needs to change, or maybe we're only going to date a few more months and once it runs its course, well, I'll know. But I don't think it will run its course in a few months. I think this is the real deal. And I'm glad we're having this conversation, even if you are aggravating the shit out of me right now, because I need you to know how much I really, truly love you."

He sucked in an audible breath, and she plowed on. "I love you, Ryan, not some fantasy guy that I dreamed up watching TV when I was sixteen. I'm all grown up now, if you haven't noticed. Old enough to know what I want. I want you. Smart, sexy, strong you. You are enough for me, but maybe I'm too much for you. And if that's how you feel, I'll deal."

She waited a beat, but he said nothing back. Her heart stumbled, but she dusted herself off and kept going. "I don't want you to be with me because I asked you to be with me. I want you to be with me because you want to be with me. So find me when you figure that out."

Ariel left without looking back, waiting until she was well clear of his office to let out a shaky breath. Her hands flew to her cheeks. They were dry.

Chapter Twenty-Six

Sawyer's Cove: The Reboot
Episode 309: The Wedding Planner

INT. THE BAR - NIGHT

LILY: This isn't another false alarm,
is it?
AMY: Nope. I'm well and truly knocked up
this time.
LILY: And how do we feel about this?

Amy bursts into tears.

R yan was pretending to answer emails—in reality, staring blankly at his computer screen—when Selena popped her head through his partially open office door.

"Hey, Ryan. Is now a good time to chat?"

"Sure." He got up and his knees popped. How long

had he been sitting, staring after Ariel, hearing, "I love you, you idiot," on a loop in his addled brain? He pulled up a chair for Selena so they could sit on the same side of the desk. He could function like a normal person. He found some words and managed to ask, "How's your visit going?"

"No surprises, so that's good. I'm being reminded that *Sawyer's Cove* has the absolute best crew. I'm totally jealous. The team we have on *Gunsmoke* are pros, but they aren't a family, you know?"

He allowed himself to relax minutely. "How is *Gunsmoke*, by the way?"

"Oh, it's all right. I have a diva for a leading man and a hypochondriac in the number two slot. Managing them is a bit of a headache, but the scripts are tight, and we're under budget, miraculously. I think we're being true to the book, which is what I care about. But it's hard. I miss Misty Harbor, believe it or not."

"How's Warner doing?" Ryan had never met Selena's partner, but he knew Warner was the man whose book she was turning into her next hit show.

"He's a little homesick, too, but at least our schedules are compatible. He's working on the third Jake Wilton novel, and when he's not writing, he comes to the set and his suggestions are not the worst in the world."

"Lucky."

"Yeah, we collaborated on the script, but that wasn't a guaranteed good time. Working with your significant other doesn't always turn out well. As you know."

Ryan started. What did Selena know about him and Ariel?

"Sorry to bring up your ex," she said after he didn't respond right away.

"Oh. Right." She was talking about Heather. They had been coworkers, not at first, but they'd developed a show together, brought it to life together, though they kept their roles separate. It was less a collaboration and more that they each kept to their lanes and did what they did best. It wasn't like it was with Ariel—where he found inspiration in her performance, in her *existence.* "It's fine."

Selena brushed past the sticky moment. "Well, anyway, let's talk about *Lost Stars.*"

"It's rough," Ryan said quickly. Talking about a first draft was scary enough to get his mind off the mess he'd made with Ariel for a moment. "I didn't realize Cami was going to share the script with you, and I have a lot of fleshing out to do."

"Yeah, it's fairly rough," Selena said matter-of-factly. "You'll have to figure out the secondary characters. This first script is almost a two-person play, which is cool, but for longevity we need to think long-term about arcs, which means more of an ensemble. And I also want to pitch you on the location."

"Wait—what are you talking about?"

"I loved it. Like, started reading it and couldn't stop until I was done loved it. It's the best television I've read since—well, since the *Sawyer's Cove* reboot. Franny is an incredible character. Flawed but strong, smart but obtuse about some fundamentals about her life. I have to say it —you write women so damn well, Ryan Saylor. It's annoying."

Ryan took the praise for what it was. Selena didn't bullshit. If she said she liked it, it meant she liked it. And she'd said she loved it. He valued her opinion more than almost anyone else. "Thanks," he said awkwardly. It was inadequate, but it was a start.

"So, the studio will be an easy sell if we pitch it the right way. And if we get the right person to play Franny. Someone bankable and reliable, but with the chops to get the emotion across. This is a home run. If you want me and Cami to take it on, we can have a contract drawn up right away. And we can talk numbers, of course. But I want to ask if you're open to something."

He stopped himself from saying "anything," tried to remember he had an agent and he didn't have to agree to anything right away. "What's that?"

"What about shooting here in Misty Harbor? We'd have to work hard not to replicate too many *Sawyer's Cove* locations, but it's really important to Cami that we keep our base of production in Misty Harbor when it makes sense for the project. *Gunsmoke* doesn't work, obviously, since it's a city story, but *Lost Stars* is set in Hometown, USA. It could be anywhere, and the sets we can build from scratch. You wouldn't even have to be here most of the time if you didn't want to. Unless you want to be the showrunner instead of only write. We'd have to talk about that." She wasn't giving anything away for free. Smart woman.

Ryan thought it over, his mind racing with everything she'd just calmly spit out. He'd written the script because he'd had something inside him that needed to come out. And now she was talking about making it a reality, giving him another job in this fickle industry. He didn't get offers to produce a new television show every day of the week.

Making it in Misty Harbor made complete sense if

Selena and Cami were to produce. They both had strong ties here, especially Cami, whose partner was a local boy who cared strongly about the health of the community. A project like this would keep up the momentum of television production as a local industry. And he could see Franny here, licking her wounds after a yet-to-be-figured-out debacle in the city drives her home, where she encounters demons she thought she'd put to bed long ago, where she builds a new life and grows into maturity.

He thought about being in charge of another show, writing it, shepherding it from conception to execution, just like *Sawyer's Cove*. Only this time he had two decades of hard-earned experience to help him, plus the dynamite duo of Selena and Cami at his back.

"It all sounds rather too wonderful to be true."

"Well, I'd love to work with you again. But think about it. And think about casting. I know you'd like to get Ariel for Franny, and she'd be absolutely ideal—"

"Ariel Tulip?"

She gave him a confused smile. "No, Ariel the mermaid. Yes, Ariel Tulip. Didn't you write it with her in mind?"

"I—" Ryan faltered.

"You wrote her name a couple of times instead of Franny in the script, that's all. So I figured she was your first choice, which tracks. She'd be fantastic."

"Fantastic," he repeated dully. He'd been aware of the parallels, of course, but hadn't let himself truly picture her in the role, but then again, his subconscious must have done the work for him if he'd accidentally written her name into the script. But of course she was perfect for it. He let himself imagine for one fleeting second working with her that closely again, going home together at the end of the day. Would it be suffocating? Would it burn them out? Or would it just deepen the connection they already had?

If they still had a connection after the fiasco of their earlier conversation, that was.

"Look, I know you still have to finish up here, and I'm going to be busy with post on *Gunsmoke* for months. I'll talk to Brad at the studio about it the next time we're in the same room, feel him out, and we'll go from there. You know how many steps there are from idea to green light."

"Ten million," Ryan said. "And all of them shaky."

"But you keep working on the script in the meantime. It's a special one, Ryan. Okay?"

"Okay. Thanks. I'm glad you like it," he said. "And I'm glad you're here."

"I wish I could stay longer. But I'm going to try to come back for the podcast thing Ariel's set up. It sounds super fun, and I don't want to miss out. So I could be back soon."

Selena left as assertively as she'd come in, leaving him reeling. She wanted to make his show. The show he'd written for Ariel. Ariel, who might have given up on him because he was too stupid to see what was right in front of him.

Like a riddle that only seemed impossible until you heard the deceptively simple answer, he wondered why he was only now realizing why he felt the way he did when he was around her.

He was in love with her.

He'd been in love with her for weeks and hadn't known what to call it—because for all his writing about the subject since he was fifteen years old, he knew now he'd never actually experienced it for himself. The kind of love that dummies like him claimed to represent in TV and movies and books and songs. But what had he really known of it before the girl with the gray eyes that were beautiful when filled with tears—happy, sad, and in-between—had looked at him and made the heavy cloak wrapped around his heart disappear?

She was right, about everything. And he'd hurt her by being too slow on the uptake.

She'd told him what to do when he figured it out. He might be nine years older than her, but she was obviously wiser when it came to seeing what they were to each other. He had to find her and fix this.

But when he visited her dressing room, it was empty, and she didn't pick up when he tried her cell. Was it too soon to panic? He had visions of her packing up her car and driving to New York just to get the space he'd forced her into wanting by being monumentally stupid. He didn't care how far away she ran; he'd follow her. He'd figure it out, do whatever it took to prove to her that he loved her back, that soulmates or not, he would gratefully be with her as long as she allowed him to be near her.

But he had to find her first.

Chapter Twenty-Seven

Sawyer's Cove: The Reboot
Episode 309: The Wedding Planner

INT. THE BAR - NIGHT

AMY: Is it possible to be so happy that it makes you sick?
LILY: That might be the baby hormones, sweetie.
AMY: I'm riding a cocktail of morning sickness, excitement, and paralyzing fear. What if I'm a bad mom? I didn't exactly have a stellar role model.
LILY: Impossible. You're my favorite woman, Amy Green. You've got this.

"You should really try a milkshake," Ariel urged her dining partner.

Erika Rainwater, one of the hosts of *The Sawyer's Cove*

Rewatch Project Podcast, sat across from her in her favorite booth at Melba's, the one by the window that overlooked Main Street. Erika was about her age, with pretty pale skin, seventies-folk-singer-long blonde hair and generous curves.

"You know what? I love milkshakes, but I had a banana split here once that was life-changing."

"Oh wow, I haven't had a banana split in forever," Ariel said. "Is it weird if I copy you and get one, too?"

"It would be weird if you didn't," Erika declared.

They ordered identical banana splits and grinned at each other when Loretta promised they'd be up in a jiffy. Ariel knew the banana split wouldn't exactly make her achy heart feel better, but it probably couldn't hurt.

"So, what else do we need to cover?" she asked.

"Kate's got all the technical stuff worked out. She wouldn't normally come on-site for something like this, but I know she wants to see you, so she'll be here in person."

"She's a sweetheart. And her son's old enough now for her to take more time away from him."

"Oh, he's the cutest. Maverick, right? I met him when I was in L.A. with Henry a few months ago."

"How are things going with you two?"

"Good. Really good." Erika smiled. "To tell you the truth, though, we're both looking forward to the end of *Sawyer's Cove.*"

"Seriously? You're the first person I've heard say that. I'm freaking out about shooting being over in like a week."

"It's different for us—we weren't part of the original run. I mean, I watched it, but that's not the same thing.

But Henry doesn't want to keep acting as a job. And I love doing the podcast, but to be honest, I'm tired of the grind, producing content week in, week out."

"I guess that makes sense. So, what are you going to do?"

"Henry's been getting his teaching credentials, and I've been writing. My agent just put my first book on submission."

"Oh my gosh, that's fantastic. I remember you mentioning you were writing a book. A young adult novel, right?"

"Yep. I'm staying in my lane of angsty, sexually precocious teens with a book set at a Seattle private school. We'll see if anyone bites."

"I have no doubt editors will be fighting for the rights."

"I hope so. So, once this chapter, so to speak, is over, we're going to settle down in Seattle. No more long distance. I'm really looking forward to it."

"I bet," she murmured. Even if Ryan got his head out of his ass and realized they were supposed to be together, they still had to figure out the whole living-on-two-coasts thing. Why did life have to be so complicated? She wanted what Henry and Erika had—two people in love, building a life together, in the same geographic location. Was that too much to ask?

"Don't get me wrong," Erika said as Loretta brought the banana splits. "*Sawyer's Cove* has changed my life for the better in so many ways. I'll always love it. But there needs to be change."

"Change is good." Ariel tried to mean it as she poked her spoon at the whipped cream on her dessert. She sort of wished they could just keep making *Sawyer's Cove* forever and never have to think about the future. But she'd miss New York, her apartment. If nothing ever changed, she wouldn't get to see Cami's baby, or Mimi's, or cry her eyes out at Darren and Crosby's wedding. Weddings were peak tears events. She wondered what kind of wedding she and Ryan might have—then remembered he'd actually have to decide to be with her before they could get married.

She shook off her malaise. "Well, we're really looking forward to doing the podcast. It's going to be a lovely way to cap off the season. The series, too."

"It's going to be epic," Erika enthused. "Almost as epic as this banana split. It's even better than I remember. I forgot about the candied pecans."

"Is that what's making it extra decadent?" Ariel asked, taking a bite with all the layers—ice cream, whipped cream, banana, chocolate syrup, and the candied nuts scattered on top. She moaned as the flavors mingled on her tongue. "Fuck, that's good."

"Seriously fucking good," Erika said with feeling.

She was about to ask more about Erika's book, but was distracted by a ruckus at the entrance to Melba's. It was the dinner rush, and people had been streaming in and out all evening, but the noise level had just risen dramatically. She looked over and saw Ryan waving apologetically to a large family he'd brushed past at the host stand as he barreled in their direction.

"Is that Ryan Saylor?" Erika asked.

"It sure is," Ariel said. "What the—"

Ryan came to a halt in front of their table, while Loretta played interference with the family.

"Ariel, I found you."

"You did," she said, taking in his feverishly bright eyes, disheveled hair, and the fact that he didn't have his trusty messenger bag with him. "Uh. Do you want to join us?"

"No, what I mean is I wasn't looking for my soulmate, but I found you anyway."

Oh.

"You fell out of the sky and into my life and you made me realize everything I didn't know I was missing—love and joy and emotion and sex and laughter and caring about people. Being a family. You let me in, you practically forced me to be part of this fucking amazing family that we have here, and you were right, I was too stupid to see what was going on between us, but I see it now and I love you too and please tell me it's not too late. Is it too late?"

Ariel got out of the booth and faced him. He was breathing hard, as if he'd run all the way from the sound-stage. She didn't know how he'd come to the conclusion that he loved her, but she wasn't going to make the same mistake he had by assuming he didn't mean it or that it wouldn't last. She'd take what he was offering with pleasure.

"It's not too late," she swore. "It's never too late." She wrapped her arms around his waist. "We did it, Ryan. We found each other."

"We found each other," he agreed. He tipped her chin up and kissed her, and it was as romantic and perfect as any kiss in the history of kisses, Ariel thought, just as perfect as the first time Sawyer kissed Lily, his true soul-mate, the one who complemented and completed him.

But that was a television show. This was their life. And she swore she could feel something in her heart click into place as he held her and kissed her and loved her the way she'd always been afraid she'd never be loved.

Now she was.

Now they were.

And it was glorious.

Someone cleared their throat and Ariel eased away from the love of her life and looked behind her.

Erika was staring at them as if they'd spouted extra heads. "Excuse me, was that some kind of a reenactment from the show? No spoilers, please."

"No, that wasn't from the show," Ariel said, laughing a little. "That was real life, thank goodness. Although that speech was pretty good. You might want to write it down, Ryan, while it's still fresh—wait, you didn't actually write it down ahead of time, did you?"

"Completely off the cuff," Ryan said, smiling. "Although I did practice the 'I love you' a couple of times out loud. I didn't want to screw that part up. Again."

"You nailed it."

"Wait—so you and Ryan are...wow." Erika's eyes were the size of Melba's coffee cups. "Did I just see that?"

Ariel cringed. "Sorry. TMI, probably. But it's fitting." She glanced at Ryan. "I started falling for you at Melba's. Remember the first time I ran into you here before we even started the season?"

"Same. The prettiest girl I'd ever seen told me she was going to find me a date."

"Oh gosh, I was trying to do what I thought made sense. Obviously, I was already battling my attraction to you." She laughed self-deprecatingly.

Ryan's gaze dropped to her mouth, and he said throatily, "Oh, totally obvious in retrospect."

"Uh, maybe I should go," Erika cut in.

Ryan waved at her. "Sorry to crash your dinner. I'm Ryan."

"I know. I'm Erika," she said, her face scarlet. "I'm the host of—"

"The podcast. Can't wait to do your show."

"Jesus. This is completely surreal. Ryan Saylor, creator of the best TV show of all time, can't wait to do my podcast. How is this my life?"

"Tell me about it." Ariel laughed.

"I'm going to head out," Erika said, grabbing her purse. "Henry's waiting for me at the inn."

"What about your banana split? You didn't get to finish it."

"I don't need sweets after a display like that," Erika said dryly.

"I'm so sorry to cut our evening short," Ariel said.

"No problem. It's not every day you get to see a superstar actress and the superstar showrunner declare their love for each other in a retro fifties diner. Hardly ever, actually."

"Erika, could you do us a favor and not mention this on the podcast or anywhere?" Ryan asked.

Erika nodded swiftly. "Of course. Although..." She looked around, reminding them they were very much in public.

"You know what? It's okay with me if it's okay with you, Ryan. We don't have to make a big announcement or anything, but it's okay if people know we're together." They'd find out eventually, Ariel figured.

"Are you sure?"

"I want people to know how lucky I am."

He kissed her again, right there in front of everyone eating dinner at Melba's. "How lucky *we* are."

"Exactly."

Chapter Twenty-Eight

Sawyer's Cove: The Reboot
Episode 310: The Last Ride

INT. CLOUDY COVE COURTHOUSE - DAY

PARKER: You guys didn't think you were
going to get hitched without us?
AMY: You know how stubborn we are.
WILL: Besides, if you were trying to do
it on the down-low, you shouldn't have
tried to do it at my place of business.
NOAH: Being nosy has its perks.
SAWYER: You are the stubbornest, nosiest
friends in the world.
LILY: And we love you. So come on, we're
getting married!
SAWYER: Just to be clear, not all six
of us.
PARKER: Whatever you say, man.

A riel loved him. She loved him. And he wasn't going to mess this up. Not when he loved her back.

The walk from the diner to her apartment was a blur of elated glances, the brush of her fingers against his ass, a stolen kiss while she fumbled to get out her keys. Thank God she didn't live far. He needed to show her how much she meant to him, how far he'd go to keep her, to make her happy for as long as he drew breath.

They stumbled inside, drunk on love, bleary with joy. Her bedroom was too far. He took her to the couch, lowered her down onto the cushions, cradling her like she was something precious, fragile. She wouldn't break, but he'd never be careless with her again.

"I love you," he said against the elegant column of her neck as she sighed. Her heart fluttered under her sweater. The couch was a tight fit, but being closer was a bonus, not a negative. She threw off the sweater and kicked out of her jeans and panties while he slipped out of his jacket with a practiced shrug, then pulled off his shirt. He attacked his pants with single-minded vehemence until he was naked between her legs. Deliberately, she ran her hands over his shoulders until her left hand clutched his upper arm and her right hand cupped his stump. Like always, she made him feel seen, feel cherished.

"I need you, Ryan." She spread her legs for him sweetly, easily, her fragrance rising between them. She'd left her bra on, pink silk encasing her full breasts.

Who was he to deny her anything? He sank into her without delay, not even checking if she was wet enough first, knowing she liked the stretch. She was so tight, and yet so welcoming, the slide into her pussy so satisfying he could almost live on this sweet feeling alone, no orgasm necessary.

"Yes," she gasped when he started rocking in and out of her. She twined her legs around his waist, urging him closer, deeper, harder. "God, I love you so much."

"Fuck. Darling. I'm going to—" Despite feeling this was enough, forever and always, he was suddenly close. He didn't remember ever being told he was loved while having sex. The idea that this woman, this real, dangerous, sensational woman, loved him—it was heady, to say the least.

"It's okay," she said, breathless, plucking her own nipples as he drove into her. "Come in me. I want it. We have time, Ryan."

"Time," he repeated. She felt so goddamn good he thought he was going a little bit crazy.

"Tell me again," she begged, her eyes nearly closed, her heels digging into the back of his thighs, her hands on her own tits.

"I love you." The truth of it settled in his bones to stay. "I love you, Ariel."

"Yes." She threw her head back and came.

He let himself enjoy the sight for a few precious seconds before his own orgasm overtook him, nearly incapacitating in its intensity, blanking out everything around him for a moment except the sound of her saying it back to him.

"Ryan. I love you."

He kissed her through the comedown, her legs clamping him in place, keeping him inside her.

"I don't want to crush you," he said a few minutes later. She made an adorable grumbly sound and released him. He offered her a tissue to clean up with, took a moment to disentangle his boxers from his trousers, and put them on.

"What a day," Ariel said, sitting up on her elbows. She looked debauched and lovely, mostly naked on her rented couch.

He looked at her and shook his head. "What a day," he seconded. It had started with all those bombshells from her—their—friends. Then Selena's visit. His ill-advised attempt to break up with the love of his life. Oh yeah, and they'd both done work somewhere in there. Which reminded him—

"By the way, I had an interesting conversation with Selena today."

"Oh?" She patted the sliver of couch in front of her, and he lay down dutifully, pressing his front to hers. The configuration put his mouth close to her breasts, so he nibbled on the flesh just above the scalloped edge of her bra. "What did she say?"

He stopped tasting her to answer the question. "Right. Well, I didn't tell you this, but I started writing a script. For another show. I showed it to Cami, just to get her initial thoughts, and she showed it to Selena, and she liked it. She really liked it. She and Cami want to develop it and pitch it to the studio."

Ariel let out a happy noise. "Ryan, that's unbelievable. I didn't know you were looking to do another project so soon."

"I didn't either. This idea popped into my head. I hadn't felt inspiration that strong in a while, so I wrote it fast. It's rough. The secondary characters need a lot of fleshing out. But I have the main character pretty strongly defined. Her name is Franny. And Ariel, darling, I wrote the part for you."

"For me?"

"I'd be honored if you'd read it and tell me what you think."

"No one's ever written anything for me before," she said quietly. He shifted so he could look her in the eyes.

"I don't want you to think you have to play her, or that you can't tell me you hate it, or, hell, anything. But she's a strong, vulnerable, capable woman, and I couldn't help modeling her on the strongest, most fearlessly vulnerable woman I know."

Her eyes began to water, and Ryan couldn't help it, his heart swelled at the sight. "God, you're so beautiful when you cry," he said. "Especially happy tears."

She sniffed. "And you didn't think we were soulmates."

He shook his head. He was still a bit overwhelmed by the implications of the fact that they were both in this one hundred percent. But they didn't have to have everything in their relationship figured out in the next sixty minutes, like on a TV show. They could keep taking things one step at a time, as long as they tried to take the steps together, or at least waited as patiently as possible for the other to catch up.

And maybe, if they were lucky, they'd have the next sixty years or so to keep figuring it out together.

"Oh, and I forgot to tell you the other part."

"What other part?"

"If it gets to this stage—which is a big if, obviously— they want to film the show right here in Misty Harbor."

Ariel laughed until tears were streaming down her face yet again.

"What's so funny?" Ryan asked.

Ariel swiped her cheeks and grinned. She looked so happy his heart expanded with joy. "I'll have to renew the lease on this place, after all."

Chapter Twenty-Nine

Sawyer's Cove: The Reboot
Episode 310: The Last Ride

EXT. CLOUDY COVE BEACH - DAY

LILY: The best is yet to come, Sawyer.
SAWYER: I want to believe you.
LILY: Then do.

"She's not going to get here in time," Ariel wailed, checking her phone for the seventeen bajillionth time in the last hour. Selena had been caught in traffic coming from the airport, and they were going to have to start the show without her. Four hundred eager ticket holders were sitting in the Misty Harbor Inn ballroom waiting for the Cove crew to take the stage. Ariel had been planning this for months, had known something would inevitably go wrong, but she still wanted it to be flawless.

"She can join us when she arrives and it'll be a cool surprise for the audience," Cami said reassuringly. "That'll work, right, Kate?"

Kate Treanor nodded. "Of course it will. Don't worry Ariel, everything else is set. I'll have someone meet her and bring her out when she gets here."

"Yeah, but—"

"Ariel, can I talk to you for a second?" Ryan cut in, pulling her gently by the elbow into a corner of the green room.

"What is it?" Ariel looked into Ryan's eyes and instantly felt calmer. "I'm being extra, aren't I?"

"You've done all the work to make this happen, darling." He lowered his voice on the endearment, saying it with throaty subtlety.

They were slowly rolling out their relationship to the wider world. Everyone in the *Sawyer's Cove* crew and cast knew because they hadn't been able to keep their hands off each other at the wrap party. Jay had closed his bar for the event, and Ariel had gotten a little tipsy on champagne and accidentally-on-purpose made out with Ryan on the dance floor while the DJ spun a mashup of "In My Life" and "Freefalling." She'd instantly declared those "their" songs. Ryan had laughed and said it was like her to claim two songs instead of one. And then he'd kissed her so hard her toes had curled, so that was all right.

"It's time to relax and have fun," he said, trailing a finger over the back of her hand. She shivered and allowed herself to be distracted. What was the point of having a boyfriend if you didn't take advantage of the perks, like letting him soothe your anxiety and turn you on at the same time?

"All right." She squeezed his hand once, gratefully, then kept hold of it. To Kate she said, "Let's do this."

A few minutes later, she was taking her seat on stage as a voice on the PA system said, "Welcome, one and all, to the first-ever live *The Sawyer's Cove Rewatch Project Podcast!*"

The enthusiastic crowd erupted into cheers and applause.

Erika Rainwater and Jules Thompson, the hosts of the podcast, were installed on stools on one side of the stage with mics set up in front of them, while the guests sat on stools behind a long table. Cami was nearest the hosts, with Jay next to her, followed by Nash, Darren, then Crosby. Ariel sat between Crosby and Ryan, and the last chair on the stage stood empty for Selena.

"We're going to dive in because I've been dreaming about this ever since Ariel approached us about doing it, and now that it's here, I kind of want to pee my pants with excitement," Erika said as the audience roared their appreciation at her signature brash style.

Jules picked up where Erika left off. "We promise we won't pee our pants, but we won't promise not to gush. Let me start with Ariel. What made you want to black-mail—I assume blackmail was involved—all these fine folks into doing our goofy little podcast?"

Ariel laughed. She was already having fun, which was a relief. It had been a lot of work to get everything lined up, and even though Selena wasn't there, her hopes for this event were already met. They'd raised a bunch of money for the new teen center that Mimi and Nash were spearheading, and she'd kept the crew together for one last hurrah. "No, I'm saving my blackmail material for something really important," she joked. "Actually, it was pretty easy to get everyone to sign on, because we're all such big fans of your podcast. And we love talking about the show with people who really understand it and what we're trying to do with it."

"Flattery will get you everywhere," Jules said. "So let's talk about the show. You just finished filming the third season of the reboot, and I know we've all signed our life away so we can't discuss specific plot points, but you can put this anxious fangirl's heart at ease by giving us some clues that we're not in for any major tragedies. Cami, you're the one who made us sign the NDA, so you know where the line is."

Cami took the question on graciously and explained they were excited to share the last season in less than two months, but they wanted to keep the storylines a surprise. "But I can tell you that you'll need tissues for happy tears, not sad ones."

"Whew, that's all I wanted to know," Erika said. "Let's hear some non-specific favorite moments from the set this season. We want the inside dirt. Darren, you want to start?"

Darren launched into a funny story about a seagull messing up his takes when they were filming on location at the beach that had the live crowd in stitches.

While he spoke, Ariel let herself take in the faces of the audience. These were die-hard fans, some of whom had traveled long distances to see them in person. Everyone looked so happy, and she was reminded again why she loved what she did for a living. She loved the personal challenge of acting, of becoming someone else, and she loved collaborating with everyone on the stage and beyond, but it was always gratifying to remember that what she made was then consumed and enjoyed by countless people. It felt so good, and she had her fingers crossed that they'd end up making another show here, together.

"Oh yeah, and my other favorite moment from this season was when this guy said he'd marry me—in real life." Darren grabbed Crosby's left hand and held it up to show off the glittery diamond-studded engagement band on his ring finger.

The crowd gasped, and Jules let out a fervent, "Holy shit."

Ariel internally fist pumped. She'd wanted this to be an epic event, and Darren had just sealed the deal by making their first public announcement of their engagement.

"To be clear, Sawyer and Noah aren't running away together, despite the copious amounts of fanfiction that posit that idea," Darren added.

"I'm more of a Parker/Will shipper, TBH," Jules said.

Jay and Nash exchanged amused glances while the audience laughed. "I know, Parker is so vanilla," Jay said indulgently. "But that's where the fans get really creative."

"Keep it coming. Will and Noah are my OTP, but we love to see all the fan art and fan vids that you guys make," Nash said expansively. "By the way, I really appreciate all of you who are in the audience today. All of the proceeds from this event are going to a new teen center here in Misty Harbor. We've all pitched in to get this place off the ground, and I'm so proud of the Cove family for helping out. It should open by next summer. So just wanted to say thanks."

"Thanks, Nash," Jules said, then steered the conversation back. "Wow. So many congratulations to bestow. This show has spawned so many real life love stories—both behind the scenes and between fans. We get letters all the time from listeners who knew their partners were the one because they loved *Sawyer's Cove*, too."

"Speaking of," Erika started. She made eye contact with Ariel, and for a second Ariel worried she was about to be put on the spot. She and Ryan weren't a secret, but the engagement and baby news were probably enough to blow fans' minds for now. "Oh, we interrupt this regularly scheduled broadcast with a special guest. Please welcome to the stage writer-producer-all-around-amazing-person Selena Echeveria."

Ariel glanced over her shoulder to see Selena, looking calm and professional in a red sweater and linen slacks as she waved to the audience and took the remaining seat next to Ryan, who gave her a quick hug before she adjusted her mic and said, "Sorry I'm late everyone." Ariel let out a sigh of relief. Everyone was there, and the timing snafu had not been the disaster she feared.

"Since Selena and Ryan are now both here, we have the unique opportunity to hear from the brilliant minds behind this show. I, for one, want to repeat a question that Ryan answered about a decade and a half ago—but with the benefit of being more recently involved in the storytelling of the new show, I wonder if your answer has changed at all. Why did you create *Sawyer's Cove*, and what does it mean to you now, all these years later?" Erika asked.

Ariel leaned forward, as eager to hear his answer as Erika and the fans.

Ryan cleared his throat. "It's a good question, Erika, and thanks for asking it. It still thrills me that so many people connected with the show on such a deep level back then. To see the endurance of the show's legacy—it's really special and I'm so grateful to have been able to be a part of it, twice. I'm also really glad Selena got a chance to run her own show, because she's a treasure and we need her helming shows." He shifted so he was facing Selena, but the mic still picked him up loud and clear when he said to her, "You started as a writer's assistant in the early days of *Sawyer's Cove*, and seventeen years later you turned around and gave me a job, and I couldn't be happier about that. You rock."

The audience burst into ecstatic applause, and Selena got up and hugged Ryan. Ariel sniffed. Her boyfriend was magnificent.

"Thanks, Ryan. I knew I could trust you with this final season, and you've done an absolute banger of a job," Selena said. "We were lucky to get you back. Cami and I breathed new life into it, but we owe the heart and soul of *Sawyer's Cove* to you, truly."

"Hear, hear," Ariel cried.

Ryan shook his head. "I think you're giving me too much credit. I had an idea about a world where the dorky kid could get the pretty girl. As a team, we spun that into something so much more. It took on such a life of its own, and I'm proud of that. I also want to say I'm really touched by the changes in the new show.

"I was always an observer, not a participant. I watched people; I figured out what they wanted and why they wanted it by watching them, because I wasn't having those experiences for myself. *Sawyer's Cove* was about writing all of those experiences I didn't have because I was the weird smart kid with one arm who didn't do sports and liked to watch movies and read.

"I think being born with a visible disability made me appreciate that everyone, even the most seemingly normal person, has something that makes them a bad fit for the world. Each of us is a square peg in our own way. I bet the roundest-looking peg actually feels like a misshapen lump on the inside at least some of the time. I know the show has made a lot of people who feel like square pegs realize there are others like them. Maybe they've become friends with other square pegs because of the show, and that's amazing."

He glanced down the row of actors, smiling at each one in turn. "It's so Hollywood to offer you beautiful, talented people as examples of not fitting in, but all of the characters embodied by the folks on stage have gone through a lot of adversity. They're all survivors. Every last one. And we made a difference, because all these years later the show features a young woman with a limb difference, and she's seen as beautiful and desirable, and she has people fighting to spend time with her, which is no less than she deserves. I wasn't able to put someone like that on the screen the first time. But Selena was brave enough to do it. She saw the value in it. And Stephanie Mae is a beautiful person and I'm proud to know her and have her on the team. So I thank her, I thank Selena for bringing her onto the show, and I thank our fans for embracing her like one of their own. Because the fans of *Sawyer's Cove* know that it doesn't matter what you look like, it's what you do, what choices you make, what you choose to believe about the goodness of other people even when you have very little evidence that goodness exists. A familiar refrain from the show is 'I want to believe you.' We use it in a lot of contexts. It can mean many things. But to me, it means having hope. It means being willing to suspend fear and defensiveness and maybe even logic to trust that something better could be possible. Hope is a powerful emotion, and it's one I never want to lose."

Ryan stopped talking and Ariel realized she'd been holding her breath for the last half of his speech because she suddenly needed to suck in air. She clapped wildly, joined by the rest of the room, everyone showing just how much they appreciated Ryan's beautiful speech.

"Sorry for getting on my soapbox," Ryan said sheepishly to the hosts. Jules was openly sobbing, and even Erika looked a little misty-eyed.

"No, Ryan, it's okay," Erika said. "I think you spoke for everyone here. That's why *Sawyer's Cove* has endured, you're a hundred percent right. All of us square pegs want to believe the world can be a little better, a little warmer, a little more accepting of us, and when we meet others like us it helps keep that hope alive, and maybe even make that better world right here, right now."

"Well said, Erika." Ryan smiled at her warmly.

There was a second while eyes were wiped, then everyone settled down. Tension took over as no one seemed to know how to follow that up.

"See why I brought him back?" Selena said. The audience laughed, and the strain was broken.

"I was hoping someone could talk about the legacy of *Sawyer's Cove*. It's ending again, but does anything really ever end in this era of recycled content and new generations discovering past hits?" Jules asked.

"I can talk about that a little," Jay said. "I think you're right. Even though the show itself is ending, it's not over. I think it's cool that new people get to discover the show all the time, whether or not they were even alive when the original show aired. It's a little surreal, and sometimes it's strange that I basically get to live in Cloudy Cove all year long, but real life is hard enough, why not make some fun by incorporating our made-up world into it a little."

"I never thought about it that way, but that is pretty cool," Erika agreed.

"On a personal note," Ariel put in, "Someday the show might be forgotten, but I'll never forget how much fun we had making it or how much we all mean to each other." She gestured to her friends on stage. "We're a family, and families stick together. I thought I'd be so sad to finish the run of the show—and I am, don't get me wrong, I've been crying buckets for a week—but it doesn't matter if we all go our separate ways. We'll always come back together because we love each other, and that doesn't go away just because we're not working together any longer."

"Speaking of working together, I know it's not exactly a *Sawyer's Cove* reunion, but won't some of you be working together on a new project soon? Tell us about that, Ryan."

He laughed. "Oh, it's early days, but Cami and Selena aren't going to let me rest very long. They are the best producers I've ever worked with, and they have some exciting ideas. I'd be lucky to get to work with anyone on this stage again."

"Very diplomatically and vaguely put, Ryan," Erika said with a wink. "We've gotta wrap this evening up, but let's end with everyone telling us what's next for them after *Sawyer's Cove* so we can support your future endeavors. Let's go on down the line and start with Cami."

Cami patted her belly. "Well, I'm going to finish growing this little bean." She beamed at Jay. "And we'll probably take some time off when the baby gets here. Meanwhile, I'm working on *Gunsmoke* with Selena, which will be out next summer. After that—" she glanced at Ryan "—who knows? But something will turn up, I'm sure."

Jay made a plug for The Cove and next summer's Harbor Fest. "Come see us in Misty Harbor," he said. "We're always happy to meet fans."

Nash mentioned the teen center again, and that he was working on a new album. "Mimi and I are a couple of months behind, but we're going to have two little Orlando cousins here pretty soon, so that's my main focus right now."

The audience cooed.

"I'm lined up to direct a TV movie super soon," Darren said. "In pre-production right now. So I'll be sure to let you all know when you can catch that flick. Oh, and wedding planning, I guess? Unless you wanna elope, babe."

Crosby rolled his eyes at the endearment and at the audience's collective, "Awwww," but he couldn't help smiling, either.

"I'm sure our parents would love that," he said dryly. "But we'll have to wait until after the run of the play I'm doing. I'll be in previews early next year for a brand-new show called *Legendary*. And if you're in New York before then, check out our castmate Trevor Kendrick in *Clown Car*."

"We love Trevor," Erika put in. "And his show is hysterically funny. I caught it a while ago. See it before it ends, people. How about you, Ariel?"

Ariel looked at the audience, at the happy faces of people who were having an amazing time at the event she'd instigated, then down the line at her friends, her family, who all had such exciting things to look forward to. She glanced to her left at Selena, who looked rosy with pride, and at Ryan, who was an endlessly lovely surprise. She'd been so despairing of her own future only a few months ago, afraid it held nothing but ever-diminishing returns after the career and personal high that was *Sawyer's Cove*.

But it was funny how life turned out sometimes. She had gained a partner who was equal to the task of loving her and who made loving him a pleasure, as well as a renewed appreciation for her job. She wasn't afraid of being too much anymore.

She grinned. "I don't have any firm plans right now, though I'm expecting to work with some of these incredible people again, which makes me happy. I'm so proud of us. And as for what's next? You'll have to tune in and watch."

Epilogue

JULES: This is such a bittersweet moment for us.

ERIKA: I promised myself I wouldn't cry. Too late!

JULES: It's okay to cry. Just don't blow your nose into the mic. Our producer won't like that.

ERIKA: It's our final episode of this podcast. What a ride it's been. I can't even fathom how to express our appreciation for all the listeners who've been with us the past few years, from the first episode when we were figuring out how this podcasting thing worked, through the reboot news, to us getting a home on a network, getting to meet the fabulous, sexy people who make the show, through our live pod and beyond. Thank you.

JULES: *Sawyer's Cove* was always first and foremost about friendship. I want to thank my friend Erika for going on this journey with me. I love you.

ERIKA: [crying] I love you, too.

JULES: Here's to the next chapter, babe.

First days never went smoothly. It wasn't that Ryan was terrible at his job and no one should ever have put him in charge of a multimillion-dollar television show that would be the centerpiece of the fall schedule. It *felt* like that, but, no, it was just the usual first day jitters, snafus, and delays.

Ryan dropped his forehead to the top of his desk with a satisfying, if slightly painful, clunk. "Ow."

"Hey, be a little nicer to my boyfriend, would you?"

He raised his head off the desk and took in the vision standing in the doorway of his office. Ariel Tulip was still dressed in her Franny costume, black turtleneck, faded jeans. Her hair had been cut for the role—no longer Lily's waterfall, but a pert chin-length bob that still managed to be sexier than it had any right to be. She looked beautiful as ever, but she'd transformed, even if she was still Ariel.

"Rough day, baby?" she asked sympathetically as she walked into the room.

"Just the first day of shooting. Tomorrow will be better."

"*Tonight* will be better," she corrected, alighting on the edge of the desk.

"What's tonight?"

"Tracy's birthday party. Can you believe Cami and Jay have a one-year-old?"

"Yes, because I know how long it took to get this show off the ground."

"But you and Cami and Selena did it and it's going to be a huge hit."

"I have to get through the shoot first." Ryan loved his job, but, man, it was a lot of work.

"I'll help you through it," Ariel promised. She went around the desk, swiveled his chair so she could plop herself in his lap. She was reassuringly warm and soft when he wrapped his arm around her waist, and she smelled like peaches.

He buried his nose in her hair and breathed her in. They'd had some ups and downs since the production on *Sawyer's Cove* ended. They'd had to be apart for a while right after, when he went to L.A. to work on postproduction and she returned to New York to attend to her life there. But, eventually, she'd traveled west to shoot a small movie role that had come up unexpectedly and they'd felt out what their relationship was like in Los Angeles. The bloom didn't wear off the rose. Rather, each day he spent with her felt like a gift. It helped him to have a reason to get up in the morning that wasn't work-related, and she was endlessly supportive of the work he had to do on both *Sawyer's Cove* and on the new project, *Lost Stars*. The studio had wanted to see the first season's worth of storylines before they'd take a meeting, so as soon as *Cove* post was finished, they went back to New York, where he moved in with her and spent his days writing and his nights making love to her. If that was all he did for the rest of his life, he'd be a happy man, but then there was promotion and rounds of interviews to do for *Sawyer's Cove*.

He didn't renew the lease on his L.A. apartment when they decided to make New York their home base. Even now, after *Lost Stars* had been green lit for a twelve-episode season and they had started up the Misty Harbor production unit again, they were still feeling out the edges of their relationship. It was tempting to block out the rest of the world and live in a bubble with Ariel at the center, but not realistic.

She'd worked intermittently on small projects until it looked like *Lost Stars* would be a go, then she'd lobbied hard for the role of Franny. The part was meaty and complex, and she was completely right for it.

But *Lost Stars* wasn't *Sawyer's Cove*. Would *Cove* fans be disappointed at the tone and themes of the show? Or would it find its own audience? Ryan couldn't do anything but create the very best television he knew how to make, and with the team Selena and Cami had assembled, he was in the best possible hands.

"You are way overthinking," Ariel said, bopping him on the nose. "Come on, you need some recreation. I'll go change and meet you at the car."

He responded to two more emails, shut down his computer, grabbed the birthday present for Tracy he'd picked up at the bookstore a few days ago, and walked out of the soundstage building to the parking lot. It was spring, and the air was cooling off rapidly now that the sun was going down.

He gazed at the building, allowing himself a moment of reflection. God, he was so lucky. He was with a terrific woman, who he loved working with, even when it got difficult. They weren't always going to be on the same projects, but although their romance had been born from sharing their work, what they had built over the past year and a half transcended what they did for a living. They knew who they were, independently and together. As hard as they worked, they'd learned how to play together, too.

A moment later, the most stunning woman he'd ever encountered came strutting out of the slate gray building, wearing a fuzzy cream-colored sweater, dark linen slacks, and wedge boots. She walked right up to him, wrapped her arms around his torso, and nestled her face against his chest.

"You want to go celebrate our honorary niece's birthday?"

"I want to go anywhere with you," Ryan said, kissing the top of her head.

"Then let's go."

Tracy had her father's brown eyes and her mother's blonde hair. She was on the cusp of walking, but she might never learn, since sometimes it felt as if she was passed from one adoring pair of arms to the next without being put down.

Ariel clucked and grabbed Tracy from Darren the moment she came in the door.

"Hey, I just wrestled her away from Trevor," Darren protested.

"Look, this is my only chance for baby cuddles. You'll have your own in, like, four months." After a fairly long process, Crosby and Darren had found a surrogate, who was due in July with their baby girl.

"Which is why I need the practice," Darren argued.

"Where's Dawson? Practice on him."

Two months after Tracy had been born, Mimi and

Nash had welcomed Dawson. The newest generation had kept everyone on their toes for the past year, but somehow they'd also found time to promote *Sawyer's Cove*, celebrate the success of *Gunsmoke*, which was not only a ratings hit but had been nominated for a bunch of awards, and get the green light for *Lost Stars*.

"I think he's in the kitchen with the mamas."

"Well, let's go see," Ariel said.

"I'm going to get a drink," Ryan said, heading toward a table next to the fireplace in the big open living room of Cami and Jay's house, behind which Jay was playing bartender. She spotted Warner and Selena over there, along with Trevor and Nash.

"Get me something with bubbles?" Ariel asked. "I'll come get it in a minute."

Ryan kissed her cheek. "Yes, darling."

"So, how is baby prep coming? Did you guys find a place yet?" Darren and Crosby had been switching between their separate apartments for the past few years, and had spent several months looking for a bigger place for their growing family—but New York real estate being what it was, it had been a frustrating process.

"Fingers crossed we have—I haven't had a chance to tell you yet, but it's like three blocks from you and Ryan."

Ariel squealed. "That is the best news I've heard all day."

She and Darren found Cami, Deb, Mimi, and Mimi's friend Pauline in the kitchen. Dawson was there, too, being held one-handed by Mimi while she counted cupcakes with her free hand. The other women were busy prepping trays of food.

"Darren needs a baby to hold," Ariel announced.

"Take him," Mimi said, thrusting her ten-month-old son at Darren. Dawson had light eyes and barely any hair, but he was still tied for first with Tracy for the cutest baby Ariel had ever seen, including her own sister's kid.

Pauline frowned at the counter full of cupcakes. "I don't think these are all going to fit on this platter."

"There's another one above the fridge," Deb said. "But I think you girls made too many."

"No such thing as too many cupcakes," Darren said, bouncing Dawson up and down. "Except I guess this little guy isn't going to be helping out."

"No, he hasn't had sugar yet," Mimi said.

"What about this beauty?" Ariel looked into Tracy's round, happy face. The girl was a pleasant weight in her arms and her gut lurched with baby envy. She and Ryan had talked about how they both wanted kids, but the timing wasn't right. Soon, though, maybe they'd have a little one of their own with Ryan's shifting eyes and her red hair. "Has she had sugar yet?"

Cami laughed. "Well, the other day in the Bakeshop she stole a croissant off my plate and shoved it in her mouth before I could stop her. Does that count?"

"Croissants are mostly butter," Zelda said as she arrived in the kitchen in time to hear Cami's tale of woe. "Hi Ariel."

"Hey, Z, how are you?" Ariel felt lucky to count Zelda among her true friends now. She'd even joined Zelda and Danica's book club, video calling in when she couldn't make it in person.

"I'm really good, thanks," Zelda said, smiling broadly. She and Alphonse, the butcher, had been married for six months now, and married life seemed to agree with her. "Ooh, what kind of cupcakes?"

"We made chocolate with chocolate frosting, vanilla with vanilla frosting, and red velvet with cream cheese frosting," Cami said, pointing to the three different types Mimi and Pauline were trying to fit on an entirely too small serving tray. "I guess I went overboard. Sue me, I'm still nesting."

Cami looked like she was about to audition for the part of retro domestic housewife, her blonde hair up in a tidy bun, her blue eyes sparkling, her cheeks round and rosy. She was even wearing a dress, a casual pink spring number. She hadn't acted since *Sawyer's Cove* ended, and had happily embraced producing full-time, along with motherhood. She and Jay were planning a wedding, too, a small affair when the weather got warmer, but before Harbor Fest.

"Hey, I'm not complaining about having flavor choices," Zelda said. "Want some help?" She took over for Mimi, plating the cupcakes with the efficiency of a pro.

"Wow, you are good at that," Pauline said.

"Thank you, Zelda," Mimi said gratefully. "I haven't entered my nesting era yet, apparently."

"You're too busy changing lives over at the library. How's the teen center going?" Ariel asked, as she gently extricated the lock of her hair that Tracy had grabbed and was trying to put in her mouth.

"Can you believe we've almost been open for a year? So far, it's been really positive. A few bumps here and there, but the kids have really taken ownership of it. Colin's helping organize a film festival. And Nash is sponsoring a friend of ours to come in and give the kids guitar lessons. He learned as an angsty fourteen-year-old, so we figure it's a good outlet for some of them."

"I was never angsty," Nash contradicted as he came in and gave his wife a kiss on the cheek. They'd married in a quiet ceremony in their backyard about a month before Dawson was born, Mimi wearing a peasant-style dress and looking radiant with magenta streaks in her hair, Nash in dark jeans, bolo tie, and cowboy boots. Ariel and Ryan had counted themselves lucky to be included in the tiny guest list.

"Whatever you say," Mimi said with a fond eye roll. "Is everyone ready for food?"

"More than ready, we have a lot of hungry friends and relatives," Nash said, stealing a red velvet cupcake from one neatly arranged platter.

"Hey, dinner before dessert," Mimi protested, swiping it back.

"Then let's eat," Nash said.

"Here, take this out and get started," Deb said, pushing a huge salad bowl into her son-in-law's hands.

"I'll help get the ball rolling at the buffet table," Zelda offered, leaving with Nash.

"What do you think, Dawson? Time for dinner?" Darren asked the burbling baby.

"He already ate," Mimi said. "Here, let's find a place to put him down so we can try to scarf down some food in the five minutes before he's going to want to be held again."

"Why don't I take Tracy, too?" Deb suggested. Ariel handed her over only slightly reluctantly—her arms were getting tired. She made a mental note to increase her upper body strength training.

They walked out of the kitchen, leaving Ariel alone with Cami.

"How did it go today?" Cami asked as she rinsed some dishes in the sink.

"Oh, the usual first-day hiccups, and I'm still getting the feel for Franny, but it's a good challenge. Lily was like a comfortable pair of boots, and Franny is like a new pair of heels. I have to step more carefully, but I know I'll break her in, and she'll feel more natural soon."

"And how's Ryan?"

"Ryan's wonderful." Ariel sighed happily. "He's so brilliant, and his writing is so damn good. Every day with him is better than the one before."

It was true they'd had to learn how to make their relationship work and were still working on it, probably always would, but it was worth it. Once they'd started living together, Ariel's eyes had been fully opened to the daily challenges Ryan faced with his limb difference, and she'd realized how much about her life she'd taken for granted. She was more grateful than ever for every day she got to spend doing the thing she loved, with her friends close by, and a partner who understood her by her side.

"You know, I used to think I was too much for people, but Ryan, and you, never make me feel like that. Have I thanked you for that lately?"

Cami smiled, dried her hands on a dish towel, and hugged her. "You don't have to thank me for being your friend."

"Are you quoting *The Golden Girls* theme song at me?"

"Unintentionally, I swear!" Cami laughed. "Now, let's

go eat. Tracy's bedtime isn't that far off, and I want to sing her 'Happy Birthday' before then."

Ariel left the kitchen and found Ryan by the bar, still talking to Jay and Selena. He had a glass of bubbly in his hand, which she took from him with a smile.

"Hey, sorry, got talking to Selena and Jay about some logistical stuff," Ryan said apologetically.

"No worries. Hey guys." She smiled at Jay and gave Selena a hug. Selena and Warner were holing up in Misty Harbor for the duration of the *Lost Stars* shoot, and she was looking forward to spending more time with the couple. "Your showrunner rocked it today, by the way, Selena."

"I don't know about rocked it, but it felt a little rocky," Ryan joked.

"First days always are," Selena agreed. "But it'll all even out. We have the best team in television working on this project."

"We really are the dream team," Ariel said.

"I'm so glad you two have enough confidence for all of us," Ryan said. "I'll relax after we get the first episode in the can, when I'll know we can deliver the rest."

"You've got this," Ariel said, "because I'm dynamite as Franny and she's the best character you've ever written. So there."

Selena lifted her eyebrows above the rim of her over-sized glasses. "I like this energy. You have an exceptional leading lady here, Ryan."

"Oh, I'm aware." Ryan lifted Ariel's hand to his mouth and grazed her knuckles with a kiss. Her skin tingled. She wanted to drag him to Cami and Jay's guest room and ravish him, but it wouldn't have been a good look at her honorary niece's first birthday party.

Collecting herself, she asked Ryan if she should get them something to eat.

"Sure."

Ariel found a spot to leave her drink, then loaded up two plates with chicken and salad and sourdough rolls from the Bakeshop. She grabbed seats at the long table Jay and Cami had set up for the occasion, then beckoned for Ryan to join her. "These rolls are amazing."

"*You're* amazing," he said.

She shook her head at his silliness, but blushed at the simple compliment, anyway. "You're a dork," she teased.

"I know," he said. "And you love me."

"I do love you." Her chest felt warm and light.

"I love you, too." Every time he said it was a small miracle.

They kissed, surrounded by their friends, their family, the people they loved, the people who loved them in return. They kissed for the past they'd shared, they kissed for the future that lay in store, and they kissed for that single moment, which was full of all the love they could ever want.

The End

Thank you so much for reading *Take Me Over* and the entire Sawyer's Cove: The Reboot series! I hope you loved it!

For more steamy, funny romance and an endearing group of friends, check out my Never a Bride series! Scan the code to learn more about the first book in the series, *Can't Help Falling in Love.*

xoxo,
Libby

Acknowledgments

I honestly can't believe that Sawyer's Cove: The Reboot has come to an end. So many people supported me through the creation and publication of this series. For their inestimable assistance bringing *Take Me Over* to life, thank you to Sara Kettler, Tracy Finistrella, Dar Albert, and Jessica Snyder.

For moral support, brainstorming, blurb help and so much more thanks to the SALT plotters and the KBR crew. Sara, Isabel, Annette, Mary-Ellen, Nicole, Arell, and Taylor—you all know how much you helped me get to the end of this series. Thank you.

Thanks to Gabi Coatsworth for her generosity with advice, to the supportive staff at the Westport Writers' Workshop, and to my ever-inspiring students.

Thank you to the Star Readers on my ARC team—you're awesome!

To my boys—you're the best and your support means everything to me.

Thanks once more to the *Dawson's Critique* podcast for inspiring me to write this series in the first place.

Finally, to all the readers who have let me know they enjoyed this series, thank you for reading!

About the Author

Libby Waterford is the author of the Sawyer's Cove: The Reboot and the Never a Bride series. She's obsessed with her pollinator garden, DIY fermentation, and writing swoony first kisses and hopeful happily ever afters. Her steamy contemporary romances mix witty banter and all the feels with a solid dollop of good old-fashioned sexual tension. Libby wrangles her two ever-growing sons and a husband in Fairfield County, Connecticut.

Get a free story at libbywaterford.com and email Libby at libby@libbywaterford.com.

- facebook.com/LibbyWaterford
- instagram.com/libbywritesromance
- bookbub.com/authors/libby-waterford
- goodreads.com/libbywaterford
- amazon.com/author/libbywaterford
- tiktok.com/@libbywaterfordauthor

Milton Keynes UK
Ingram Content Group UK Ltd.
UKHW011120180424
441376UK00004B/83

9 781963 910018